A Lady
of the Line

PHILIP McCUTCHAN

A Lady of the Line

A NOVEL

Weidenfeld and Nicolson
London

Copyright © 1992 by Philip McCutchan
Published in Great Britain in 1992 by
George Weidenfeld & Nicolson Limited
91 Clapham High Street London SW4 7TA

British Library Cataloguing in Publication
Data is available

ISBN 0 297 84055 X

Typeset by Deltatype Ltd, Ellesmere Port
Printed by Butler & Tanner Ltd
Frome and London

1

Bella often thought back to that day, long before hostilities had begun, the day she had first seen the great Rock shimmering under the heat haze, standing out gaunt and grey-brown from the Mediterranean blue. From that time onward, until the night the Land Port barrier had been shut, Bella could have asked for nothing better than the glamorous, ceremonial-filled life which had so surprisingly become hers. A young girl of nineteen, she had been married for just over a year when her husband, Colonel the Lord Kilkieran, had been summoned to Whitehall and had received personal orders from his Royal Highness the Commander-in-Chief to embark his regiment, the 74th Foot, aboard Lord Howe's fleet at Plymouth and sail to join the troops in garrison at Gibraltar.

From the moment that the Fleet had entered Algeciras Bay and the great ships of the line had backed topsails to lie off under the lee of the towering Rock of Gibraltar, Bella Kilkieran had warmed to the prospect which her new life held. Her hot Irish blood had thrilled to the sound of the drums and fifes echoing in the still, hot air along the Water Port, bringing tears to her eyes as the 74th had disembarked to march, behind the charger carrying her still-handsome, unpredictable husband, to Hargrave's Barracks. Thenceforward she had given her youthful vitality fully and wholeheartedly to the social life of the garrison while such had lasted through the months of peace.

And then in the following year – 1779 – everything had come to an abrupt stop, very suddenly and almost without warning.

The first public sign of this change had come on the evening of 21 June, when a sergeant's escort of the 12th Regiment had marched to the Land Port, the great north gateway out of the fortress facing Spain. The day had been one of those when the Levanter – that humid wind from out of the East – had been blowing: a day of low cloud and stifling heat which depressed the spirit. The marching men sweated into their tight red coats, the high stocks biting into brown necks and the muskets feeling deadly heavy as the sounds of the drums and fifes, muffled by that Levanter atmosphere into an unbearable sadness, beat about them, resounding off the close buildings and filling the air with martial noise.

As the sergeant's escort approached, the Land Port sentry, a private of the 12th, challenged them.

'Halt! Who comes there?'

The sergeant filled his lungs, felt the sweat trickle down below his tricorne hat. 'The Keys!'

'Whose keys?'

'King George's Keys.'

There was a pause. The sentry presented arms. 'Advance, King George's Keys,' he called. 'All's well.'

Stickily, the sergeant of the guard advanced; while the drums of the battalion beat out their background tattoo from Casemates Parade, he did something that he'd not been called upon to do before: he turned the massive key in the lock of the Land Port gate. This done to the accompaniment of much sweating and grunting, the sergeant turned about and called throatily.

'God preserve King George!'

Waiting first for the escort's loud 'Amen', the sergeant moved smartly to rejoin the soldiers. 'Escort o' the Keys . . . about – turn!' A pause. 'Guard an' escort . . . quick – march!'

The drums rattled out again and the men marched away into Water Port Street, a dwindling splash of red moving through the sand-coloured buildings of Irish Town . . . a small group of infantry who had locked the gates of Gibraltar against the might of Spain, not then realizing that it would be more than three years before those gates would once again be opened for their peaceful purposes. Lady Bella – she was always known as Lady Bella, Lady Kilkieran seemed somehow to be too formal for so gay a child – was one of a small crowd of officers and their ladies who had been watching from a balcony in Casemates – watching, and few of them realizing the full horror of what was to come. Bella now lifted her lovely dark head and turned blue eyes upwards to her husband's face, dimpling a little as she did so.

She said mischievously, 'It seems that my Lord Kilkieran may have his chance to show his valour in the field! Does the prospect frighten him?'

'Tush, Bella.' Kilkieran moved irritably, his long, determined chin jutting. 'How like a woman, to ask meaningless questions at a time of danger and difficulty!' He laid a hand on her shoulder. 'I *am* frightened, but only for you, my dearest.'

'Why?' She seemed amused. 'What's going to happen, Charles?'

He shrugged, muscles rippling under the fine red cloth. 'You must ask His Excellency . . . though even he cannot forecast the future. But from all I hear, the years of peace are coming to an end – '

'Clearly!'

' – and you will see no more banquets for a while. My own suspicion is the Dons intend to lay siege to us. That's the way they've always attacked Gibraltar before, and they'll do the same again.' They were walking away now, across Casemates Parade. 'If it were not for the dangers of the sea passage in present circumstances – for the Spanish Fleet will be watching for any English sail – I would send you home to England, Bella.'

'Oh, la!' She laughed lightly, gathering up the silken dress against the dust. 'You'll not be getting rid of me as easy as that, my Lord Kilkieran! I shall stay here, as you will.'

Kilkieran frowned, the dark brows coming together in a flash of anger. 'You'll do as you are bid – if I bid you!'

She held his eyes in her mocking glance and the frown relaxed into a deep laugh. She said, 'But you are not going to bid me. Are you?'

'I have already hinted that the sea dangers are too great a risk – and so I shall not bid you go. Are you satisfied?'

'Yes, Charles.' She took his arm, holding her body tightly

against his. 'Or I think I am . . . Tell me – what will things become like, if the Dons bring up a siege train?'

Kilkieran spoke with unwonted seriousness then. 'Bella my dearest, they will become severe if the Dons are able to mount a long and effective siege. You must be prepared for that. The garrison has not rations for any extended period, and the Dons have all in their favour. We shall have to eat anything we can find . . . mice, rats, the horses possibly. But let us hope it will not come to that,' he added on a more cheerful note. 'Myself, I do not believe it will. The Dons are no match for our English regiments.' He stopped, there in Water Port Street, and took her face in his hands. He said, 'Whatever happens then – you and I will see it through together?'

'No Englishwoman will leave her man,' she answered stoutly. 'Do you wish it said that an Irishwoman runs away?'

He gave a great laugh. 'That's my Bella, then!'

As they made their way home to their quarter, Kilkieran spoke little. He was much preoccupied. He knew that the Governor, General Eliott, had been seriously worried; His Excellency had had private information that the court at Madrid had been playing for some time at power politics and he had heard that their ultimate objective was indeed none other than the re-conquest of Gibraltar after a period of quiet which had lasted since 1727 – more than fifty years of peace and tranquillity. And then, only two days after His Excellency had paid a ceremonial visit to the Commandant in the Spanish lines, and had been most cordially received into the bargain, the mail from Gibraltar was refused entry into Spain. Discreet enquiries had revealed to His Excellency of Gibraltar that the Military Governor in the Spanish coast town of Algeciras had received orders from Madrid which, by command of His Most Catholic Majesty of Spain, had decreed that all com-munication between Spain and Gibraltar was to be discon-tinued forthwith; and after that Eliott could no longer be in any doubt that trouble was on the way.

As Kilkieran had remarked to Bella, the Dons had every-thing in their favour; the fortress was peculiarly susceptible to attack, for the Spanish shore, which sweeps in a half-circle round the western side of the Rock, commands the bay and all seaward approaches through the Strait; while an attack by land along the narrow isthmus of the neutral ground connecting the Rock with Spain was a very distinct possibility.

Although no openly hostile act had occurred, Eliott, after the stopping of the mail, lost no time in making prudent preparation for defence. After the Land Port barrier had been shut, he ordered the northern guards fronting on the neutral ground to be reinforced immediately, and the pickets were cautioned to be alert in case of an alarm to arms. An officer of artillery was ordered to present himself at Willis's Battery to protect the Devil's Tower guard and observe and report upon the movements of what was already being regarded as the enemy. Admiral Duff, commanding the naval force consisting of one ship of the line, three frigates and a sloop-of-war, was told to move his vessels away from the Water Port anchorage, where they were liable to come under the fire of the enemy's shore forts, and anchor them off the New Mole to the southward. During the next few days, though no attack came, the Spanish were seen to be drawing down cannon from San Roque to animate the coast forts – and that, His Excellency decided, was a definite pointer to what was to come.

Urgent preparations were going ahead in the fortress when, on 5 July, a Spanish squadron hove in sight from the westward and lay-to off the garrison, and the 12th and 72nd Regiments were ordered to stand-to, while the Captain of Europa Guard, found from Lord Kilkieran's regiment, was ordered to join his command at once and not to wait for the beating of Retreat; and that very afternoon, the first gunfire of hostilities crashed out from the southernmost tip of the Rock as the Europa Battery opened fire on a schooner which stood across from the enemy to reconnoitre three British privateers arriving from the westward. This fire caused the Spanish ships to drive to the eastward, and next day, after the packet had come in with despatches from England, the Governor made a public announcement to the effect that he had received word that hostilities had officially commenced between Great Britain and Spain.

The fourteenth siege of Gibraltar had begun – though so far

only Lord Kilkieran had voiced the suspicion that it was in fact to be a siege; the general expectation was rather for imminent and all-out attack from land and sea. From that time onward, great activity prevailed in the garrison; the engineers erected new batteries on the heights of the North Front overlooking the neutral ground; some land before the town was cleared and levelled to encamp the regiments should the enemy fire upon the town. A new battery of twenty-two guns was begun in the Navy Yard. And meanwhile, though the enemy batteries remained silent, the blockade started; as the weeks passed the grim spectre of real and urgent hunger began already to stalk the Rock. Prices rose tremendously, and Lord Kilkieran's household had to tighten their belts with the rest. A few ships came in, and these all left again with a full load of townspeople who preferred a residence in Barbary or Portugal to remaining in besieged Gibraltar. Those civilians who had nowhere to fly to, and so were forced to remain, grew daily more clamorous and complaining, and there were a few dangerous incidents.

Lady Bella had gone out one day to buy bread for the household, and as she crossed Grand Parade and came into Water Port Street, she was met by a howling mob who, themselves besieged from without, had evidently determined to lay siege to the bread shops. Her eyes flashing, Bella tried to force a passage through the mob; it was a foolish thing to do, and she had already been seized by a big ruffian who was making obscene remarks and trying to force his hand beneath her dress, when there was a shout from behind and the man let her go, slinking back into the crowd. Turning, Bella saw two files of redcoats coming up at the double under a corporal.

The corporal saluted. 'You'd best get home, milady. You'll do no good here today.'

'Go home, is it!' She stamped her foot. 'Sure, I'll do no such thing! I've come to buy bread, and buy bread I will – '

The corporal interrupted unceremoniously, sweat streaming down his leathery face. 'You'll have to do as I say, milady. If I leave you here, His Lordship'll have my head.'

'You cannot escort me through?'

The corporal shrugged. 'With four men – against this?' He waved his hand towards the menacing throng, only temporarily halted. He was having to shout to make himself heard. 'Come now, milady. A file will escort you – home.'

He detached two men, and Bella, furious, was led home between them. Kilkieran was in, and she told him what had been going on. He snapped, 'I know all about that, Bella.' As he spoke, he was buckling on his sword. 'I'm going to see His Excellency now. Keep indoors – d'ye hear me?'

He stalked out of the house, strode off across Grand Parade. He was admitted to His Excellency's room, and some half-hour later he was riding out from Hargrave's Barracks at the head of the 74th Foot, leading his men towards Water Port Street. Reaching the edge of Grand Parade, he halted the troops. For a moment he surveyed the fighting throngs, some of them, the luckier ones, tearing at hunks of bread with ravening fingers, stuffing it into hungry mouths. He listened to the shouts and screams of those who had not been so fortunate, saw the mob turning upon its own members to rend them tooth and nail. He stood in his stirrups, called an order to the drummers. They advanced slowly, beating out a tattoo. The deafening noise lessened a little, and Kilkieran tried to make himself heard – but in vain yet. He tried for some two or three minutes but the noise grew to a crescendo again and the mob started towards the soldiers. Kilkieran wheeled his horse off the street, barked an order to his sergeant-major. Each man of the front rank of the 74th went down on one knee; they, and the rank behind, brought up their muskets and fired a volley, point-blank into the crowd.

Water Port Street ran with more than a little blood that day; but in the long run, many lives were saved – and so, perhaps more important, was much of the bread.

That day His Excellency commanded that in future bread would be issued only under guard. Then, at the end of November, the bread ran out altogether and the Governor ordered rice (a prize laden with this commodity had recently been taken) to be used as a substitute.

On 12 January of the following year, the Dons' Fort St Philip fired into the town and four days after that the garrison was somewhat astonished to be joined by a deserter from the enemy's Walon Guard, a mercenary who informed His Excellency, when brought before him, that the enemy had everything prepared in their lines to bombard the town. And then, hard upon the heels of this news, came a rumour that Admiral Lord Rodney was on his way to relieve the hard-pressed garrison.

Next day, Lord Kilkieran was killed.

2

'But my dear girl – you shall not remain alone and unprotected in a garrison under siege! It is unthinkable, really unthinkable.'

A shaft of hot afternoon sunlight stole through the long windows of the official residence of the Governor; it fell across His Excellency's shoulders, bringing up the scarlet coat and the fine lace at his cuffs and neck, glinting on a silver snuff-box which stood open on the leather top of the desk before him. General Eliott was looking in growing concern at the flushed, dark face of the girl – she was little more than that in his eyes, even though she had been the somewhat unlikely wife of one of his colonels – sitting at the other side of that desk; he had noted the heaving breasts, the small, clenched fists, the determined, obstinate set of the red-lipped mouth. Untamed and wild was what she was, he thought ruefully . . . an impetuous Irish girl from County Wexford whose mother, so rumour had it, had had good blood in her veins even though she had married a farmer and, disliking the life, had preferred the more exciting one of near-prostitution in Dublin . . .

Eliott sighed and said, 'With all respect to a very gallant officer, Kilkieran should never have brought you to the garrison.'

'Your Excellency,' she pointed out tartly, 'the 74th joined the garrison some time ago. My husband was not to know at that time that the fortress would be isolated – or that he himself would be killed yesterday.'

Eliott inclined his head to hide the sudden unseemly twinkle that came into his eyes. The girl had plenty of spirit – there had been fire in her voice; she had dared even to deliver a rebuke, there was no doubt of that! He said, 'I am well aware of that, child.'

'Child, sir?' The hot blood, rising angrily, brought up her youthful beauty. 'Is that how you think of me, then?'

Eliott laughed aloud at that. 'Come, come,' he said. 'You cannot appear other than a child to me, my dear!' Then, again, he gave a faint sigh; his sensitive face, tired and heavily lined after seven months of siege, showed his consuming anxieties but yet remained firmly resolved. He went on, 'Lady Bella, a young woman of your years cannot remain, alone and unprotected as I said, in a garrison which is undergoing every imaginable privation – and is in imminent, indeed hourly, danger of its very life. Conditions must become very much worse as time goes on, even if there is no attack. It was your husband's last wish that you should leave the fortress.' He raised a hand, and the white lace cuff fell back over the scarlet to show a lean brown wrist. 'I am only trying to carry out that wish – '

'Then, sir, if you please, stop your trying!' The clear blue eyes blazed at the Governor, almost ferociously, and once again he was struck by this girl's beauty – and her courage. He was forced to admit that she seemed perfectly capable of looking after herself. 'That it was my husband's wish I do not dispute, for I heard him utter it, but he spoke only from a natural concern lest I might be killed or wounded and he no longer here to help me either recover or meet my God! He did not propose that I should run away,' she said with passionate contrariness. 'Your Excellency, the Kilkierans do not run!'

Slowly, Eliott shook his head. 'I know that, Lady Kilkieran. But in the case of a woman one can, I think, scarcely make that a point at issue. Besides . . .'

'Besides what, Your Excellency?' Bella gave a light laugh, but it was a laugh with an edge to it. 'You were going to say that marriage does not give a woman the Kilkieran blood, were you not? Or – were you going to be even blunter, Your Excellency?'

Eliott frowned. Rumour could be a lying jade, of course . . . but Colonel the Lord Kilkieran was precisely the type of man to despise conventions and take for his second wife an impetuous young beauty like Bella without giving so much as a thought to the mother's easy morals. Eliott had no intention in the world of speaking of this now; but he had it very much in mind. Like father, like son . . . like mother, like daughter. And Gibraltar under siege was woefully if necessarily short of women! A girl like this, all alone, could play havoc with the garrison. He said distantly, 'Lady Kilkieran, have you any very special reason for wishing to remain in the fortress? You know very well that it is my duty to put you aboard the first blockade-runner which is able to reach us – '

'And consign me to the possibility of being taken by the Spaniards at sea, or of being drowned?' The girl's dark eyes flashed again, and she leaned forward so that Eliott could see the deep cleft between her breasts. 'Not that I am afraid of *that*. Yet you have asked for a reason, Your Excellency, and it is this: it was my husband's dearest, most precious dream to be with the 74th at the moment when the siege was finally lifted by might of England's arms. He never doubted that that day would come.' There was, Eliott thought, something incongruous in the way the girl spoke, her wild yet so curiously virginal appearance, and the light voice, not dovetailing with the precise military sentiments; and she seemed to be aware of this herself, for she flushed slightly. But she went on, 'He wished for a Kilkieran to be present throughout what he had begun to feel in his bones was to be a long siege, and he wanted a Kilkieran to be present when the tenacity of the regiments was rewarded with the prize of victory. Now that he is no longer able to be present, I, Your Excellency, shall stand his proxy. He did not give me the Kilkieran blood, no – but he gave me the Kilkieran name! I shall not dishonour it. Through my eyes, he shall see the redcoats come ashore from the Fleet to reinforce the garrison and then to march against Spain . . .'

'Enough!' The Governor stood up, frowning somewhat testily. 'It is not for women to speak of men's work, though I confess I admire your spirit.' When she looked like making a scornful interruption he hurried on, 'To put no finer point upon it, it is my duty to conserve all possible supplies of food for my soldiers. This is a fortress, and you know very well that food is woefully short. You have my decision, Lady Kilkieran. I shall give orders that you will leave the garrison when Lord Rodney's fleet weighs for England.'

A smile seemed suddenly to touch the corners of the girl's blue eyes, as though she had been waiting for this. It was a smile which brought the Irish mischief fleetingly into her face and turned her eyes to glowing pools of deepest Mediterranean blue. She said demurely, 'Sir, Lord Rodney's ships, which in any case are a mere rumour, have not yet even entered. Whether they do so or not is scarcely in your hands, but in those of God – and the King of Spain!'

'Ha – hrrmph.' Eliott looked away in irritation. What a baggage this was! 'And in the hands of Admiral Rodney, who is not without his resources, ma'am. His ships will enter shortly, as published this day in Garrison Orders – '

'Which I have not yet had the pleasure of reading.'

Eliott glanced at her sharply. 'Then I shall tell you what is in them. It is confirmed that Lord Rodney is proceeding to our relief with twenty-one sail of the line . . . and is in addition bringing in a convoy which he took from the Dons whilst it was sailing from Bilbao to Cadiz. This news comes from the captain of a brig which put in yesterday – and we expect Lord Rodney daily. He will not fail to bring in the greater part of his fleet, my dear, whatever the Dons may do to stop him! Lord – '

'And he will be bringing much food, Your Excellency?' she suggested hopefully and with a suspicion of cunning which made the General smile to himself. An irritating baggage she might be – but by heaven she was young and pretty!

He said, 'As I trust.' Then he hesitated. 'But, I fear, few soldiers – so the siege will continue against us, at least until the next force enters, and as I have already said, we shall have to conserve our food carefully for fighting mouths – however much food Lord Rodney brings.'

'So I shall have to go?' Bella asked miserably. She sounded compliant at last, but the submissive lowering of her head concealed her eyes from the General. 'That is your last word, sir?'

He nodded, but gently. 'You will have to go with the assurance that England is grateful, and that the name of Colonel the Lord Kilkieran will ever be remembered in the garrison with pride . . . and will be a lasting inspiration to his own regiment.'

'Thank you, Your Excellency.'

Without waiting for Eliott's dismissal, Lady Bella got up; she walked swiftly and imperiously from the room, her dark head held high, her small feet making no sound on the thick maroon carpet. As she walked angrily down the passage, an officer – the Governor's aide-de-camp, a haggard and hungry-looking Captain of Highlanders whose kilt was flapping unbecomingly round skinny shanks, came out of a doorway and Bella all but bumped into him.

He jerked himself backwards and bowed. 'Your pardon, Lady Bella.' He gave an awkward cough, but his eyes gleamed curiously at the sight of her young body. 'Will you permit me to offer you my condolences, ma'am?'

Preoccupied as she was, she seemed, though she had stopped, scarcely to have noticed the ADC. 'Your condolences?' she repeated vaguely.

'Aye, ma'am . . . on the loss of the Colonel. A fine, brave man.'

She inclined her head. 'Thank you, Captain Frazer. As you say . . . a brave man.'

'Who will be sorely missed. And – the General – I understand that we are also to lose you now?'

The girl's cheeks flamed anew. She had never liked this man; perhaps considering her needful of sex with a husband three times her own age, he had once tried to press himself on her. Once, and once only. He had never forgiven her for her cutting rejection of his advances. Now, she looked directly into his eyes, at the spare, angular frame bent towards her with such spurious solicitude, and she made a sudden angry gesture of fury and defiance. 'Then you understand wrong!' she snapped in that fresh, light voice. 'I do not propose to leave the fortress . . . never, never, never! Good-day to you, Captain Frazer.'

Gathering her skirts she ran swiftly down the passage and out into the brilliant, stifling sunshine, where a mangy dog snuffled up to her skirts, his eyes filled with a desperate pleading for food. 'Och!' she cried, 'Away with you, you foolish fellow, or it's eating you for his dinner that great Highlandman'll be! Sure they can't spare food for my mouth at all, let alone yours. Come now, and we'll just see what we can find for you at home.'

Girl and dog went off together, into the heat and the dust and the ravening flies. Gunfire rumbled across from the Spanish shore, from before the mysterious, purple-tinted Andalusian hills. Puffs of white came from the direction of La Linea, there was a curious sighing whistle, and the shot began to fall by the South Port, kicking up the sunbaked earth. From a window in His Excellency's residence Captain Frazer looked after Bella with his eyes narrowed, eyes into which another gleam had come, a gleam of sadistic hatred. This gleam had first appeared when she had said so definitely and so defiantly that she wouldn't leave the Rock. Lady Bella was a girl of fire and spirit and vitality aged no more than twenty – and for two years now she had been married to a man of fifty-eight and now she was widowed. She, by birth nothing more than a common Irish peasant, had rejected him once. Frazer felt instinctively that she would do so again – if she was given the chance. And all the time that she was upon the Rock she would disturb him, would never give his cavorting thoughts a rest. Frazer looked after her still, watched the play of her rounded buttocks beneath the thin dress as she walked. His mind felt aflame with desire, his body gave him no peace. Then, after a few moments, Captain Frazer shrugged and walked away towards the Governor's room with almost an old man's gait himself. The siege was turning the whole garrison into a collection of haggard, ageing scarecrows already . . .

She could still hear distinctly Kilkieran's words as he'd lain in the dust by the Devil's Tower, his red coat showing the heavy, sodden stain of a darker red.

'You're young, my Bella. You'll marry again, but not a soldier next time. Wives become a cursed nuisance to the regiment after a while, and . . . damme, Bella, but you're far too good to become the horror of the barrack square and the misery of the Mess!' Just for one moment the magic of the old smile stole through the pain and overlaid the twisted, agonized features and then, with increasing difficulty, he went on, 'And get away from here. You must . . . do that at the first opportunity. Old Fitzmaurice'll look after you until Lord Rodney's fleet enters. When . . . when he's sober . . . he's a fine officer and a gentleman too – but keep away from him when he's been at the brandy.' The fact that Major Fitzmaurice had been present and was tugging in some confusion at his somewhat grubby and unpowdered wig, hadn't inhibited Kilkieran in the very least; he'd simply grimaced up at the fat, red-faced officer and winked an eye at Bella. 'By the way . . . there's no money, my darlin' girl. We Kilkierans . . . had all the money in the world once, but now 'tis all spent, every penny. So perhaps after all you'd be doing better . . .'

Bella never knew what he had been going to say, for that had been all and the voice had broken off and then those clear Irish eyes had darkened on a spasm of pain which seemed to rattle his very teeth, while the skin of the handsome, aristocratic face itself had taken on a fearsome transparency beneath the tan, and her husband had died (without a priest to speed him, but that didn't matter for Bella knew that Kilkieran would have given a priest short shrift anyway, and in fact the very presence of such a one would have been nothing but a vexation to hasten his going). So Kilkieran had died out there on the dusty, rough roadway beneath the Devil's Tower, the extended and unprotected outpost which commanded the approach across the neutral ground separating the Gibraltar fortress from Spain . . . a thousand miles away from the remote and lovely mountains of his beloved Connemara. A volley of musketballs from the advanced sentries of Spain had taken him clean through the stomach. Of course, a rider had gone at once for Bella, and for the surgeon; but there was little the latter gentleman could do except try to staunch the life-blood which was flowing from the colonel's body into the baked ground of the Devil's Tower guardpost. Soon after Bella's arrival, Major Fitzmaurice had dashed up on his scraggy, ill-nourished horse – one of the very few now remaining in the garrison – his red coat covered with dust and himself shaking all over and breathing hard, reeking already of brandy and somewhat bleary of eye. Bella hadn't cried over her husband's body. Bella had felt loyalty and gratitude towards Kilkieran; and she had admired him, and her admiration had come very close to love, but though she enjoyed his embraces and gave herself to him without reserve, she had stopped short of whole love. It was in her nature to enjoy the physical expression of love but she still had not loved him in quite the way that she felt her vital young body to be capable of love, which should be a thing of passion. And so the tears would not come, however sorely she knew she would miss the comfort and protection of his dashing, devil-may-care presence. Dimly she had felt, even in that first moment of widowhood, that the best memorial to Kilkieran – indeed the only way in which she would be able to mourn him as he deserved – would be to watch over his beloved regiment, to remain now the only Kilkieran on the Rock, to see it all through to the bitter end whatever Kilkieran's wishes to the contrary – wishes which, indeed, were no more than any dying husband would feel obliged to express in the circumstances of the siege.

A few minutes later old Fitzmaurice had called for a commissariat cart and had helped her into it, handing over his own mount to an orderly; and then, the colonel's body in another cart behind, they had trundled off over the rough ground, bumped and shaken, and then through the Land Port towards Hargrave's Barracks. Fitzmaurice, dabbing at his rheumy eyes with a piece of lace, had held Bella's hand and pressed his gross, sweating body a little too close to her slender, youthful one. Mistakenly perhaps, she had not protested, but had sat inert, her mind in the past. She had not protested until later – when, that night after the officers had dined frugally and she was alone in the quarter where she had lived with Kilkieran, Major Fitzmaurice had come to her, staggering with drink and incoherent, and had tried, in his clumsy, drunken fashion, to seduce her.

Tight lipped and white, she had struck out at him, leaving the imprint of her small, capable hands on the coarse, vein-seamed face. There was indeed something wild and untamed about her, and Fitzmaurice had recognized defeat instantly. Some glimmering of belated chivalry, perhaps, had penetrated the brandy-soaked brain of the soldier and he had desisted, even mumbled some kind of an apology, and then he'd gone away with his cheeks wet with silly, maudlin tears of contrition.

And after that Bella herself had cried also, and then fallen into a troubled sleep. When she woke she couldn't decide whether those tears of hers, which had left her face stiff where they had dried, had been for herself or for her husband; at all events, she now had to face the day, and after it a succession of days, alone in a beleaguered fortress.

But whatever happened, she wasn't going to leave.

She was no less sick of life under siege than anyone else in the fortress, but she would not give in any more than they would. There would be no giving in at all, ever.

There was something stormily unrelenting in the Irish blood that flowed so strongly through Bella Kilkieran's veins and whether it had been given to her by her solid farmer father or her feckless mother she couldn't tell: but she did know that her mother had come from the West, from County Galway . . . from that same Connemara that had bred the Kilkierans, where the wild purple hills run down to the bogs, where the rocky Atlantic shores are washed by the roaring rollers sweeping in white and green from the New World . . . from a far and remote countryside, desolate and filled with the softly falling rain which runs like tears down the face of a sad land to fill her salmon rivers and her lovely loughs. A land which, when the rains lift from it, shows a sparkling fresh face beneath wide blue skies broken by little puffs of white cloud speeding along on the wind, bathed in a light which defies description, light which beckons the Irish home across half the world. A land where neighbours are wonderfully few and far between, where a magnificent style is kept up in the great houses and where whiskey flows like water – and where the poor are very, very poor but still finely and proudly independent. So perhaps it was her mother's blood that was telling her that she was going to see this siege through right to the end even though she knew quite well – and had been given some very practical knowledge by Fitzmaurice during that night – that Gibraltar under siege was no place at all for an unprotected and strikingly beautiful girl.

★

After her interview with General Eliott, Bella walked across Grand Parade and went home to the quarter which would remain hers until Fitzmaurice, who had taken over command of the Regiment, moved in. After a while she went out again, and left the fortress by way of the South Port. She climbed a little way up the great Rock to a point above the Red Sands from where she could look out across Algeciras Bay towards those blue-hazed hills of Spain . . . the hills where the huge siege train, the thousands of men and the guns, the combined French and Spanish armies now, lay waiting unhurriedly and in patience to deliver the *coup de grâce* once the garrison was too weakened with hunger to resist them. The sun was dipping to the west now, and the principal impression was one of pastel colour: the deep-blue sea and sky slashed by those Spanish hills and the rearing purple heights of the North African mountains across the Strait; the sand-coloured buildings of the little town itself below her; above, the towering structure of the Rock, grey and barren except for the close-growing, once-green scrub in which now she stood. Seemingly far below, although she had not climbed for long, she could see companies of redcoats moving about stickily in the heat of the garrison, their uniforms standing out vividly; a company of men was marching out from the South Port towards Red Sands, men perhaps of her husband's regiment. Well – old Fitzmaurice was their Colonel now . . . and there wouldn't be many who would welcome the change! Bella knew that Kilkieran had not been especially loved by the men under his command, for they feared him and his wild ways a little too much for that, but he was respected as a gallant soldier and a dashing leader whose men would have gone anywhere with him – something which was unlikely to be said of fat Fitzmaurice.

Her glance shifted again to seaward, rested on the white sails of a ship making in past Tarifa and keeping just out of range of the Spanish shore batteries whose guns were kicking up spouts of water near her hull. Since she was under fire, she must be an English ship.

Was she, Bella wondered, a privateer – or the vanguard of Lord Rodney's fleet?

3

From the rocks behind Lady Bella a tall, well-set-up man with a dangerous look about him and thick black hair descending the nape of his neck below the tall head-dress of a company of Hardenburg's Hanoverians, watched the girl from a thick patch of scrub and felt the hot blood leap in his body. Obviously the girl hadn't yet realized that anyone was near . . . he studied her. The soft dark hair falling over the pale shoulders, the tiny waist, the swelling firm breasts which he saw as she turned her body slightly, the pride – the arrogance, almost – of her bearing . . . it all added up to an urgent quickening of the pulses of the man in the tattered, dusty Hanoverian sergeant's uniform.

He knew who she was, of course; after seven months of siege everyone in the garrison knew the Lady Bella Kilkieran. He had seen her many, many times. It had appeared to him (and he did not stop to reason that she was young enough to hold such things harmless) that she had not been above flaunting her charms before a garrison kept well at bay by her exalted rank – and by her husband. A corsage which slipped on occasion, a little white flesh titillatingly displayed as if by accident, a mocking and provocative glance – these things played havoc in barrack-rooms and camps. In looks, and probably in temperament, she was in fact most oddly like the husband who now lay buried in the cemetery before the neutral ground, that ever-growing little patch of consecrated earth where the victims of the siege lay like a kind of motionless advanced guard to the fortress. Lord Kilkieran, so far its most illustrious freeholder, had been an arrogant and imperious man, and his widow looked to be much the same, with those flashing blue eyes and the high cheekbones and the determined jaw. And now she was on her own, one of a mere handful of women, all of the others much older than her and with their husbands still alive, marooned by war in a garrison of some five thousand woman-starved soldiery.

The hidden man moved a little and made some small sound which carried to Lady Bella's ears. Startled, she turned her head from the sparkling blue prospect of the sea which was gently ruffled by a breeze blowing through the Strait from the westward to bring a welcome touch of Atlantic cool. Head thrown back, chin high, she revealed the long, slim throat; her hair streamed down her shoulders, pointing up the curve of the neck rising from the valley made by the twin mounds below. A girl fresh as her native hills as well as arrogant.

Seeing the man now, she recognized the uniform. Hardenburg's Regiment was composed of mercenaries from Hanover who had taken service under King George against the designs of France and Spain. Bella looked coolly at the man, noted the flush on the sun-darkened cheeks, saw the twitch of a tiny muscle beside the cruel mouth. Perhaps feeling herself safe yet as the widow of Kilkieran, she made no attempt to conceal her charms, and the movement of her body sent provocative waves of perfume winging towards the soldier as she returned his lingering look haughtily.

Speaking with a guttural accent he said, 'Good afternoon, milady.' The sound grated, but he spoke English well enough.

She inclined her head but did not speak.

'You are the widow of the English colonel who commanded the 74th. The regiment whose command now passes to Colonel Fitzmaurice. Is that not so?'

A spasm of something like pain crossed her face for an instant, but she nodded equably enough and the clear blue eyes held steadily to the coarse Hanoverian face. One eyebrow went up, quizzically, at this presumption by a non-commissioned officer and a foreign mercenary at that. She asked icily, 'And what, pray, has that to do with you, Sergeant?'

'Nothing, except . . .' He shrugged heavily, wetted his lips with his tongue.

'Except – what?'

'Except that you, like me, are nothing now.' The soldier

heaved himself to his feet, came out from the scrub and brushed dirt off his torn uniform. He said indifferently, 'I care nothing any longer for any of the regiments, nor for what any of the fools who compose them may do.'

'I understand. You are a deserter.'

He laughed. 'Let us say rather, that I am in process of becoming one. It would be a fool indeed who would consider his act accomplished, milady, until he had delivered himself from this accursed Rock.' He added abruptly, 'I left the Middle Hill Guard last night – and I brought someone with me.'

He called over his shoulder. 'You, Englishman. Come out, and meet the lady.

Bella stared. No Englishman, surely, would have left his post, joining this Hanoverian mercenary as a deserter? When nothing happened in answer to his call, the sergeant turned away and disappeared into the scrub. There was the sound of a blow, and then a sharp cry of pain, and the head and shoulders of the sergeant loomed again above the bushes, and a moment later a slim young man lurched out into the open to confront Bella.

She started, genuinely shocked. She had recognized the facings on his red coat, and her lips set hard. The Hanoverian sergeant, coming up behind the young man, said roughly, 'Milady, one of Lord Kilkieran's regiment . . . Private Carter of the grenadier company of the 74th, who has joined me in my desertion.'

The young man, whose face was a greyish white and streaked with dirt and dried blood, gave Lady Bella a bow. It was odd, that courtly bow, coming from a private of foot and in such strange surroundings – and he a deserter too. He started to speak, but he was not allowed to go on, for the Hanoverian grasped him by the shoulder and flung him back to fall in a crumpled heap on the ground. The sergeant looked at the girl with a leering expression, and she met his eye, though her heart faltered now.

She said calmly, drawing herself erect and looking at the man with contempt, 'You will not be at large for much longer, my friend.'

'You will inform my commanding officer – and Colonel Fitzmaurice?'

'Of course,' she said frigidly. 'I am well acquainted with Colonels Dachenhausen and Fitzmaurice.'

Grinning, the man lunged towards her, his eyes bloodshot, filled with something more than the signs of hunger and lack of sleep. 'Of course! I am quite sure you would . . . if it were not for certain things which I have in mind.'

Bella kept her gaze on his face still, but she didn't speak. She felt stifled in that atmosphere which somehow seemed composed of blood and sand and heat. The sergeant went on, 'You will be very useful to me, milady, for the deserter without friends would not last long on this damned Rock! With your help, I shall be all right. Now listen. I said just now that you are nothing, since you no longer have your husband to give you the authority of his presence. That is true, and very well you know it. But – they are acquainted with you in the garrison, all of them from the Governor downwards. They will trust you absolutely. They will not question where you go nor what you do – and they will never suspect you of aiding deserters.' He drew a deep breath. 'After dark, you will go down to your quarter and you will gather food, and pistols, and ammunition, and all these you will bring to me at this spot.' His face grew darker, more suffused, as he went on, 'We shall live together after that, your sweet young body and I, for perhaps a day or two . . . and when the time is right, my girl, you will find me a rowing boat and my friend and I will go to sea and embark aboard one of any such ships, not British ones, as may be sailing through the damned Strait – never to return to Gibraltar!'

Her tone was cutting, her laugh contemptuous. 'You really believe I will do that?'

The man's black brows lifted in a sudden guffaw. 'Why, that you will go down into the town I am quite sure! That you will collect such food as you can from people by your charming smile is equally certain . . . and that you will provide yourself with the protection of weapons against the attentions of your gallant and chivalrous British officers,' he added sneeringly, 'is also a very logical assumption.'

'And then?'

He gave a mocking bow – a bow very different from that of the young Englishman. 'That you will return here to me, unescorted and with all the things I need – which at the moment you may think the most doubtful proposition – of that also I am perfectly sure. Even if I were not quite so certain, I would take the risk, for I am facing death in any case and I can be none the worse for taking necessary chances now.'

'Why,' she asked coolly, 'are you so certain I shall return alone – and not inform your Colonel of your whereabouts?'

He was close to her now and she could feel his breath hot and gusty on her face, could catch the strong tang of bodysweat as he moved. She felt a dreadful repulsion, a shrinking of the flesh, as he reached out and caressed her throat, staring into her eyes as he did so. He said softly, 'Girl, I know the pride of your race, of all officers' women everywhere, the pride which will crack and fly to the winds – for it cannot bend – as soon as you have lain with a rough, coarse Hanoverian peasant, and felt his arms about your body . . . the pride which, before it goes, my lovely, will tell you that you have been sullied and disgraced for ever by such intimate contact with a common foreign mercenary such as I. When I have done with you, you will never wish to show your face to the officers who knew your husband – if ever they should find out what has happened to you, that is. If I am captured, I shall talk – you understand? Remember, I can die once only. So you will speak to no one and you will return alone.'

His eyes blazed at her, set teeth showed for a moment between the full lips, and a moment later clumsy hands were pulling at her dress, tearing and ripping at the flimsy material. Then suddenly Bella saw the redcoat in the background jerk upright, and the pale face of the young English soldier became visible over the Hanoverian's shoulder.

He said hotly, 'Leave her alone. Lord Kilkieran was my Colonel. You shall not touch her.'

For an instant Bella saw the anger in the sensitive face, saw the courage, saw the hand stretched out towards the sergeant. Then the Hanoverian swung round and a bunched fist smashed viciously into the private's mouth and the

Englishman fell to the ground, hitting his head on a jagged rock. He lay there, dead white beneath his own pouring blood. A moment later Bella felt strong, calloused fingers grasping her back and thighs. She screamed once, and the hopeless cry was lost in the vast, grey barrenness of the Rock, awoke only the insect life of that sun-scorched scrub. And then the coarse red mouth was pressed to hers and she felt herself sink away into the mists as she was crushed into the virile body. The Hanoverian picked her up like a child, held her close to smother any more cries.

He muttered, 'Girl, you'll take some taming – but you're mine now!'

It was not until Bella heard her own moans filling her ears that she realized she was coming round from a dead faint. She found that her body was bruised, racked with pain and torment. For a time she scarcely knew where she was nor what had happened to her. She felt thorns pricking into her naked flesh, and, lifting her head, she saw her own clothing in a heap beside her and half under her head, and as remembrance returned in a blinding flash of cruelty she felt she must go out of her mind. As her sobs broke into the still, quiet air, a figure in a red coat, a piece of shirting tied round the head, moved to her side, and a hand came out to smooth her brow.

The voice – and it was a cultured one – whispered urgently, 'Lady Bella, thank God you are recovered. I was greatly worried . . . now listen, please, for I have only until the sergeant returns, and I dare not speak aloud. Will you listen to me . . . milady?'

She gave a barely perceptible nod, the effort sending fresh waves of pain and nausea through her body. 'You may speak.'

He whispered, 'I am no deserter. I was forced by the sergeant to join him, because had he left me I would have given the alarm. I wish to rejoin my regiment, but now they will surely not believe what I say. Milady, I throw myself on your mercy . . .'

It was beyond her in her present state. She broke into a wild torrent of sobs as she thought of the dreadful predicament she was now in – and perhaps, for the young man's sake, it was just as well she had broken down, for it made him stop talking just in time as the Hanoverian came round a big boulder. The sergeant took a few paces towards her and stood watching her with an exultant smile on his face. She tried to hide herself and her shame in the gathering shadows, tried to shrink away from the man's dark gaze.

The sergeant said curtly, 'Englishman, you can get away from her. She does not need your help. She's known a man now, a real man.'

The private of foot got up slowly and edged away, his face a controlled mask now. Presently the sobbing ceased, and the sergeant pulled Bella roughly to her feet, his fingers sliding lasciviously down her cringing flesh.

He said, 'You can cover yourself now, girl. Cover that lovely skin of yours . . . and go! It will be full dark by the time you reach the South Port. Make yourself look decent,' he added with a leer, 'even though you do not feel it! Do what I told you, and return here quickly. I shall be watching this spot from a distance and from cover, and I have my musket, and this man's musket. If you are escorted, then you and your friends will die. But – I do not think you will be escorted.'

She said nothing; almost mechanically she obeyed his order. Under the watchful eyes, she pulled on her garments, tidying herself as best she could. There was no looking-glass to show her the tear-stained, blood-drained face nor the marks on her body where the man's grip had held her, the bruises where the mingling sweat of their joined bodies had caused flesh to stick to flesh so that their movement had brought out the discoloration; but she felt the dreadful trembling in her limbs.

When she was ready, the sergeant pulled her to him again and kissed her mouth. He said, 'I have taken you, Bella, and you are mine. We shall go forward together now. Do you understand?'

Saying nothing still, she made as if to free herself, and then she became aware of the redcoat, Carter. He had picked up his musket, was coming up behind the Hanoverian's back, and he had the maddened, red glint of the killer in his eyes. Involuntarily, Bella screamed. The sergeant swung round and moved aside. Carter fired, and missed, his ball zipping a fragment of material from Bella's full skirts, and then the Hanoverian went for him with his fists. As a crashing blow swung in Carter's direction, the younger man leaned sideways and the Hanoverian, off balance, lunged his fist into a jut of rock, splitting open the knuckles. Swearing with the pain, he recovered himself quickly, but Carter was quicker. The young private was upon the sergeant in a flash and Bella saw the shining steel of his bayonet poised ready, failed to look away in time, saw the sharp weapon buried deep in the Hanoverian's neck. The sergeant fell back, a curious rattling cry coming from the torn throat, and then, staggering as Carter withdrew the steel, he dropped in a widening pool of blood.

Bella's face was ashen as she leaned her trembling body against a rock.

Carter stared back at her, the blood dripping from his bayonet like a butcher's knife; and then, dropping the weapon, he fell to his knees, burying his face in his hands.

4

As she struggled down the steep track leading from the rock through the South Port into the fortress and the town, Bella was haunted by more than that terrible death which she had been forced to witness; the pale young face of Private Carter kept rising up before her. What he had said about being forced into an act of desertion by the Hanoverian sergeant had sounded to Bella like no more than the simple truth, truth which rang in her ears together with the young man's stammered and somewhat melodramatic explanation that he had sought to avenge the honour of the widow of his Colonel by killing her attacker – truth which forced itself into her heart and brain despite the dreadful, searing experiences of that day.

And those experiences had left their mark, left it in the pale, strained face, the shadowed eyes, the trembling body. Bella found her mind going round and round in circles of misery in which she saw so cruelly the full horror of the stark change which had taken place in her position within the compass of so short a time. It was scarcely more than twenty-four hours since Kilkieran's death, and yet now she was a branded woman, raped, dishonoured, almost demoralized.

But – not so demoralized nor so distrait that she was incapable of beginning to think this thing out or, within a short time of entering the town, of steadying herself. She had enough of her mother in her not to regard her plight as entirely desperate. That sergeant had miscalculated – had he lived, she would in fact have gone, once she had calmed herself, straight to Colonel Dachenhausen, would even have been prepared to guide the armed escort to the rendezvous and take the consequences to her own safety and reputation . . . for there would be plenty of malicious tongues to say that she had been a willing cooperator in that rape.

But now everything was changed by Private Carter.

Bella absolutely believed his story; there was no duplicity, no cowardice in that fresh young face. He certainly did not look or act like a deserter. He had the stamp of the dedicated soldier despite his youth . . . and yet he didn't speak like a common private of foot. But what was to be done? No one else in the garrison would believe him, or could allow themselves to believe him, of that Bella was quite certain. To believe him, to let him go free after what was in fact an act of defection (for he should, according to the military code, have chosen to die before he allowed himself to be forced into desertion) would only be to encourage similar defections in the future. And now he had killed a comrade – had in fact killed the one man who could, perhaps, have been forced into a confession which would have cleared him of the major charge of outright desertion . . .

Bella urged her aching body on. There was really only one thing to do now. She must collect rations, and return to that hideout on the rock. Private Carter had thrown himself upon her mercy – and he had acted in her defence.

She would not let him down now.

When later that night the Lady Bella knocked at the door of Colonel Fitzmaurice's quarter she was shown into his presence immediately. The colonel levered his gross form out of a chair and came to meet her, arms outstretched. He appeared to have forgotten his repulsed advances of the night before.

'My dear Lady Bella! Delighted to see you, m'dear – delighted!' His small eyes glittered. 'But tell me – what brings you here?'

His gaze roved over her body, lingeringly.

She smiled at him, her face innocent, careful not to let him see her repugnance at the desire which so clearly possessed him as his eyes sought the outlines of her figure, at the smell of brandy harsh on his breath as he came nearer, at the little, bleary, red-shot eyes which told of an evening's hard drink-ing. He was, in truth, even a little unsteady on his feet.

Well – so much the better, perhaps! A man whose brain was befuddled by drink could the more easily be handled in the way she meant to handle him now, could the more readily and painlessly be made a fool of.

Bella said demurely, 'Sir, I trust I do not incommode you – '

'Oh no, no – by no means, m'dear – '

'You see, I – I knew of no one to turn to for help. No one but you . . .'

Fitzmaurice laughed throatily. 'Tush, ma'am, pray do not apologize.' His fleshy hand, draped with its linen cuff, came down on Bella's arm, lingered for a while on the firm flesh. Meeting his eye, she gave him a slow smile and then gently removed his hand.

Still holding his gaze in hers she said, 'You are a little premature, Colonel Fitzmaurice. Later, perhaps – who knows? But first – I am in need of help.'

He raised his eyebrows in a query. 'If you will tell me how I may help, ma'am?'

'I am in desperate need,' she told him in a low voice. 'There is no food in the house.'

'None?'

She shook her head, making the dark hair dance provoca-tively. 'None whatever. I . . . a woman in my forlorn position has great difficulty in securing even her modest entitlement.' She allowed her warm red lips to form a pout, her corsage to slip a little. Already she could see the reaction in the soldier's face. 'You must know how the people fight in the streets for crumbs, so bad have things become.'

'Yes, indeed I do.' Fitzmaurice frowned heavily. 'I am sorry. I had not thought. You may rest assured that I shall do whatever is possible, but you must also understand the difficulties, m'dear.'

'The difficulties?' Bella lifted an eyebrow. 'The Colonel of the 74th, confessing to – difficulties?'

Fitzmaurice looked uncomfortable and disconcerted. 'Yes, certainly,' he said. 'Er . . . a man in my position, to seem to be showing favouritism, don't you know, especially perhaps to a young widow of rank.' He coughed.

She said meaningfully, 'Difficulties exist merely to be over-come, do they not? And – if you are afraid of gossip, I, at least, am not.'

He coughed again, his face going a deeper red. 'Yes, well. Well, well. There are, naturally, always ways and means – but they are not easy, you must realize that.' He looked at her narrowly, calculatingly. 'I am sure you have heard of His Excellency's strict orders regarding the garrison rations?'

'Naturally.'

Fitzmaurice's look became almost one of pleading, but she said nothing further to help him. Frowning, he turned away and marched up and down the room in silence, hands clasped behind his bulky back, red neck bulging over his high collar. After a while he stopped and turned to face her. He asked, 'What precisely is it you want, m'dear?'

She said calmly, 'A requisition in your own hand, and signed by yourself, made upon the garrison quartermaster so that I can be supplied with a fortnight's rations in advance, in order that I shall not have to go out into the streets daily to be jostled by the mob.' Her eyes flashed with their old imperiousness. She was beginning to enjoy this. 'I have been nearly trampled underfoot by the townspeople! That is an ordeal and an indignity for a young and unprotected woman – a woman of your own regiment, Colonel Fitzmaurice, and it is up to you to see that a stop is put to it!'

'Yes, yes,' Fitzmaurice muttered. 'I quite understand that, of course. Yes – of course.' Once again he coughed, seemingly embarrassed despite the drink that was in him. 'It may be possible, it may be possible. I may be able to use my influence.'

'Which I know is very great.'

'Ahem.' There was a silence then, during which Bella, watching her man, saw the colour flooding into his face, saw the twitch of his fingers and the beat of a small muscle in his cheek. His little eyes seemed redder, more bloodshot than ever as they feasted upon the exposed flesh of her arms and décolletage . . . lowering her gaze, and bending forward just enough to reveal further the deep valley made by her taut breasts, she said, 'It is a great favour which I ask of you, I am not unaware of that. But it is one which, I assure you, need not go unrewarded . . . if you so desire, that is?'

He nodded, the heavy jowls shaking as he did so. He ran his tongue over his lips, moved towards her. His breath was coming in short, sharp jerks now and he put out a hand to caress the girl once more. This time, she let it stay, and her lips parted a little.

He said huskily, 'But – last night – I understood . . .'

'This is not last night, Colonel Fitzmaurice.'

The soldier expelled pent-up breath, and gave a long sigh. Their glances met again, and his face suffused with blood as he drew her towards him.

Laughing lightly she held herself back and there was a harder quality in her voice as she said, 'First, the requisition – the rations to be delivered to my house tomorrow morning. And there is something else. A woman, alone in a garrison such as this, needs the protection and security of – arms. So, you see, it would be as well if you wrote another requisition also, this time upon the armoury, for the provision of two pistols and the appropriate ammunition.'

'Gad! That's a lot to ask of me, m'dear!'

She shrugged. 'If you do not wish – '

'I did not say that. But cannot you use your husband's pistols?'

'I could have done,' she said sarcastically, 'had they not already been requisitioned for the garrison by one of your own officers. How either you or he had the impertinence to give or to obey such an order, I shall never know. So kindly make good your actions, Colonel Fitzmaurice, and do as I ask.'

Fitzmaurice gave her a long look; and then, mounting desire getting the better of prudence, he moved heavily across to his desk.

Later, as she submitted her young body to the clumsy embraces of the ageing officer, Bella was unable to do other than hold herself rigid and unresponsive for the most part, enduring the exploring fingers, those clutching eagle's claws, enduring the obscene fumblings of old Fitzmaurice and his brandy-sodden breath and balding head which shook with the desires that racked his near-impotent carcase. Hating what she was doing, Bella found herself at the same time glorying in a new awareness of a woman's power over men, men whose Achilles heel was hers to attack . . . whenever she should wish to do so.

Early next morning Bella took Fitzmaurice's requisitions to the garrison quartermaster and to the armoury and arranged for the food stocks to be delivered under guard by the commissariat wagon on its rounds. And that afternoon she went out of the fortress by the South Port, past the sentry who knew her well and showed no surprise that she should be going for a little exercise alone, taking the way which she had so often taken with my Lord Kilkieran so short a time before when they had walked upon the Rock. The pistols, and such of the food as she could safely carry, were well concealed beneath the skirts and petticoats whose slight extra fullness was altogether unremarked by the sentry, who was concentrating most of his attention upon those portions of the Lady Bella's body as were more seductively exposed. If she took the precaution of skirting back above the town, and re-entering the garrison by the northern end, and thus confusing the sentries' recollections of her comings and goings, she would be well able to bring up more food for her young private as occasion demanded.

An hour or so after leaving the South Port she saw, as she toiled up to the rendezvous, the redcoat ahead of her and half-concealed in the scrub. There was no sign of the corpse. She called out and a moment later the young man emerged and smiled at her shyly.

He said simply, 'The Lord be praised that you have come back, milady.'

Hot and panting, the girl drew level with him. She saw how tattered his uniform was, torn even more than before with the wild brambles, and still encrusted with blood.

For the time being, she preferred to keep off the subject of the Hanoverian's death at this young man's hands; but all the same it was very much in her mind, as was the reason why he had done it. She looked away from him, not wanting him to see the expression which she felt was in her eyes, windows of the deep feeling which had suddenly almost overwhelmed her, suddenly and astonishingly. To cover her confusion she said shortly, 'The rations. I have them with me.'

He looked at her, evidently puzzled.

'If you will have the kindness to turn your back,' she said, 'or go away, I will give them to you.'

Her voice was a little sharp and she could have sworn she saw a blush on the young soldier's face before he turned quickly away. She felt her cheeks flaming for an instant, and then she gave a low gurgle of laughter . . . really, this decorum was quite ridiculous considering the state in which this young man had seen her already – and yet, even now, it was natural for her to shrink from lifting her skirts dispassionately before a man . . . she fumbled with her clothing, and set her precious burden on the ground, and then called out to Carter to turn around.

He did so, and took a step forward, fell to his haunches to examine her offerings, gaunt cheeks covered with stubble, and flushed again, this time with a ravening appetite. His eyes feasted on goat's-milk cheese, eggs, bread and rice and some ship's hard-tack which had been landed from a blockade-runner. Then his hand went out to caress the pair of pistols which the girl had brought to him – pistols which were so much handier than a musket for a man on the run.

Softly, his eyes shining, he said, 'Milady, this is a miracle. I do not know how to thank you, and I do not know why you have done this for me.'

'I think you did rather a lot for me! But we will not talk of that now. Eat first.'

He still looked at her, gravely now. 'No one saw you come, milady?'

'No one.' She sat down on the rough ground and smoothed her dress across her lap. 'Now – eat your fill. And one thing more,' she added impulsively. 'We are going to be comrades in distress for a while, I'm thinking, so you can stop calling me milady. A man who has . . . killed for my sake shall not call me that. My name is . . .' She hesitated, but only for a moment. 'Yes, I think Bella will do very well.' She looked at him mischievously. 'And yours?'

'Carter . . . Roger Carter, ma'am, at your service.' Then he added with a curious touch of arrogance which made Bella look at him sharply, 'Private of the 74th Foot.'

She nodded. 'That much I knew, Roger.' She found she could use the name easily enough. As strong white teeth bit into a loaf of bread, Bella studied the soldier. She saw that there was a refinement in his face and bearing, remembered what she had thought about him the day before, that he was a distinct oddity for a private of foot – that his speech alone was not that of the customary run of private soldiers. There was indeed something about him that was unusual, something that spoke clearly of some intriguing story; but her curiosity would have to wait, for he was hungry.

When he had finished, and was sitting back against a big rock, and sighing his satisfaction for a full stomach, she smiled at him gently. She said, 'After the feast – sleep, Roger!' She had noted the red-rimmed eyes, the pallor of the face, the difficulty which he had, even when eating, in keeping his eyelids from falling shut. 'How long is it since you have slept, Roger?'

For some unformulated reason, she wanted to keep repeating that name.

He said, 'Two nights, mi – Lady Bella. All this while I have had to be alert for the search parties, if such should be sent out. You heard nothing in the garrison?'

'Nothing.' She thought: search parties! Perhaps I can arrange with Fitzmaurice that there will be no search parties, but then I must not rush Fitzmaurice *too* much . . .

'They may well not search,' Carter was going on, 'for they will expect me to give myself up before very long, as others have done before me. Thus the soldiers' strength will be preserved to fight against the Dons. But I have remained alert in case, and when I have dropped off the smallest crackle in the scrub has at once aroused me.'

She said almost tenderly, 'Then forget your cares, and sleep now until you are refreshed, and I shall be your sentry.'

'No, Lady Bella.' His good-looking face was strangely troubled. 'You have fed me, and now you must go back, or there will be much trouble for you.'

'Indeed,' she said shortly, 'I am not going back! At least, not yet. I shall have to return before full dark, or they may search for *me*, but later I will come back to you again. We are both in this now, Roger.'

He shook his head in puzzlement, but a moment later his eyelids, as heavy as lead weights, closed; his head drooped sideways and he was asleep under the shelter of the bushes. Bella sat there, in the open beneath the hot sun, smiling at the sleeping soldier in his bloodied, torn uniform, the uniform of her husband's beloved regiment. After a while she moved into the shade of some rock, and sat there watching Roger Carter, her unaccustomed fingers holding one of the pistols pointed down the track.

Overhead, vultures wheeled disappointedly and then flew off. There would be better pickings in the town, where already some of the older inhabitants had succumbed to starvation and their relatives too weak from hunger to bury them.

5

Four days later Bella temporarily deserted Roger Carter and remained in the fortress, for the place was agog. There were crowds of the military along the Line Wall, infantry and artillery, Highlanders and engineers – all, indeed, who were not presently required for duty. There was a handful of down-at-heel civilians, men and women, scraggy, half-starved, verminous, stinking, to bring a sombre note to the still-colourful soldiery, civilians who shook with fear but who had been drawn from their holes and hovels in the bombarded town by some force stronger than themselves, some force which had driven them to witness what promised to be a great and inspiring spectacle.

For Lord Rodney's fleet was wearing into Algeciras Bay.

The ships were rounding Europa Point past which, a couple of days earlier, they had been driven on the current. In the glare of vivid lightning, the wind had failed them suddenly off the Rock as they were approaching through the Strait from the westward.

Now, under the hot Mediterranean sun, the great ships came in, the English sail of the line nosing into the bay under a spread of canvas gleaming white in the harsh sunlight, pushing the still, blue water into foam which creamed up below the great figureheads to sweep aft along the sides of the ships, below the open gunports where, as the Fleet came nearer, the noses of the cannon could be seen, and behind them the sweating, half-naked seamen gunners who stood by along the gundecks ready to rake the Spanish shore or any foolhardy Spanish ship which might stand across to intercept them, and to watch the big ropes which would check the cannons' recoil before they loaded again. The enormous line-of-battle ships, the seventy-fours with their towering bulwarks, and the smaller frigates stood guard over fat-bellied, deep-laden merchantmen from England and the Spaniards which Lord Rodney had seized off Finisterre while on his way to relieve the garrison.

As a breeze took the convoy and carried some of the ships to the westward until they were almost under the shore batteries of the enemy, the watchers on the Line Wall heard the distant tattoo of the drums. Bella, who had gone down alone to watch the entry of the Fleet, and was now standing wedged in between the soldiers, asked a sergeant of artillery what the drums intended.

He said, 'It's the Dons beating to arms, me lady.'

'They mean to open on the Fleet?'

'That'll be so, me lady.'

Bella felt her heart constrict with fear for the sailors; she, along with all the others, had seen the results of the spasmodic Spanish fire into the town, but those big ships, those wooden walls, were so vulnerable, so much nearer the coastal batteries now . . . as she was about to speak again to the sergeant she saw a line of white puffs appearing beneath San Roque. These were followed almost at once by a series of explosions. Great spouts of water leaped up from the sea alongside the British ships, flinging spray over their decks and lower yards.

The sergeant shouted, 'There's one of the seventy-fours hit!'

There was a groan from the crowd as the ship of the line, His Majesty's Ship *Redoubtable*, swung over to starboard, seemingly out of control. Her mainmast seemed to lurch drunkenly and a moment later fell, bringing down a tangle of rigging and smashed yards, and torn, flapping sails. Bella could imagine the confusion on her upper deck. The ship fell out of line, swinging right round to threaten the safety of the remainder of the convoy. A little after, one of the frigates was seen to be manoeuvring to her assistance.

Every gun along the enemy shore seemed to have opened on Lord Rodney's ships, but the gunners aboard the Fleet were giving back shot for shot, and Bella saw the intermittent blaze of fire which indicated that an English broadside had found its marks on the guns of Spain, dotted around the coast and in the cork woods beyond.

Under cover of their tiers of cannon, the Fleet drew slowly clear. *Redoubtable*, whose mainmast tangle had now been hacked away with the axes, was under control once again and sailing in under such sail as she could still carry, her guns firing bravely. As the ships came in towards the New Mole to anchor off the fortress, Bella found herself cheering madly – though she was only too well aware that Rodney's arrival could mean her own departure shortly – cheering with the soldiers who were flinging their head-dresses into the air and roaring a heartfelt welcome to the relieving force.

And that afternoon the garrison itself was strengthened: The 73rd Regiment, under orders for Minorca, was detained on the personal command of His Excellency of Gibraltar, and disembarked from on board the Fleet. Bella found herself watching with mixed feelings but with a decided lump in her pretty throat as the regimental drummers beat along the Water Port and a fine-looking body of men with full stomachs marched away with gleaming bayonets to take up their billets.

She had wondered whether or not it would be decorous for her to attend the austere reception which was to be given by His Excellency in honour of Admiral Lord Rodney. After all, she had only just lost her husband; widows were accustomed and expected to remain in their weeds – and their homes – for at least twelve months after their bereavement. Kilkieran, however, would have laughed aloud at any such notion. Indeed, during his lifetime he frequently had done so, calling it morbid folly and a public parade of private grief. He, of all people, would never expect Bella to remain in purdah on his account. And Bella, for her part, had no desire to do so; she was too young, too passionate and vital for that. She was too fond of life and she cared nothing for what people might say; the wagging tongues of a small and parochial garrison community held no fears for her. So she decided to go. She wouldn't be the only woman there; except for the local population (who of course wouldn't be asked) there were few women indeed left in the garrison, but those that were would be sure to put in an appearance at this, the first slight relaxation into some semblance of a social life that had been permitted since the so-far-off-seeming evening when the Land Port had been shut against the enemy.

The reception, Bella found when she arrived, was a very muted, utilitarian affair compared with the glittering gatherings of the past, the great parties held on State occasions or when visiting British or foreign diplomats had been royally entertained at His Excellency's residence. Then the scene had been one of opulence and splendour; of handsome officers in their varied mess uniforms, peacocks who vied with the ladies for the beholder's eye; of many servants moving about discreetly as they ministered to the needs of thirsty gentlemen; of military string bands playing softly in candle-lit rooms or moon-filled gardens, and of young officers jostling one another to obtain the favour of a glance from the Lady Bella – until the arrogant, commanding figure of my Lord Kilkieran put a stop to their presumption with a single look.

This evening it was more than austere. It was frugal in the extreme. There was little indeed to drink beyond what Rodney and his officers had themselves brought to His Excellency – and nothing at all to eat. With his garrison pulling in the buckles on their belts, and his civilians queuing for bread and rice, with the very horses slaughtered to provide meat, General Eliott would not indulge either himself or his officers in any degree whatsoever.

Bella nodded at one or two of the officers, met the raised eyebrows of their ladies. She accepted their condolences, their pointed condolences, on her recent loss, and then she moved away on the arm of Colonel Fitzmaurice, who had escorted her. After a while, when Fitzmaurice had become engaged in conversation with a fellow colonel, Bella smiled provocatively at a tall young man with deep-set eyes, a man in the uniform of a lieutenant in His Majesty's Fleet.

He returned the smile boldly.

With a demure look she said, 'Welcome, sir, to our wretched garrison. Sure, I watched your ships enter this morning from the Line Wall . . . we were all praying for your success, I do assure you!'

'Then, ma'am, rest assured that your prayers were

answered.' The lieutenant gave a slight, stiff bow. 'I trust they will accompany us when we sail again.'

'And when will that be – so that I shall know when to start interceding with Almighty God?'

He said, 'In three days' time, and for England.'

'To return here with another convoy?'

He shrugged, smiled. 'Who knows, ma'am? Such decisions are in the hands of my Lords Commissioners.'

'Of course.' She hesitated, changed her tack as if quite inconsequentially. 'Tell me, if you will. Were many of your men lost in the action today?'

He nodded sombrely. 'Twenty, ma'am. Twenty good English seamen dead, and thirty-seven wounded sorely, most of them aboard the *Redoubtable.*'

'And the ship herself?'

'She will be ready for sea at the same time as the rest of our Fleet. It is merely a question of repairing the mast and the rigging, and our shipwrights and sailmakers are even now hard at work, with assistance from the Yard here.'

'I see.' Bella played with her fan. 'So she will be sailing home short-handed?'

The naval officer shrugged again. 'Unless we press some men while we are here, ma'am – though God knows, there will be few enough available for the press who are worth the pressing! Your locals will not amount to much.'

'I see . . .' Bella looked away, using her fan to shield her face from the lieutenant, for she did not wish him to see her expression. Across the room she saw Fitzmaurice, talking to a naval captain and the Governor's aide-de-camp, the Highlander Frazer, as dour and gloomy as ever, knees knobbly below the kilt. Fitzmaurice's red, bulbous face was wet with sweat which he kept wiping away with a vast blue handkerchief, only to allow more beads to gather. Sweat had darkened the high collar of his uniform coat and he had the look about him which spoke of much brandy having been consumed. Either his private store was inexhaustible or he had been royally entertained aboard the Fleet that afternoon . . . after a few more polite words with the young naval officer, Bella excused herself and moved away towards

Fitzmaurice, who broke off his conversation to introduce his companion to her.

'Sir Edward Grenville, m'dear,' he said pompously, mopping again at his face, 'whose brother is Major-General on the staff of His Royal Highness the Commander-in-Chief himself.' This was said as though Fitzmaurice was speaking of the Almighty.

'Indeed?' Bella gave a curtsey, was immediately aware of Sir Edward's penetrating greenish eyes on her breasts, of a sudden pulse in his neck as he pulled at his high-bridged nose as though to hide a sudden quickening of his interest. She also noted that the ADC was not unaware of the naval officer's reaction to her and had gone gloomier and more silent than ever. She went on, 'I have met the Commander-in-Chief, Sir Edward – when my husband was given his orders to bring the 74th out to this garrison. Indeed, I think it likely that my husband and your brother were acquainted.'

Grenville inclined his head. 'May I offer you my deepest sympathy, Lady Kilkieran?' he said gently in a deep voice. 'England has lost a fine soldier. I have indeed heard my brother speak of him, and speak highly. If you will allow me to say so, I feel it an honour that my ship has been chosen to take you home to England.'

Bella stiffened, stared back at Grenville. Two bright spots of colour showed in her cheeks. She said hotly, 'Then it is an honour of which I have not been informed, Sir Edward, and one which you would enjoy only if I intended to board your ship, which I do not!'

The ADC glowered dourly at that; Grenville looked at her in surprise, but there was a twinkle in his eye. He said, 'My dear Lady Kilkieran, I had indeed heard that you wished to remain in the garrison – and that shows courage in a woman. But I would be interested to hear you tell me why this is so?'

'My husband's post was here. I think you will understand . . . there has been a Kilkieran with the 74th since the regiment was raised. I intend that there shall be one here – when the siege itself is raised.'

Grenville nodded. Fitzmaurice dabbed again at his face and said peevishly, 'But m'dear, you must forgive me. This is nonsense. His Excellency – '

'The devil take His Excellency!' she cried, stamping her foot and taking no notice whatever of the horrified anger in the ADC's face. 'General Eliott is not the the arbiter of *my* destiny, Colonel Fitzmaurice, whether or not he commands the garrison of Gibraltar!'

Grenville chuckled and glanced swiftly at Fitzmaurice's dismayed face. 'You have a fine spirit, ma'am,' he said with some approval. 'And yet, I fear, it is His Excellency who has the power.'

She retorted crisply, 'There are other things which shape our lives besides the words of general officers, Sir Edward.' She turned to Fitzmaurice then, and laid a hand on his arm. 'A word in your ear, Colonel Fitzmaurice,' she said calmly. 'Come!' When the soldier seemed to hesitate she gave his arm a gentle pressure and looked at him with meaning.

A gleam – somewhat of puzzlement, somewhat of sudden but cautious passion – came into Fitzmaurice's eye and he bowed. 'As you wish, m'dear.' He turned to the others, pompously. 'If you will be good enough to excuse us, gentlemen. . . ?'

'Of course. I shall be delighted to make the lady's acquaintance again shortly – aboard my ship. For I fear, Lady Kilkieran, that His Excellency's will must in the end prevail. And I repeat, I shall hold it an honour to have you aboard.' Grenville's tone held all the meaning in the world but his eyelids were lowered as he bent over Bella's hand and held it tightly to his lips for a brief but vital moment.

She said mockingly, 'You are very kind, sir, and I shall be sorry to deny you the pleasure. Come, Colonel Fitzmaurice.'

She turned away and walked ahead of the soldier through the groups of naval and military officers and those few women – the women who, she could sense, were already beginning to talk about her. She made for the hall and the french windows into His Excellency's once well-kept garden. The night was hot and still, sultry, filled with the heady scents of the night flowers which still survived despite the lack of water – the precious water which had had for months past to be preserved for the exclusive use of the humans and those few animals which remained upon the Rock. There was a bright moon almost overhead, and the sky was thick, luminous, with stars that seemed to hang so low, so closely overhead, that Bella felt she could almost have reached up and brought them down from heaven . . . she led the wheezy Fitzmaurice over to a low wall from where one could look across the bay, past the great ships at anchor, towards the enemy lines along the coast, the lines where the enemy watch was being maintained upon Gibraltar, the great gun-batteries and the guardposts manned continuously, night and day.

Bella stopped by this wall, feeling a gentle breeze play lightly on her cheek. Fitzmaurice came up beside her, hot and perspiring and breathing hard, stinking of stale brandy. He reached out and put a heated, shaky hand on her flesh, slid his fingers up her arm.

She moved away from him. She said distantly, 'La! I think you presume a little too much, Colonel Fitzmaurice. It is not for that, that I asked you to come out here.' She was smiling a little in the moonlight – smiling coldly, knowingly.

He stammered, looking more than a trifle ridiculous. 'But – last night, my dear girl – '

'Was last night, and will not be repeated.'

'But – ' Clearly, he could not accustom himself to her whirlwind changes of heart.

'There are no buts, Colonel Fitzmaurice, and do not, I pray you, think of taking me by force. Remember that we are in His Excellency's garden. I have only to scream, and it will be you who is shipped to England – disgraced and broken.' Her eyes glimmered with amusement in the semi-darkness as she felt the surge of rage and frustration in the middle-aged officer's thickened body. Then she said more softly, 'That is . . . except, perhaps, on certain terms.'

He drew in his breath sharply and she saw the whites of his eyes, dulled now with brandy. 'And – those terms?' he asked in a croaking voice.

She tapped him lightly with her fan; it was a playful gesture, but her voice was sharp and incisive. 'See to it – yourself personally – that I remain in garrison with my husband's regiment, Colonel Fitzmaurice! That I am determined to do, and to that end I am willing to pay the price which I know will satisfy you. If you inform His Excellency that you will be responsible for me, that you will watch over me like a father . . . I believe he will feel easy enough in his mind about my remaining here. After all, I feel certain that he is very sensible of the undoubted dangers of a sea passage out of the garrison – with the Dons waiting for every English sail. He may discover a use for a woman, to tend the wounded . . . you could even make that point to him. He may well consider that the new Colonel of the 74th would behave more chivalrously towards the widow of Lord Kilkieran than would the Dons . . . even though both you and I know very well that the new Colonel would behave in no such way at all.'

'Ha-hrrmph.'

She gave a low gurgle of laughter. 'You may well make such a sound! I know quite well what is in your mind, and mine also for that matter. I would keep my side of the bargain, you may be sure. Well? You will agree?'

'I shall do my utmost, my dear Bella. But – it occurs to me that His Excellency . . .'

'May already have word of your reputation, which will have gone before you? Almost certainly he will, dear William! But he also knows quite well that I am capable of looking after myself should I be unwilling, and that it is my own affair if I *am* willing. He will be concerned only that I have a protector. You understand?'

'Yes, I – '

'Good!' She was conscious of a surge of triumph and joy, but she had not finished yet with her demands on Fitzmaurice. She went on, 'But there is one further condition, William, which I shall also insist upon.'

He moved restlessly. 'Go on.'

'It concerns Private Roger Carter of the regiment – '

'Who deserted the Middle Hill guard on – '

'Who did not desert from any guard, William!' she said hotly. She felt her heart flutter, not fully understanding herself why the mere thought of a humble private of foot should make her feel as she did. She had been with him in spirit, with him out there on the unfriendly rock, ever since her last visit to him. 'Oh, I'm sure you genuinely believe he did, but I assure you he did *not*, and his only desire is to be allowed to serve his king and country as he has undertaken to do. He was forced at musket-point to desert by a sergeant of Hardenburg's Hanoverians – a sergeant whom he has killed in – in the execution of his undoubted duty to apprehend a deserter. I happen to know where Private Carter is, and also that he fears to return to the garrison in case he should be charged with desertion and possibly with murder.'

Fitzmaurice's mouth was opening and closing like a fish. He gasped, 'My dear girl . . . how is it that you know all this? I – '

'I shall say no more. You must accept what I say, and do as I wish.'

'And you wish – '

'I wish,' she said with determination, 'to save the life of Private Carter. And this will be up to you – to arrange, William, either for him to be anonymously pressed for Lord Rodney's fleet in the room of one of the unfortunate seamen who were killed this morning when His Lordship entered – or for him to be received back into the 74th as a man who has done his duty. You would be well able to arrange either of these alternatives, and I suggest the latter as being much the more appropriate of the two. It is simpler . . . and Private Carter has not the look of a sailor at all!'

Fitzmaurice spluttered. 'My dearest Bella, I cannot possibly promise any such thing – I must investigate the facts first. I must speak to my adjutant, and the man's company commander. I should possibly need to consult His Excellency. I – '

'I want an unconditional assurance, William. There will be no investigation. You cannot decry the power of colonels to me, dear William. And you are gentleman enough not to break your word once you have given it, that I know.'

'Thank you.' The soldier's tone was stiff. 'And if I do not? You will not then consent to become my – my – '

'Your mistress. No, William,' she replied vigorously, her eye full of mischief, for she realized now that she had won. 'I shall not, but much more important to your career, I shall scream! Remember, *I* was not born a lady. My father was a common farmer and my mother was said to have been a whore. I can make up a story,' she went on with relish, 'that will curl His Excellency's wig! Well, William?'

6

Captain Andrew Frazer, His Excellency's aide-de-camp, was in a black mood – a black mood for which Lady Kilkieran had been entirely and directly responsible. The ADC's long, dark face had glowered the moment he saw her – though his body was telling him unmistakably that her nearness was extremely disturbing, not to say desirable, to him. It was her tongue, however, not her body, that Frazer was presently the more conscious of. The Lady Bella, coming as she did from peasant stock, had a sharp tongue, a tongue that at times could be extremely coarse. And this morning she had laid that tongue, with devilish accuracy, upon a sore spot. She had come in obedience to a summons from His Excellency, and she had started off as bluntly as the ADC had learned to expect of her.

She had said, 'Captain Frazer, notwithstanding Colonel Fitzmaurice's assurances and the fact that I could make myself of use in tending the sick, if sickness comes as come it must – notwithstanding this, I take it you have already advised His Excellency against allowing me to remain in the garrison?'

He had been shaken by that forthright statement, which in point of fact had been entirely accurate; but he did not believe he had shown it. He said cautiously, 'His Excellency will, no doubt, arrive at his own conclusions, ma'am. I confess that it is my private view that *all* women should leave the garrison when opportunity offers.'

'So that the officers should not be troubled by thoughts unbecoming to gentlemen?' She smiled coldly, arrogantly. 'Hoity-toity, Captain Frazer! That is a coward's way out. But I take it you refer more particularly to me than to anyone else.'

He raised his eyebrows, swung his kilt angrily. 'Tush, ma'am! Why so?'

Her manner had changed then. A flash of sudden anger had

come into her eyes and her hands had gone to her hips. No longer the colonel's widow, she had become the Irish peasant once again. 'Because,' she said loudly and with deliberate scorn, 'because 'tis myself that troubles you more than any other woman, Captain Frazer, and once you've got rid of me you'll no longer be troubled by those desires of yours . . . the desires you aren't man enough to fulfil!' Frazer flushed at the injustice of this statement, remembering keenly her repulse of his advances months before. She went on, 'You want to bed with me, och, I know that well! But you dare not, even now I have no husband to protect me, in case His Excellency should make objections. What real man allows his desires to be curbed by an Excellency, I should like to know? Not that I would have bedded with you had you been the last man left in the whole garrison . . . and *that* you have known too, have you not, and because of it have always been my enemy, Captain Frazer. But you will see!' She tossed her head, 'I shall remain here to keep your thoughts awake.'

Frazer, his face pale with fury at this somewhat contradictory but reasonably accurate tirade, had snapped, 'Lady Kilkieran, I demand your apology – '

'You'll get no such thing out of me, I assure you, Captain Frazer.'

The ADC held onto his temper with difficulty. When he spoke his voice was tense but low: 'You will do well to have a care, ma'am. I shall not forget what you have said.'

When she calmed down, she had been somewhat scared lest she might have proved her own prosecutor; but she had no personal fear of Captain Andrew Frazer, and in the end His Excellency had acceded to her request to be allowed to remain – and had informed her, to her joy, that Private Carter had been contacted under a flag of truce and had already rejoined his regiment in full honour. Fitzmaurice, she thought with secret amusement, must indeed be avid for his reward. He could scarcely have carried out his part of the bargain with more despatch!

Fitzmaurice said pettishly one morning, 'This damned salt cod! Y'know the scurvy's started, I suppose?'

Bella turned away from the window, where she had been looking out at the heat-haze shimmering the distant Spanish hills. 'Yes, William, I did. Is it really bad?'

'Bad enough,' he grumbled, mopping at his face. 'No damned vegetables, and the salt cod from that Newfoundland ship most damnably persistent! The regiment had a long Sick Parade this morning, I can tell you. The captains report their companies badly depleted. Ah, well.' He sighed, and dropped heavily onto a chair, fanning himself vigorously with his tricorne hat. His collar stood open, revealing black hairs curling below a thickly bulging neck. Like one of the Rock apes, Bella thought disgustedly. She had become revolted by him over the long weeks. 'Those of us who survive the enemy fire will be so weak that we shall be moving about on crutches before long, m'dear, to support ourselves to our duty.'

She nodded and left the window. As she moved she passed a long looking-glass, and glanced critically sideways. She thought, I'm certainly slim enough, but I'm ageing in this climate and with this hunger gnawing constantly at one's entrails it's no wonder . . . her mind went back over the past weeks, the weeks which had lengthened into months now, since Lord Rodney's fleet had sailed for England without her. Daily things had grown worse in the fortress. Rodney's fleet had replenished the food stores, certainly – but in spite of His Excellency having maintained the ration at full stringency, they had all too soon emptied again – apart from the interminable salt cod which had sickened the whole garrison. If this accursed siege, which had now lasted well over a year, went on much longer . . . but that scarcely bore thinking of! The Spaniards had shown no signs of having relinquished any of their intentions as a result of the successful arrival of that relieving force, indeed more men had been moved into their lines from time to time. Certainly their guns had remained silent of late, and no one knew the reason for this – but no one doubted that they would open again one day. There had been much sickness in the garrison apart from the scurvy, and Bella had had her hands full. She must, she had insisted, take her share of the work. She would not be an idler, a parasitic mouth to be fed, and besides that, she had promised His Excellency she would make herself useful. She had not enjoyed the work, going about the stinking hovels where the civilians lived, or around the barrack-rooms and camps where the military sick lay on their palliasses, some of them vomiting, some of them gangrenous from wounds received earlier and improperly cared for by the overworked surgeons and surgeons' mates. She hadn't liked it but she had stuck to it and had indeed become an angel of mercy. His Excellency himself had been warm in his praise of her and there had been no more talk of sending her home, in spite of the arrival and departure of a handful of blockade-runners in the months since Lord Rodney had sailed away.

Turning now from the looking-glass she caught Fitzmaurice's meaning eye and sighed. Despite the short commons – admittedly only comparative in Fitzmaurice's household – the terrible privations, even the lack of brandy now, one thing had never altered or suffered in any way: Fitzmaurice's appetite for her body. Despite bouts of impotence which, when they occurred, maddened him, this appetite had never dimmed, and she knew very well what he wanted at this instant. That afternoon and night he would be on duty, riding round the many outposts, maintaining at command level the vigilance of the fortress. He had to take his opportunities when he could; these were frequent enough in all conscience and Bella had sickened of him. Those coarse hands roaming her white body, exploring, gripping, the hot breath rasping in his throat, the thick body pressed urgently against her flesh . . . they revolted her, gave her a sense of nausea. Nevertheless, she had entered into a bargain and she must play her part in that bargain however much she might detest it; so she sighed again and nodded and went through into her bedroom. Some while ago now she had given up the old quarter, handing it on to the Colonel of the 73rd who was senior to Fitzmaurice, and had herself moved into Fitzmaurice's own household. Here, at any rate as far as His Excellency and garrison convention was concerned, she was amply chaperoned by Fitzmaurice's soldier servant and his housekeeper, an elderly local woman who was as deaf as a post and in fact spent, as it seemed, most of her time sleeping.

Afterwards, Fitzmaurice resumed his uniform to go down to Hargrave's Barracks and before he went he said officiously, 'By the way, m'dear. I've arranged the usual detail to escort you shopping this afternoon. You'll – um – be interested to know who's been detailed this time.'

'Yes, William?'

'Private Carter.' He laughed. 'Your precious deserter.'

'Who did not desert . . . indeed, I well remember him, William!' Her heart gave a curious lurch. 'But why – why him?'

'Why not? Someone has to do the duty, and it is his turn, as decided by his sergeant.' Fitzmaurice was too preoccupied, too sated with his recent and successful love-making, to bother about the topic any further. As he took his leave Bella found a strange thrill running through her body at the thought of the young private. He had been a well-set-up man, tall and straight – and very good looking. Shy possibly – but manly and honest certainly. There was something very intriguing about him, too, and, being honest with herself, Bella realized that she had indeed thought too much about him on and off during recent months. After rejoining his regiment, he had attended upon her to express his thanks and gratitude personally for her intervention, and many times she had seen him marching to and from the Devil's Tower, which was still manned by the 74th, or at work with his comrades helping to restore some of the shattered masonry in the town, the result of the earlier bombardments. She did not think he had seen her, but she had taken more than a passing interest in him, and had found herself wanting more and more to have a chance of speaking to him again. This, she told herself now, was no more than natural – considering what he had done for her and also what she had done for him! Indeed, she thought with distaste as Fitzmaurice came into her mind, she had paid a heavy price for his life and would go on paying it indefinitely so far as she could see . . . at least until this siege was lifted. Fortunately Fitzmaurice had a wife in England; had that not been so, Bella felt that he would have badgered her into marriage and that would have been a prospect not to be contemplated on any account. Better by far to leap from

Windmill Hill, or from the embrasures of the Grand Battery into the Land Port ditch, as had one or two genuine deserters in their vain attempts to get away from the fortress . . .

Bella wandered into her dressing-room and began to brush her hair with long, slow strokes. There was a curious light in her eyes and she looked very much more alive than she had looked for weeks. Fitzmaurice had begun to make her feel like an old, old woman.

7

He was the same as she remembered him that day so long ago outside the town. Still shy, still diffident, still handsome and upstanding and manly, though with older lines on his face and as thin now as the rest of the garrison except Fitzmaurice – so thin that his elbows stuck sharply from the ragged holes in his uniform, the uniform itself hanging upon him like a sack. But she responded at once to his youth, felt herself blossoming into life like a flower too long under grey skies, felt the desire to be pleasing to a man rather than merely compliant.

He said stiffly and formally, as though he had determined not to be other than entirely impersonal, 'My lady, I am ordered by my sergeant to report to you for duty.'

'So I have been informed, Private Carter,' she said with an inward smile at the young man's gauche awkwardness. She added coquettishly, 'What experience have you, pray, of escorting ladies on shopping expeditions?'

He hesitated for a moment, looking straight ahead over her shoulder. There was a brief glint of merriment in his eye and then he flushed. He said, his face wooden again, 'Very little, my lady.'

'Other than, perhaps, your mother or sister?'

'Yes, my lady.'

'You have no girl at home, Private Carter?'

'None.'

His reply was so quick, so unstudied and natural, that she knew he was telling the simple truth; and, though it seemed a curious truth for so personable a young man, Bella felt a funny little flutter of gladness. She looked again at the soldier, who was still standing rigidly at attention, a shaft of late afternoon sunlight touching up that deplorable red coat. She was as convinced as ever that this was no ordinary private of foot. He had none of the customary look of the men who took the King's shilling, of the heavy, bovine yokels drummed up from the villages of England by the recruiting sergeants and the military bands with their specious promises of glamour and glory. And yet at the same time he had somehow the look of a young man who had led a disciplined life, and a sternly disciplined life at that. If he wasn't a smocked yokel, then he certainly was no pale-faced clerk either. Indeed he had the carriage, the manner, of a gentleman, and he spoke like one also. It was all very intriguing and Bella longed, with a woman's curiosity, to get to the bottom of it; but she sensed that whatever it was, he did not mean to talk about it to her or anyone else. He was a reserved young man and he would never let her into his life – at least, she told herself with a degree of hope, not until they knew one another a great deal better than they did at present.

And all at once, biting her lip, she determined that they were indeed going to get to know one another better . . .

She said, 'I am ready to leave now for the market.'

He bowed. 'As you wish, my lady.'

'You know what is required of you?'

'To act as your escort.'

'And carry home the fish,' she said airily. 'That will not be so pleasant, I'll warrant! I warn you, it smells.'

He didn't smile; he stood aside as she went to the door. As she passed by him she brushed close to his body, provocatively, sensed the shiver that ran through him like a wave, an involuntary movement of his sinews. She hesitated for a fraction of time and then went on. Carter followed her. They went out into the street, making for the free market in Irish Town, just inside the Land Port; the market where they would be able to buy little beyond that wretched salt cod, and other fish if they were lucky, and a few handfuls of rice, to eke out the official ration. Hot overhead, the sun blazed down upon them, raising the sickening smells of dirt and decay from the sand-coloured buildings, so many of them nothing now but heaps of rubble and the ones that were standing showing cracks in the masonry, and flaking plaster which left great bare patches. They pressed on along the dusty, filth-littered streets, past the morose, bone-thin inhabitants of the town. Distantly they could hear the Spanish drums beating out a tattoo to convey some order, and once a bugle blared out, savage and triumphant, echoing off the Andalusian hills behind San Roque. Roger Carter kept one pace in rear of Bella and slightly to her right, as befitted a soldier attendant upon his Colonel's protégée; and Bella, not wishing to risk the possibility of embarrassing him just yet, kept silent, though she would dearly have liked the young man by her side; indeed nothing would have pleased her more than to feel him striding proprietorially along with her where Fitzmaurice would have waddled pompously and fussily.

Reaching the market, feeling her heart beating much more rapidly and pleasurably than was customary on these expeditions, Bella made such purchases as she was able, and Roger Carter carried the smelly basket of fish which she bought, the scaly wickerwork bumping against the tattered tails of his uniform coat and the stink rising to his nostrils.

'The Colonel,' she said after they had returned to Fitz-maurice's quarter, 'will not be at home tonight.' She spoke off-handedly, on impulse, though her heart was still drumming against her ribs.

'No, my lady.' There was tension in Roger too. 'I . . . am aware of that.'

She gave a little sigh and studied him with some amuse-ment. 'Tell me,' she asked suddenly, sitting down so that he could see her ankles beneath the dress, and the slim legs, 'you will obviously remember how last we met? I do not refer to the visit which you paid me to thank me for what little I had been able to do on your behalf . . . but to that earlier occasion . . .'

He said stiffly, flushing as he recalled what the Hanoverian sergeant had done to her that day, 'It was a very great deal you did for me . . . and yes, I remember, my lady.'

'I embarrass you?' She laughed, lightly. 'For that I apolo-gize, but pray do not be embarrassed, Roger. I am not! What I intended to ask you was this: Do you remember that I asked you not to address me as "my lady" on that occasion, Roger?'

'I do, but – '

'There are no "buts", she said quietly and sincerely. 'My name is Bella. I should like you to use it, and to use it unadorned, if it please you. I shall be hurt,' she added, 'if you do not.'

He protested, 'I am a mere private of foot. It is not fitting – '

'It would, perhaps, not be fitting if Colonel Fitzmaurice were to overhear,' she said slyly. 'Otherwise it is very fitting. Tush, Roger! I am a lady only by marriage, not by birth. You, if I mistake not, were born a gentleman – and are living presently in a low degree only by reason of your marriage to the army. Am I right?'

'I have nothing to say about that. I'm sorry.' His voice had hardened and he had gone pale. 'I would prefer not to discuss such things.'

'Very well,' she said, laughing. 'A bargain, Roger! I shall say no more if you will be sensible and call me Bella. And . . . remain here with me a little longer. Do you agree to that?'

He started a little; but he looked down into her animated, vivid face and his own features relaxed. He smiled and said, 'Yes, I agree. Bella . . . it is such a pretty name.'

'Thank you, sir!' She got to her feet agilely and gave a mock curtsey, her cheeks dimpling and eyes alight with fun. 'And how long, pray, will you stay with me, Roger?'

The invitation was obvious. Roger didn't answer at once; then he said slowly, 'I am not required for duty before midnight, when my platoon takes over the Devil's Tower guard.'

'The Devil's Tower . . .' That spot held memories for her and for a while she was silent, thinking of Kilkieran and easy, gracious days. How different such a man had been from the gross, over-importunate Fitzmaurice. Almost Kilkieran had been an older image of Roger Carter – what Roger Carter would be in thirty-odd years time, perhaps. She roused herself from useless reverie and asked, 'Roger, what is life like in the garrison, for such as you?'

'For a private soldier?' He shrugged. 'Hard enough, in all conscience – but bearable until we attain victory.'

'Hard for you particularly?' she asked, still probing.

'For us all, La – Bella, for us all. Yet there are few real complaints, except from the shirkers – and the handful of men who have tried to desert.'

'You have faith in His Excellency?'

'Absolute faith,' he said with conviction. 'All of us have.'

She sighed. 'You're lucky, Roger. Lucky to have someone whom you can have such faith in.'

'You do not feel the same way about General Eliott, then?' His handsome face, his eyes, suddenly became withdrawn.

'Oh, yes,' she said, and meant it wholeheartedly. 'I do, of course. But Roger, a woman . . . oh, never mind. I doubt if you would understand if I tried to tell you what I meant.' She shook her shoulders as if impatient, and turned away. She crossed to a window and looked out towards the Line Wall and behind it to where, fairly recently, the Spanish had stationed chains of small cruisers across the entrance to Algeciras Bay, cruisers whose job it was to keep off any blockade-runners who made the attempt to enter. They had been remarkably successful; since their appearance in those deep blue waters, nothing whatever had entered the Water Port. It was all so hopeless, she thought drearily, they were to have to live out all their lives in this stifling, negative business of mere existence. Yet she still would not have been elsewhere than in Gibraltar at this moment of history . . .

Suddenly she became aware of Roger Carter behind her and she half-turned and looked into his eyes. She gave a low gasp at what she saw there. It was naked desire, desire for a beautiful woman which gave his features, not the twist which the same desire gave to Fitzmaurice, but a mature glow of determination, of male strength and virility. It was gone in a moment, and she saw him trying to find the words of apology for what had been a momentary weakening, a self-revelation of his innermost feelings.

Tears trembled beneath her eyelids and she felt a yearning in the pit of her stomach. She put out a hand and touched his cheek. She said very, very softly and unsteadily, 'Roger, I didn't know . . . I didn't know.'

'Bella, I – '

'No, please. Please don't go on. This is so precious. This

moment . . .' She turned away, went past his outstretched arms, went out of the room and across the small landing to her bed-chamber. Her heart was thudding, thudding painfully, and she felt stifled, then suddenly cold, and found that she was trembling violently. After a while she called out to Roger and he came to her, hesitantly, slowly, as if unwilling yet obviously eager, and with a great hunger in his eyes and a great tenderness in his arms as he held her close to his body.

8

Bella felt that her body was on fire, was being consumed by flames of passion which would never burn themselves out. Private Carter knew how to make love, how to bring out her deepest desires; he was instinctively in tune with Bella, understood her needs and gently ministered to them. Afterwards, as she lay there with her eyes closed, still lost in a wonderful experience, feeling his kisses on her lids, her hair, her breasts, she was overcome with tenderness and love for this young soldier of whom she knew nothing. She knew that she was going to have to see more of Roger Carter, that she would henceforward be quite unable to exist without him now that she had once given herself to him.

After a while he roused himself. He murmured gently, 'Bella my love, I must leave you. I must report back to the barracks.'

'Oh, my dearest . . .' She held fast to him, not letting him go. With immense tenderness he freed himself and stood up, then bent again and kissed her, running his lips along her body.

Next day – after a night of unexpected gunfire during which an English ship-of-the-line broke through the Spanish cordon and entered – there was a hanging.

It was published in Daily Orders that a sergeant of the 12th Regiment of Foot had attempted to jump over the Line Wall into the sea and swim across the bay for the Spanish shore. It was a mad endeavour and though the sergeant had jumped successfully enough he had been taken in the shoulder by a ball from a musket and had then been brought back and handed over to an armed guard and a surgeon's mate by two strong swimmers who had dived from the Line Wall.

It was further published in Orders that His Excellency required the attendance of every person in the garrison, the women as well as the men, at the public hanging which was to be held at eleven o'clock that very morning on Red Sands.

Bella said, '*Must* I go, William?'

Fitzmaurice nodded, his heavy jowls sagging over his collar and his face tired from a night's duty. 'The Orders are perfectly clear. There are no exceptions, m'dear, none at all, except for the seriously sick and those on duty elsewhere.'

'But – *Why?* Why the women?'

The Colonel shrugged. 'To discourage the others by making a very public shame of it. Men do not like humiliation before women. There have been too many desertions. If a public example is not made, we shall lose half the damned garrison, Bella.'

So shortly before eleven o'clock Bella went to Red Sands, and stood among the silent, overawed crowd of spectators being marshalled by a corporal's guard at the northern end of the great arena in rear of the paraded troops. The regiments and batteries were drawn up along three sides of a square and, a separate entity within, the deserter's own regiment was drawn up in hollow square around a makeshift gallows where a commissariat wagon was standing. When all the regiments were in position the arrival of His Excellency and the staff was heralded by the General Salute. Eliott and his officers took up their positions on a raised wooden platform. Then, at a signal from the Fortress Commander, muffled drums, wrapped in black cloth, began beating out the Dead March and the prisoner, who was in full uniform, was ordered forward under escort and marched right along the assembled ranks of his regiment, with his hands tied behind his back. Bella looked on with growing anguish and horror, feeling that all this must be some terrible dream, a fantasy of extended cruelty of which she would never until this moment have believed His Excellency to be capable – though she was forced to admit he had to take a strong line, as Fitzmaurice had suggested. The sergeant was a youngish man, little more than thirty, a strong-looking man and handsome, and he was carrying himself proudly, even arrogantly, as though utterly scornful of his tormentors. When he had been paraded he was led towards the gallows and halted beside what Bella now saw was a coffin, his own coffin ready open upon the ground. The Regimental Sergeant-Major of the 12th of Foot then stepped forward and, with his sword, slashed off the prisoner's buttons and chevrons and after that the Colonel of the regiment read out the crime and punishment in a strong, clear voice.

This done with full ceremony, the man – a sergeant no longer – was marched towards the commissariat wagon and pushed up into it. Its position was adjusted until the man was immediately below the gallows and then the noose was set in place round his neck, the hangman's knot drawn taut below his ear. A chaplain said a few quiet words to him; he seemed entirely impassive still and he went to his death without a murmur. As the order was given and the mules whipped away, lurching the wagon suddenly out from beneath his feet, the body dropped and jerked on the rope and hung there twitching convulsively; a low moaning sound broke out from the crowd of civilians and Bella found tears streaming down her cheeks. Deserter or no, this had been a man; now he was suddenly a mere lump of dead but still twitching flesh, a piece of carrion which would continue to swing there on Red Sands as a warning to the others until the flesh had all been picked from the bones by the circling vultures, profitably scavenging out of Spain . . .

One or two of the former sergeant's regiment had fainted during this gruesome ceremony; now, they were kicked onto their legs by the sergeants and corporals, some of whom were themselves looking pale. It was not every day of a man's service that he was made to witness a hanging; death in action was a different thing altogether. Bella, too, felt deathly faint as the bands swung into a quickstep and the regiments were marched off in column. The crowd got on the move, carrying her along past the swinging corpse, willy-nilly in the mass; and after a few minutes of this she was beginning to feel real alarm when she saw a tall, brown-faced figure in the blue and gold of the British Fleet bearing down upon her through the crowd and she saw the pleased smile on his face, a smile of recognition. It was only after a moment of uncertainty that she saw that this was Sir Edward Grenville who had been at His Excellency's reception the night of the arrival of Lord Rodney's ships so long before. She returned his smile and saw him shouldering the mob determinedly from his path to her side.

Reaching her he said, 'Lady Kilkieran! This is a pleasure, ma'am, truly. I had hoped to see you, but scarcely dared to hope that it would be so soon after my arrival.'

She was breathless by this time. She said, 'For me also, Sir Edward, it is a pleasure! If you would be so kind as to support me through the crowd, I would be more than grateful.'

'That, too, will be a pleasure!' He took her arm and forced a clear passage, using his voice and his elbows unmercifully until they were able to walk on in comfort towards the South Port.

She looked up at him curiously then. 'When did you arrive, Sir Edward?' she asked. Then she recollected what the hanging had put out of her mind: the gunfire early that morning, and the word that a line-of-battle ship had engaged the Spanish cruisers. 'It was *your* ship we heard – was that it?'

He laughed. 'I trust my gunners did not wake the entire garrison, Lady Kilkieran. Yes, it was my ship. I have been detached from Lord Rodney's command to proceed eastward to Naples to strengthen the Mediterranean Squadron, and I have brought some provisions and despatches for His Excellency.' He broke off then and added in some surprise, 'But you are surely not alone? Fitzmaurice is not with you?'

'Should he be?' she asked lightly, dimpling with amusement. 'He is not my husband, Sir Edward.'

'My apologies.' The naval Captain bowed, but there was a glint in his eye and a kind of throaty gruffness in his voice. 'I understood . . . that you were accommodated at his quarters. I meant to convey no more than that.'

'Then you understand rightly, Sir Edward. Come. You may escort me home, if it please you. Colonel Fitzmaurice will be back directly the regiment has returned to barracks. He will be delighted to meet you again, I am sure . . . and I shall be glad of conversation to take my mind away from that terrible entertainment on the Red Sands.'

Grenville nodded sombrely. 'You have my sympathy, Lady Kilkieran. A disturbing spectacle for a woman to witness. Yet His Excellency was right. Strong measures are needed at a time like this, and it takes a strong man to enforce them for the ultimate good of all. You in the garrison are lucky in General Eliott.'

'Would you,' she asked, 'treat one of your sailors similarly, if he should desert?'

Grenville gave a grim laugh. 'It is difficult for a man to desert from one of His Majesty's ships-of-war! But if he did, and was caught as he would be . . . yes, he would hang from the maintopmast yard in full view of his mates – who would indeed be hauling on the rope which swung him up! Some captains might order the men to be keel-hauled first and then hanged, or possibly to be flogged round the Fleet, in which case he would receive upwards of four hundred lashes from the cat before he hanged.' He shook his head. 'When serving His Majesty in time of war, one can show no mercy to those who fail in their duty, or are cowards.'

Soon they reached Fitzmaurice's house and Bella, taking Sir Edward into the drawing-room, sent the old housekeeper to prepare coffee. She said, 'It will not be of a very high standard, Sir Edward. We who live the life of the besieged have to make the best of what we are fortunate enough to get.'

'Naturally. Please do not apologize. To be truthful, I feel that I should not accept your hospitality at all, Lady Bella – and indeed would not do so had I not brought a few bags of provisions as a present for you personally.'

She looked at him in pleased surprise, smiling. 'Why, that is kind of you, Sir Edward! But – why me?'

He smiled back at her, his weatherbeaten face falling into heavy but kindly folds. 'My dear, you will learn, if indeed you have not already, that a pretty face attracts such attentions to itself. I remembered you well from my last visit. I was greatly disappointed that you did not in the end honour my ship with your presence back to England.' He added, 'Tell me, Lady Bella – do you regret not leaving this benighted garrison when you had the chance to do so?'

'Not in the very least,' she said with decision. 'Why should I?'

'You ask why?' He raised his eyebrows. 'The rigours of life, surely, are not for a mere woman? And the more particularly not for a young woman who should be enjoying all that civilized life has to offer.'

She gave him a somewhat disdainful look. 'I should be bored to death with the life that is usual among young ladies in England. I have known hardship, discomfort, enemy fire . . . I would have nothing in common now with my softly living contemporaries in England with their petty entertainments and parties and the young men thinking of nothing but card-playing.' She laughed. 'I would grow into someone to be avoided at all costs, someone who bored everyone else by talking of what she had seen and done out here in what, after all, is a small community of precious little interest to anyone outside it.'

'You are wrong,' he said gravely. 'The eyes of all England are upon Gibraltar in her hour of trial. And remember – you will have to return home one day.'

'One day,' she said pointedly. 'But not a day before the siege is lifted.'

'You are a spirited young woman, ma'am, and a brave one.'

'Nonsense, Sir Edward! I am selfish, perhaps. I am prepared to remain here as an extra mouth to be fed out of slender rations, rather than face the boredom of the social round!'

'I think,' he murmured, 'one need scarcely be bored anywhere . . . in congenial company.'

She shrugged. 'Perhaps not. You do not get bored at sea, then?'

He gave a loud laugh at that, his eyes twinkling. 'The weather and the enemy both conspire to see that that does not often happen. There are, however, certain aspects of the shore life which one misses.'

'Such as?'

He considered her demure face gravely. 'I think that it would perhaps be indelicate of me to elaborate further. And yet possibly I may be permitted to say . . . that we sailors are apt to miss feminine company, and when we make port it is the ladies who are our first consideration. Especially,' he added with a slow smile, 'one who attracts the senses as much as you, Lady Bella!'

'La, sir, you are over gallant!' She spoke demurely still, but there was a wicked look in her eyes. Sir Edward Grenville was an attractive man, tall, slim for his age, and with a commanding manner which she much admired in a man. Kilkieran had had it, His Excellency had it, Roger Carter even – so oddly – would have it when he was just a little older. Fitzmaurice lacked it, was merely fat and pompous and loud. She looked at the sailor from beneath lowered lids, calculatingly, saw the vein pumping away in his neck as she had seen it that evening at the reception, saw the flushed face and the now urgent manner. Grenville licked his lips, seemed to force her to look into his face, and then held her gaze. She breathed faster; there was something compelling, something magnetic in this hard, lean man's personality. Post-captains in His Majesty's Fleet were accustomed, she knew, to getting what they wanted; it was obvious what Sir Edward Grenville was presently bent upon.

He said softly, 'Bella, come to me.'

She gave a small, sighing breath and then his arms were around her, holding her close, his fingers fastening upon her breasts and cupping them almost savagely. Fiercely his lips came down on hers and she felt that she must be crushed. Her head swam, she felt light as air. His hands, rough hands now, were exploring her body when the door opened and Fitzmaurice's housekeeper came in with the forgotten coffee.

Behind her was His Excellency's aide-de-camp.

9

Captain Frazer came into the room, his face black as thunder. In silence he waited while the old woman agitatedly set down the tray with the coffee cups and then, thankfully, scuttled out of the room, muttering away to herself.

Frazer said icily, 'Ma'am, your pardon for my intrusion upon a . . . private occasion.'

Bella's lips were pressed tight, bloodless. She sensed the swelling anger in Grenville, the torrent of words building up inside him, and she reached out a hand as though to entreat him to quell them. She said, 'Captain Frazer, will you kindly tell me what brings you here – private occasion or no?'

Frazer bowed ironically, the dark, bitter eyes shining with passion. He said stiffly, 'Of course I shall tell you, ma'am. I am commanded by His Excellency to bring a despatch personally to Colonel Fitzmaurice.' His gaze swept insolently round the room, lingering on Grenville. 'I see, however, that the Colonel is not at home.'

'You are right, sir, he is not. I am, however, expecting him at any moment.'

'Indeed? I would have thought that you were not, ma'am.'

'Captain Frazer – '

'Your pardon, Lady Bella.' Grenville had heaved himself to his feet; he now strode across towards Frazer, his hand on his sword-hilt, broad shoulders towering over the ADC. His face was set and angry. He said, 'Captain Frazer, I must ask for your instant apology for your insinuations.'

The ADC glared. He snapped, 'Sir, I have made no insinuations – '

'Not directly perhaps, but they were in your tone and your manner.'

'I can scarcely fail to see what my eyes tell me, Sir Edward.'

The sailor's tone was contemptuous when he went on, 'It is no part of a gentleman's duty to follow hard upon the heels of the servant who announces him to his hostess. If he does, then he must expect to be – embarrassed.' His jaw lifted dangerously. 'I am waiting, Captain Frazer.'

'For what?'

'For your apology.'

Frazer shuffled, looked away, swallowed. Then, his voice ugly, he said, 'Very well. I have no quarrel with you, Sir Edward. I apologize most humbly if I have allowed my tone to betray my . . . misgivings in regard to Lady Kilkieran. I have no doubt that you were not yourself responsible. I shall, however, make further representations to His Excellency that Gibraltar is no place for a lady to remain – '

'What, pray, do you mean by that?' Bella broke in hotly.

Frazer bowed again. 'What I say, ma'am. No more, no less.'

'No more, indeed!' Bella's cheeks were flaming. 'You are in effect accusing me of – of being no better than a common harlot, Captain Frazer!'

'Lady Bella, I – '

'One moment.' Grenville, his eyes bright, addressed the ADC harshly. 'Captain Frazer, do I understand that you are going to influence His Excellency to have Lady Kilkieran removed from the fortress?'

Frazer nodded. 'I have already stated my intentions, Sir Edward. And allow me to add, that I consider it my duty to advise His Excellency of anything which in my opinion is prejudicial to the well-being of the garrison and hence to the conduct of the defence of Gibraltar against the enemy. I think you must fully understand what I mean, Sir Edward.'

Grenville's jaw thrust forward. 'You will now allow me to state *my* intentions,' he snapped. 'They are these: If news should ever reach me that His Excellency has acted upon your advice, I shall take steps to see that you yourself follow in the wake of Lady Kilkieran . . . I swear to you on my honour as Captain of a ship of the line that I shall see that you are relieved of your heavy responsibilities in Gibraltar and recalled to London for an easier task.' Grenville was breathing heavily now, his nostrils flaring. 'I believe I am right in saying that a recall from the firing-line would not greatly enhance your prospects of promotion, Captain Frazer – and it will not have escaped your notice that my brother is Major-General on the staff of His Royal Highness . . . the Commander-in-Chief. One word from him . . .' He shrugged. 'I think I need say no more, Captain Frazer. And now goodday to you. I shall usurp Lady Kilkieran's prerogative and ask you to leave this house at once.'

While he had been speaking Grenville had been advancing upon the ADC, and as he spoke his final words he reached out and opened the door behind the soldier's back. He almost pushed Frazer out, and then slammed the door viciously. When he turned round, he was smiling. He asked, 'What is the point of having relations in high places, if one cannot make use of them upon occasion?'

Bella said, 'Sir Edward, you astonish me. I thought you yourself were of the opinion that I should return to England.'

He nodded. 'I was, and am! But not in that way, and not at that fellow's behest. Besides, I cannot help but respect your own wish to remain until victory is ours, my dear. I trust that you will see that day shortly.' He added roguishly, 'There is another reason also.'

'And that is?' she asked, dimpling.

'A selfish one, Lady Bella! I hope myself to return to the Rock from time to time. I confess I should be much distressed to find you gone.' He came across the room and took her in his arms again, ran his fingers up and down her back, crushing her to him. He asked fiercely, 'And now, my dear – a reward?'

She pulled her head back and looked into his eyes, shaking her head a little as if to clear it. Her eyes were misty, full of longing . . . but she said gently, 'And risk Fitzmaurice, Sir Edward? No, we must not. Not now.' She smiled faintly. 'Contain your appetite, Sir Edward. There will be other opportunities – if Captain Frazer allows!'

Grenville snorted. 'You need have no fear of the Scot. His teeth are drawn, I assure you. Rest easy – there will be no more trouble from that quarter!'

But Bella could not feel so certain as that. She had seen and interpreted the look on Frazer's dark, lowering face. Frazer was a Highlandman born and bred, a fey man with an instinct and even a liking for trouble. Highlandmen did not forget or forgive, ever. Compliant now, he would, she knew well, simply wait for a more fortunate wind to blow in his direction – and she sensed that one day such a wind would surely come. When that happened, Frazer would remember; and he would be implacable . . . and she felt in her bones that she would never see Sir Edward Grenville again. It was, indeed, on that morning, the morning of that terrible hanging that Bella had her first intuitive glimpse of the future. It was no more than a shadow, a distant black cloud, but it was there and from that day forward it was never to leave her entirely. It was as though the hanging itself, that convulsive figure black against the sky, had in some way presaged her misfortune.

When Fitzmaurice came in a little later from Hargrave's Barracks he greeted Grenville cordially; but he had bad news.

He said, 'The garrison'll be damned glad of what your ship's brought in, Grenville, damned glad, though it's little enough to go far, as you'll be the first to admit.' He gnawed at his upper lip, worriedly. 'The scurvy's getting a grip – a damned tight grip! Poor turn-out for the hanging of that damned scoundrel today . . . half the garrison reported sick this morning. Four of the men at O'Hara's battery manned their posts on crutches – on crutches, d'ye hear that, Grenville?'

'Brave fellows. I am sorry.' Grenville had said that with sincerity, but Bella felt that he was contemptuous of the fat Colonel and his so obvious agitation at an expected hazard of any siege. 'A vicious thing, the scurvy. It is, of course, not unknown at sea. However, it may be short lived this time, Fitzmaurice.'

'Oh? How's that?' The voice was eager, anxious for good news, anxious to be reassured.

His eyes slanting down his high-bridged nose, Grenville said, 'Before I left England, I heard rumours – they were no more than that I must confess – that another attempt was to be made to send in a large relieving fleet.'

Fitzmaurice's face lit up. 'Lord save us, but that makes excellent hearing!' He cocked an eye at the sailor. 'You have informed His Excellency, no doubt?'

'I have not yet had the honour of being received by His Excellency. I shall wait upon him the moment I leave here, you may be sure . . . and shall explain that I have been beguiled from my duty by the charming Lady Bella! But to return to this happy rumour, Fitzmaurice – I believe that a fleet may shortly leave Torbay under Admiral Darby, with orders for Gibraltar. He is whispered to be assembling a large formation of ships of war to sail as escort of upwards of one hundred merchantmen, all deeply laden with supplies for your garrison, my dear fellow. With a measure of luck, that stomach of yours may soon cease grumbling.'

Bella stifled a giggle, but Fitzmaurice had noticed nothing.

He was rubbing his hands greedily, small eyes glittering with pleasure and anticipation. Even though his table saw much more than the official ration at times, he had been far from happy. Already, Bella felt, he was seeing the sides of beef, the succulent joints and the rich gravy and the vegetables, and the brandy with which, if Providence was kind, he would wash down his first gluttonous repast.

That afternoon Bella paid another of her visits to the sick lines.

She spoke to all the men she could, the tears springing to her eyes as she saw the starved, thin bodies, the stick-like legs still supporting weary and wasted soldiers about their business for as long as was humanly possible until, brought down finally by the terrible scurvy, their gallant spirits were forced to give in and they could only lie inert on their palliasses, staring out into a hopeless world of heat and sand and horror, staring with hopeless, burning eyes. Bella looked with revulsion and pity upon the debilitated men with their weakened muscles, upon the spongy, bleeding gums, the loosening teeth, the terrible patches of discoloration which covered their bodies, the result of the spreading subcutaneous haemorrhages. There were, as Fitzmaurice had said, so many sick; and, until Admiral Darby's fleet came in, if ever it did, there was precious little hope of relieving their sufferings.

Bella spoke to one of the surgeons, a little round man who had once been fat and whose flesh was now beginning to sag and wrinkle horribly upon his bones. He said sadly, 'There is no hope, Lady Bella, no hope anywhere. We shall all succumb. Food, fresh food, and that quickly, can alone help us now.'

'And our prayers to God.'

'Oh yes,' he said dully, 'and our prayers to God.'

Bella sighed in frustration. What, she wondered, would become of them all if the Spaniards chose this moment to mount an offensive across the land frontier, to send their guns and their marching hordes along that narrow isthmus linking the Rock with Spain, to storm the Land Port with an irresistible surge of men and cannon-balls? Or if they should determine to assemble a great fleet in Algeciras Bay and land troops along the Line Wall and at the Water Port under covering fire from the banked naval artillery? How would – how *could* – this sickly, suffering garrison withstand any such attack? This, of course, was yet another reason for nipping any desertions in the bud – the Dons must never learn exactly how Gibraltar stood.

The very next morning Bella went, on a sudden wave of impetuosity arising from her concern for the sick, to seek an interview with His Excellency in person. First she had to deal with Captain Frazer and it was not until she was face to face with the ADC that she realized how crazy her mission was. Frazer, glad to vent his seething rage, refused point-blank even to inform the General that the Lady Kilkieran was waiting upon him.

He said sourly, hitching at his kilt, 'His Excellency has a full day. Everybody of consequence in the garrison wishes for some of his time. As it is, he leaves in ten minutes' time to inspect the batteries – all of them, from the Rock Gun downwards to the Line Wall. The moment he returns from his inspection, the officer commanding at Chatham Counter-guard will be waiting upon him.'

'Then,' she said with obstinate determination, 'I shall wait here until Colonel Green has finished with His Excellency.'

Frazer made a gesture of angry impatience. 'That is quite out of the question, ma'am.'

'Why?' she flared. 'Listen to me, Captain Frazer. My business will not take long, but it is of the utmost importance –'

'I am sorry – '

'Captain Frazer,' she broke in imperiously, her eyes flashing fire. 'You have not yet heard what my business is. You have not had the courtesy even to enquire!'

Frazer scowled blackly. 'Then pray enlighten me, ma'am.'

Stifling her anger, Bella said calmly, 'I have been making my rounds of the sick, the sick of the garrison, not the civilians. It is scandalous – scandalous!' She tapped a foot on the floor. 'The garrison is, to my way of thinking, in a very imperfect state of defence indeed, whatever the commanding officers and General Eliott may have to say to the contrary! Now listen. Of vegetables we have none, but meat can be supplied yet. I have spoken to the surgeons, but they take no notice of me – '

'And what, ma'am, do you expect His Excellency to do?'

She snapped, her hands going to her hips, 'I expect His Excellency to show the surgeons that they should be laying siege to higher authority for an increased ration of freshly slaughtered meat for the sick in their care, Captain Frazer. I expect His Excellency . . .'

She tailed off with a gasp as she saw the suddenly frozen expression on the ADC's face, and she swung round. Eliott himself was standing in the open doorway of his room, smiling at her with tired, red-rimmed eyes in a haggard face – a face, she thought with sudden compassion, every bit as haggard and strained as those of the men in the Sick Lines. Taken aback for a moment she could only stammer out,

'Why – why, Your Excellency, I – '

Frazer interrupted, 'Your Excellency, I am most sorry. This woman – '

'It is the Lady Kilkieran, is it not?' The Governor's voice too was tired, the weary voice of a very old man, aged beyond his years. 'I am pleased to see you, my dear, though I fear you have come only to add to my worries. Am I right?'

She nodded. 'I fear you are indeed quite right, Your Excellency,' she said, casting down her gaze before those saddened eyes.

'Then come in, child,' he said gently, 'and tell me what it is you want of me.'

71

The ADC said, 'Sir, I must remind you – '

'About the batteries?' Eliott gave a short laugh. 'The batteries can wait, Captain Frazer. I feel the need of pleasant company for a few minutes, my good fellow. Come, Lady Bella.'

She turned to follow His Excellency; but not before she had seen the furious look on Frazer's face . . . and not before she had been able, behind His Excellency's back, to give the aide-de-camp an unladylike but triumphant wink.

Had he been a man of fuller blood, she thought with an inward giggle, he would have had a fit of the apoplexy.

10

General Eliott crossed the long room with its tall, elegant windows, his red coat and sash adding colour to the mellow polish of the exquisite mahogany furniture. As he went past a table he seemed to stagger a little, and put out a hand to the table for support.

Bella at once went forward in concern. 'Your Excellency – '

'It is nothing. A momentary weakness. Please sit down.'

The General's voice was harsh, almost angry, at being caught in a moment of physical incapacity. Bella hesitated, then obeyed what was in effect the order to be seated. The Governor, his face grey with fatigue, was waiting for her to sit before he seated himself. When she had taken a seat Eliott went slowly forward to his desk and dropped heavily into a chair behind it. He mopped at his forehead with a fine lace handkerchief; his face was gleaming with a cold-looking perspiration and he was breathing heavily and fast. Indeed, he looked very far from well; the terrible burden of long months of complete personal responsibility for so many lives, for the safety and well-being of an outpost of England, the lonely burden of final decision in which no man could help him, as well as much hard physical driving – for he was constantly to be seen at the works and batteries encouraging the men by personal example of attention to duty – was telling at last on this gallant, self-sacrificial soldier.

Eliott rubbed at his eyes, seemed lost in thought for a moment, his head sunk on his chest. Then he looked up at the young girl and said.

'Well, my dear? What is it that you wish to speak to me about?'

'The sick, Your Excellency,' she answered with some hesitation, and she coloured. Indeed she regretted her errand in a large degree, for now she scarcely liked to speak of it in the presence of this man who was sick himself and was driving himself on by his will alone, driving himself as hard and relentlessly as any of the soldiers in the fortress – and far harder than men like Fitzmaurice . . . a man whose rations were no more than those of the most humble private in his command – indeed for one period His Excellency had lived on four ounces of rice a day in order to test upon himself what was the smallest ration on which a man could live and do his duty. But she went on resolutely, 'I have been visiting them . . .'

'I know that very well, my dear child. I have heard . . . and I have heard that you have greatly cheered them. I am grateful for all you have done.' He smiled. 'My decision to allow you to remain in the fortress has been justified, amply so – as, frankly, I knew very well it would be, Lady Bella.'

'Thank you, Your Excellency.' Again she coloured, and hesitated. 'Your Excellency . . . I have come to ask if you would authorize an increase in the fresh meat ration to the sick. The salt cod has brought them very low.'

Eliott said heavily, sadly, 'I realize that. That Newfoundland ship, with the best intentions in the world, has been no friend to the garrison with its disgusting cargo! But surely better that, than nothing at all?'

Bella nodded. She said tenaciously, 'But the meat. Your Excellency, I have spoken to the quartermasters. There is, I understand, enough fresh meat in the garrison to make some small increase to the sick. At all events, to the worst of them, that they may recover their strength in order to last out until more ships come in. Even if it means cutting the ration to everyone else – though that is small enough in all conscience!'

Eliott raised an eyebrow and shook his head in amusement. 'Cut the ration to those yet able to get about, so that we ensure that they also become sick? Come, Lady Bella, there is small sense in that! And tell me – how do you, or the quartermasters, assess our needs? For how long have we to make our existing stocks last – when will the next relieving force arrive, when will the Dons remove themselves from their lines and shift the siege? Or when will they attack, is perhaps the more pertinent question. All these are imponderables.' Eliott leaned forward, his eyes almost luminous with sheer fatigue and ill-nourishment. 'Do you know we have only forty head of cattle left with which to feed the whole garrison?'

Bella, shocked, looked at him in horrified amazement. 'Forty head!' she whispered.

Eliott nodded. 'That is all. For the rest – we have rice in plenty, a little flour for bread, but very little. As for the townspeople, whose diet we may have yet to adopt ourselves, they are existing on nuts, thistles, wild onions . . . and even rats and mice when they are to be had.'

'Would it not be possible – would it not be an act of mercy – to allow the townspeople to draw on garrison rations, Your Excellency?'

'Undoubtedly an act of mercy,' Eliott answered shortly, frowning. 'But an act of madness also. You know as well as I do that all townspeople are and have always been ordered to keep at least six months' full supply of food in hand at all times against exactly such an emergency as this – a supply which, if carefully rationed, could last throughout a long siege. I must remind you that this is by no means the first time Gibraltar has been besieged. If these wretched people have chosen, as indeed they have, to disregard the Standing Orders of the fortress, orders designed for their own good, I shall most certainly not let my soldiers suffer, Lady Bella.' He waved a hand, angrily. 'The civilians are of no account whatever in the garrison, as you are well aware. If you wish me to lend ears to your advocacy, my dear, I would advise you to confine your brief to the sick among my regiments and corps.'

Bella bowed her head. She said humbly, 'Indeed I ask your pardon, Your Excellency. That was a mere digression. It *is* the military sick who have been so much on my mind. I have seen them – '

'So have I – so have I! And they are much on my mind, too. But until Admiral Darby's fleet arrives, or a blockade-runner or privateer which can break that confounded cruiser cordon as Sir Edward Grenville broke it . . . why, my dear child, I am powerless! Do you not understand that?'

'Yes, I do, Your Excellency. And yet . . . there are those

75

forty head of cattle. Will they go far towards feeding some six thousand men, Your Excellency?'

'They will not.'

There was a pause and then Bella said daringly, 'So little meat can make scant difference, surely, to those not already sick. Why should you not order that the remaining stocks be allocated entirely to those sick from the scurvy? A little meat would work miracles, and restore many men to health – at least for the time being, until perhaps some relief arrives from England or Minorca. That is, for long enough to save their lives. Do you not agree?'

Eliott smiled. 'My dear young lady, you appear to have everything decided for me!'

'I am sorry to sound forward,' she said, 'but the sufferings of the sick have moved me greatly.'

'So it would seem – and rightly so.' Eliott tapped his fingers on the top of his desk and frowned. He went on, 'I shall commit myself to no decisions, but you may be assured that the well-being of *everyone* under my command is much on my mind, and continually so.'

'Oh, Your Excellency,' she cried at once, 'I am very sensible of that! Indeed the whole garrison is.'

Eliott nodded slowly, looking keenly at the young woman who somehow had managed through all privations to retain her youthful freshness almost unimpaired. The young, he reflected sadly, wore so much better than the ageing under adverse conditions. He said, 'Let us now consider yourself, Lady Bella. Since the loss of your husband, I have seen all too little of you. You are – er – managing well enough, I take it, in Colonel Fitzmaurice's household?'

'Well enough, I thank you, Your Excellency.'

She noticed how shrewdly the Governor was studying her, as if he could penetrate into the innermost recesses of her heart and mind. How much, she wondered, did he really know? Eliott was a soldier and a man of the world. He must obviously realize that a man of Fitzmaurice's stamp would scarcely take an attractive young woman into his quarters simply as an act of loyalty towards his predecessor and former Colonel, or indeed for any other altruistic reason. Despite what she had said that night under the stars to Fitzmaurice when she had first asked him to speak to His Excellency, Bella had frequently wondered why Eliott had ever acceded to her request to be allowed to remain in the garrison under the protection of Colonel Fitzmaurice – unless, being a chivalrous man himself, he genuinely did attribute the same chivalry to all his officers, however unlikely a proposition that might sound . . .

Still looking at her Eliott said suddenly, 'The Colonel of the 74th is the most blessed of all my subordinates.'

That startled her. 'Why so, Your Excellency?'

He smiled kindly. 'Why, my dear, to have so charming a lady to grace his table – even though there be little upon it to eat! Gracious company must make up to some extent for privation.'

'You are very kind, Your Excellency,' she murmured in some confusion. It was a confusion on two counts: Firstly because the General could not possibly have known of the comparatively fine scale on which Fitzmaurice was still able somehow to live (Bella had felt guilty about sharing in this, yet at the same time she was human enough to enjoy the extra rations thoroughly – and they did not include meat in any case); secondly because there had been a curious note in the General's voice, a note of . . . loneliness? Or envy of Fitzmaurice? Certainly Eliott, however devoted to his duty, was also human enough to appreciate a lovely woman's company.

And Bella, again, was human enough over this sort of thing as well as over the rations . . . human enough to feel a guilty thrill. Where might not *that* have led her, handled aright – if it had not been for Captain Andrew Frazer?

Next day garrison orders published the information that two head of cattle per day out of the forty head remaining, were to be slaughtered for the exclusive use of the sick. Somehow – but not through Bella's own agency – the news leaked out that the Lady Bella herself had been to no small extent responsible for this . . . and she suffered the embarrassment (and also the pleasure) of being mobbed in the streets by the soldiers, and of hearing their cheers and greetings in her ears.

And something else was noted that day, by observers from the garrison: the Dons were beginning a tremendous preparation of works in their lines.

11

The news that Admiral Darby was leaving Torbay for the Rock had been no idle rumour. Indeed by the time Grenville had given this information to His Excellency Darby was well on his way; and a few days later – on 12th April – a frigate, vanguard of the main fleet, broke the cruiser cordon under cover of a morning fog and brought the word that Admiral Darby was off Tarifa and proceeding under a light breeze slowly through the Strait.

In Algeciras Bay a little later, as the sun grew stronger and the localized fog gradually rose like the curtain of a vast theatre, there stood revealed one of the most pleasing sights that the garrison had seen in many a long month of siege: a convoy of more than one hundred merchantmen sailing into the bay, with Darby's men-of-war cruising to seaward within sight of the Rock.

But their joy was to be short-lived.

At ten forty-five the van of the convoy anchored off the New Mole and, as though this were the signal for the enemy batteries to open at last, a heavy fire immediately started from Fort St Philip before the Spanish lines.

Soon, as other batteries opened, one hundred and fourteen pieces of artillery were firing into the fortress and upon the assembling merchantmen. The Spanish batteries were blazing like volcanoes; the townspeople, panic-stricken, crowding each other like sheep destined for the slaughter-house, young and old, men and women and children, fled to the southward towards Europa, leaving everything in their urgent haste to get away from the noisy havoc of the guns.

The bombardment was kept up continuously while the merchantmen began to discharge their cargoes. It was indeed kept up for the whole of the ten days which the off-loading operation took to complete, ceasing only at noon each day while the Spaniards indulged themselves with a meridional nap; and the batteries of the fortress took a tremendous punishment from that time onward. Willis's Battery was quickly reduced; the merlons were considerably damaged and many of the cannon dismounted and wrecked. The lines were almost choked up with loose stones and rubbish brought down by the shot from the rock above, and the casualties mounted steadily. The dead lay everywhere. The town, especially at the northward, was a shambles; but repair work proceeded whenever possible, and the engineers were constantly at work upon the batteries and fortifications under the continual gun-flashes from the enemy lines.

This was war with a vengeance.

During this time Fitzmaurice was away from his house a great deal, sleeping in barracks whenever sleep was possible at all. For her part Bella helped, along with the few other officers' ladies remaining, to succour the wounded, going round the awful billets and encampments and also the batteries and outposts themselves, her ears filled with the groans and screams of the mortally injured, watching men die in torment as the surgeons strove with their primitive and inadequate resources to staunch their blood or tend their shattered limbs, limbs that all too often became gangrenous before the busy surgeons could amputate. Bella assisted at the removal of a leg one night, a gruesome operation in the light of flares below the Royal Battery; and it was a scene which she knew she would never be able to erase from her memory thereafter. The man, a sergeant of Highlanders, brought down by a musket shot in the shoulder, had then been taken by a glancing blow from a ball fired from Fort St Philip, a ball at the end of its trajectory which had smashed his femur and ploughed a deep furrow right down the leg, baring tendons, bone and muscle. While Bella held a bottle of rum to the man's mouth and let it gurgle down his throat, the sweating, blood-encrusted surgeon, looking like a fiend out of hell, took off the leg below the hip with several swings of an axe.

Strangely, Bella did not faint; but afterwards, when she had left the Royal Battery and was stumbling homeward through the rubble and the flying dust and smoke, she was violently, rackingly sick and found herself shaking and trembling in all her limbs. After that she gritted her teeth and dragged herself onward, tears streaming down her pale cheeks, stumbling and falling over shattered masonry and half-buried bodies, fearfully avoiding the scavenging, flitting forms of looting soldiery and a few townspeople who had returned to search among the wreckage for the personal possessions which they had left behind in that first panic rush for the safety of Europa.

She had gone for some half a mile when she heard her name called from the shadows.

'Bella . . . it's me. Bella!'

She stopped fearfully, her heart beating fast. Then she turned, and saw Roger Carter in the shadows. He was smiling at her, but his face was white beneath the moon and he seemed to be hurt; blood was pouring from his right shoulder and the sleeve of his coat was hanging in ribbons.

'Oh, Roger . . .' She felt a terrible fear.

'It's nothing,' he said quickly. Then he added, smiling into her eyes as she approached him, 'But my sergeant sent me to get attention from the surgeon's mate . . . and I have been lucky enough to find you, Bella, the finest and most beautiful surgeon's mate in all the garrison!'

She smiled fleetingly at the joke, then examined the wound, swabbing at it with a piece of clean material which she ripped from her own underclothing. It wasn't in fact a bad wound; it had no doubt looked worse than it was, and with cleaning and bandaging it would soon heal. As she finished her examination she looked up and saw the way in which Roger Carter was studying her.

'What is it, Roger?' she asked.

'You, Bella my dearest. You have done enough – too much. You must return to your quarters, and rest. You will do more good to the garrison in the long run, by taking care of yourself, my dear.'

'I was on my way home, as it happens. But I am all right, Roger.'

'You have been crying.'

'I have seen a leg removed, that is why. I – I helped.'

'*You* helped! Oh, my love!' With his good arm he held her to his body, his blood falling on her dress to mingle with that already there, and he felt the violent trembling which shook her. Once his arm was round her like that she appeared to give way very suddenly, as though she had found safe anchorage and could let go. Tears ran down her face again, tears of weariness and weakness, and her shoulders heaved. She said through her sobs, 'Roger, take me home. I – I can stand no more tonight.' She looked up at him. 'You have not got to be back at your post yet?'

He shook his head. 'No, Bella. Had I been at my post, I would not have troubled about so small a wound. I was wounded off duty – when the barracks was hit.'

'Hargrave's?'

He nodded. 'The Colonel is safe and sound, if that is what worries you, Bella. Now – come.'

Roger bent swiftly and, disregarding his wound, picked her up. She was as light as a feather and almost at once her head fell across his sound shoulder and she slept. He carried her home, wincing now with the pain in his shoulder, through the broken streets and the rubble and debris of the nightmare bombardment, with always in the background the sound of the Spanish guns and of falling buildings as the shot struck home on the town.

On arrival, without waking the ancient housekeeper Maria, Roger carried Bella to her bedroom and laid her, still asleep, gently on the bed. He stood there for a moment looking down at her and he had turned away and had reached the door, intending now to warn Maria to attend to her mistress, when she woke and struggled to a sitting position.

She asked in sudden alarm, 'Where are you going, Roger?'

'Back to barracks. I – do not wish to embarrass you, Bella, should the Colonel return . . . in any case I am required for guard duty at six o'clock in the morning, if my shoulder is fit, which it will be.'

'You will not embarrass me, and Fitzmaurice will not return this night. And I haven't dressed your shoulder yet. It must be washed, Roger.'

'I shall not bother you,' he said gruffly. 'I shall find a surgeon's mate.'

'My dear Roger, they are all overworked as it is with the bad cases. I shall see to it myself.' She slid off the bed and stood up. 'You will wait here,' she said, 'while I boil some water and fetch bandages. I insist, so it is no use arguing with me, Roger.'

She left the room and quickly returned with hot water and fresh, clean cloth. She bathed the wound and dressed it, and after that it was much more comfortable.

When Roger tried to struggle back into his coat she said softly, 'Roger my dearest, don't leave me . . . alone in the house but for old Maria.' She reached out and took him in her arms, rubbing her cheek gently against his. He felt the wetness of tears, felt the gentle swelling pressure of her breasts against his chest, breasts which nestled so invitingly beneath the silk of her dress. She put her head back and looked into his eyes and he saw the love, the urgent desire as her body moved against his own. Fierce desire filled his own body then. He lifted her and laid her on the bed again and, with fumbling fingers, began to undress her, pulling off the filmy layers of her clothing until she lay there naked and trembling. He ran his hands lightly along her flanks, exploring her body as wondrously as if it were for the very first time, and he felt her response, saw it in the rigidity of her nipples, in the way her thighs moved to his feather touch.

'Come to me,' she breathed. 'Oh my darling . . .' She pulled him down towards her with arms that had a sudden steely strength, and their flesh met as one, sending a living flame through their loins, an ecstasy of desire about to be fulfilled, a carrying away of the spirit into realms of shining gold . . .

It was a long, long while before they separated and then Bella lay there, passing quickly into sleep, with a small smile playing about her lips as, in that sleep, she felt his arms about her and the potency still latent in his body.

12

It was Bella who woke first.

She woke from a light but tranquil and satisfied sleep the very instant that she heard the footsteps; halting footsteps, stumbling up the stairs, the clatter of a sheathed sword and a muttered curse. She sat bolt upright, eyes wide and fearful, sheet clutched to her throat to hide her nakedness, and at once roused Roger Carter who was sleeping by her side.

He was fully alert immediately, his soldier's training bringing him quickly to the point of action from slumber. He listened for a moment, then whispered, 'It must be the Colonel . . .'

'I fear so,' she breathed. 'Roger, you must go quickly! Not the door . . . the window – see! There is a drop of some twelve feet, but – '

'But that is nothing. However, my dearest, I cannot leave you to face him alone!'

'You must, Roger. You cannot stay – I will never permit it. I beg of you not to let Fitzmaurice find you here . . .'

He broke in heatedly, 'You are not his wife, dearest – and what is Fitzmaurice to me? My family . . .' He checked himself, glanced quickly at Bella, but she did not appear to have noticed anything out of place. He went on, 'But for him to find no one – yes, of course I must leave. That will be the best service I can do you . . .'

He was already out of bed and had pulled on his trousers. She said distractedly, 'Hurry – go quickly, before he suspects anything. With luck, he will not come directly to my room. Go, Roger – and God go with you!'

As the footsteps lurched nearer, Roger Carter grabbed for the remainder of his clothing, rolled it into a ball, and threw it from the window. Swiftly he bent to kiss Bella and then ran for the sill. He was precariously balanced when the door of the bedroom burst suddenly open and Fitzmaurice, a lantern in his hand, stood swaying in the doorway. There was a strong smell of rum. Roger hesitated, seeing that in his drink-sodden state Fitzmaurice had failed to recognize him so far but had already registered that someone was there; but, after an imploring look from Bella, he let himself down from the sill, hung for a moment by his finger-tips while he judged his distance, and then he dropped expertly onto the hard, baked ground in a rear courtyard, picked up his gear, leaped for the wall separating the courtyard from a side alley, and was away.

Back in the house, Fitzmaurice lurched across the bedroom towards the window, his eyes bloodshot and bright with drink and fury, sweat pouring from his face. Bella watched him in terror as he glared out . . . glared and, apparently, saw nothing. She sent up a prayer of thankfulness for that, and then Fitzmaurice staggered back towards the bed.

Thickly he said, 'You whore. You filthy, degraded whore.'

'William, I – '

'Silence!' His coarse voice, drink-inflamed, cut her like a whip; he lifted his hand and struck her a violent blow across her face. As she gave a gasp of anger and cringed away from him he laid hold of the edge of the sheet. Viciously he jerked it back and stared down at her naked body, so white and inviting, stared down with his lips working and his bloated face almost purple. He was swaying on his feet, the sheath of his sword rattling against its buckles. He said, 'To think . . . to think that you would expect me to share that body with another man!' He reached out stubby, splayed fingers and touched her nipples, running his coarse hand over the slight corrugations, felt their erectile strength under his touch. His mouth twisting in a sneer, he ran the hand down her stomach. He watched her face as his fingers reached the cleft of her thighs, saw the way her eyes widened, whether with pleasure or fear he could not tell.

Abruptly he withdrew his hand and laughed, coarsely. 'That is all I do to whores,' he sneered. 'They can get their satisfactions elsewhere, as it seems they do! By God, Bella! When I find out who that man was, I'll run him through – or at best leave him with nothing to satisfy other women with!' He calmed himself with an effort. 'Now, my lovely – a name to him, if you please!'

She said steadily, 'I shall name no names, William.'

'Oh, but I think you will!' As he spoke his face contracted and he drew his sword from its sheath. The blade flashed in the light of his lantern, which he had set upon a table. Lifting the hilt slowly, he lowered the point of the blade until its tip rested intimately upon her body. He felt her trembling running up the steel.

He said, softly now, 'A name, my Bella, a name – or I guarantee you won't perform any more of your tricks for many a long day.'

Speechless with terror, she withdrew her body a little way; the sword-point followed. Fitzmaurice's face was a mask of sadism, and his sword-arm was shaking. She felt a sudden pain, and then the slow warm trickle of blood, and Fitzmaurice made a coarse remark followed by an insulting laugh – and it was that which made Bella suddenly lose her temper, and, in losing it, regain her courage. With a swift backward movement of her body, she pulled herself away from the searching blade and, before the befuddled soldier could follow up, she had squirmed off the bed and had reached forward and seized the sword-guard in both her hands, firm and tight.

She jerked at it, hard.

Fitzmaurice, taken utterly by surprise by that jerk, let go. The sword in her hands, Bella turned quickly for the window and pitched it out and it was then that the terrible thing happened, the thing that could never be righted. Fitzmaurice lunged for her, for the window, for his sword – she never did know what. All she did know was that he lost his balance, fell heavily against the sash, and staggered across the sill. Collecting her wits she went towards him and grabbed, but she was too late.

His heavy body, legs encumbered by the swinging sheath of his sword, tilted outwards and he dropped, head first, to the ground. He screamed loudly, once, as he fell, and then there was a faint rattle of metal and a thud, then silence. Profound, utter silence.

Bella stifled the scream that came to her own throat. Her heart beat like a wild bird, desperate in a cage. For a moment she gave way to panic and then with fumbling fingers she pulled a gown over her naked body and went to the door. She ran down the stairs as fast as she could and out into the courtyard at the back. Fitmaurice was lying where he had fallen, his limbs spreadeagled, his head thrown back at a grotesque angle to his body, which itself was lying full across his sword.

Bella knelt down by his side and felt for his heart, but even as she did so she knew very well that he was dead.

Gathering her gown around her waist, she ran back indoors and fell weeping across her bed. After a while she roused herself and woke old Maria. She sent her post-haste to Hargrave's Barracks and within the hour the body had been examined on the spot by a surgeon and a Field Officer together with the second-in-command of the 74th of Foot; after that two files of men from the 74th came to take away the body of their Colonel.

Next day a court of enquiry was convened by order of His Excellency, and it was held in an apartment of the Governor's residence under a Brigadier-General. It was perfunctory enough; it was obvious that all present were trying above all else to spare the feelings of the Lady Kilkieran, who had been a close friend of the deceased and had had the misfortune to witness his terrible death. Nevertheless, the formal proceedings were a torture to Bella. She said nothing whatever about Roger Carter; it was well known that Colonel Fitzmaurice had been the worse for drink the night before – which supported her story that he had burst into her bedroom while she was sleeping, and, in going across to the window for air, had pitched out to his death. The one mystery was the sword; Bella could find no way of accounting for the fact that it had been found unsheathed and beneath Fitzmaurice's dead body – she had kept her own counsel, for many reasons, as to the fact that it had been unsheathed against her own body. But the subject was not made much of and it was evident that the sympathies of the court lay with the Lady Bella and that no one was going to pry over-deeply into what was, in effect, an unfortunate accident whatever the cause of it might have been.

The enquiry was attended by His Excellency's aide-de-camp, and throughout Bella found her attention being drawn to that dark, devilish face and its sneering expression as she gave her evidence. She had the uncomfortable feeling that, somehow, Frazer knew . . . however illogical that feeling might be, she was convinced that he knew about Roger Carter, knew precisely why Fitzmaurice had died – knew, but for some undisclosed reason of his own, did not intend to say so to the officers composing the court.

When Bella left the court she was white and ill, and shaking throughout her body. An officer who had known both Fitzmaurice and Kilkieran accompanied her solicitously to her house; he left her there when she insisted that she would be quite all right and needed no help, that all she wanted now was to be left alone.

All that day no one came near her. She had half-hoped for, half-feared, a summons to His Excellency. But then, perhaps, General Eliott would be too busy to give even a corner of his mind to the plight of a lady of the garrison, a woman whom he had originally wished to leave the Rock and who was now, once again, a nuisance – a woman alone, defenceless and hence unwanted in the fortress. Roger Carter, she was sure, would have come to her if he could, but it was clearly wiser altogether that he should not, at least not openly. Perhaps he would come that night, secretly, if his duty permitted . . . as she thought of Roger, she found tears stinging at her eyes; her longing for him had become so intense that it was a physical pain in her stomach and secret places, those warm and tender parts of her which cried out yearningly for him, for the insistence of his eager body, the unstayed thrust of eager vitality which was his and which left her gasping, her small fists bunched, body taut and bent convex . . . and then the slow prolonged pleasure as, all passion spent, their bodies parted and they slept.

Half-expecting that Roger would come to her – though she didn't know whether or not he was on guard duty that night – she remained in her drawing room until nearly midnight; and it was just as she had decided to go to bed that the knock came at the outer door, a heavy and sustained knocking. For a fleeting second, until that knocking went on impatiently, she had a wild hope that it might be Roger, but she knew in her heart that he would not knock in such a fashion . . . and she was not wrong. Old Maria came in urgently, her fat, wrinkled face wobbling and her eyes scared and staring.

She said in Spanish, 'Milady, it is Captain Frazer . . . and a file of soldiers!'

'What!' Bella's face paled, but her chin tilted ominously and her eyes were bright with sheer anger. 'What can they be wanting, then? To throw me out of this quarter, do you think?'

'Milady, I do not know. They ask to see you, that is all I can say.'

'I see.' Bella's voice was hard. 'Then you had better show the gallant Captain in, Maria.'

'Yes, milady.'

The old woman turned away. Bella straightened her dress and sat down in a chair by a small table. A moment later she heard the thud of heavy boots, the clank of metal, and then the ADC came in alone. Sounds from outside indicated that the soldiers had been halted and stationed by the door.

Frazer, lean and lank in that tattered kilt of his, wasted no time. He said abruptly and without formality, 'Lady Kilkieran, I have a proposition to put before you. It is up to you to accept it or to reject it, and I shall ask you to make up your mind quickly.'

She studied him aloofly, hands folded in her lap. 'I presume your wishes are still the same, Captain Frazer. You desire, no doubt, to bring me to bed – this time under threat?'

He said drily but with a twitch of his jaw, 'Whatever my wishes in the past, I have now no special desire to bed with a woman who has already bedded with too many men.'

'Ah – I see! You wish only to hound, to be the dog in the manger over what you cannot have yourself.' She smiled, but it was an acid smile and her eyes were hard as glass. She went on, 'Nevertheless, the devil in your loins will not be denied, Captain Frazer. That much I can see for myself.'

'Your pardon.' He bowed mockingly. 'An uncommon sight for Lady Kilkieran to witness, she would have me believe. However . . .' His voice hardened. 'Allow me to explain in some detail. I have come here to give you a free choice of two courses of action. Either you remain in the garrison, when I shall represent to His Excellency that not only is your quarter required for the accommodation of officers whose own houses have been rendered unfit by the bombardment, but also that you are an undesirable person whose conduct has led indirectly to the death of Colonel Fitmaurice – a valued commanding officer who can ill be spared by a garrison under siege – solely to facilitate my Lady Kilkieran's illicit amours – '

'Captain Frazer, I – '

He lifted a hand peremptorily. 'A moment. I have not yet finished. I was, as you know, in court today. I have no doubt in my mind as to why Colonel Fitzmaurice met his death, or why he found it necessary to draw his sword in your bedroom. The officers forming the court also had no doubt in their minds, if you ask me, but they wished to spare you, Lady Kilkieran. As for me,' he added contemptuously, 'I have no such wish. I do not wish to spare the nice feelings of a harlot, the cursed of the Lord, a – a Delilah!' Bella wondered how genuine his righteous wrath was; somehow it had a sincere ring, as though he had spent the siege telling himself that his own natural desires were wicked too but that luckily they were housed within a body for the most part strong enough to withstand them. She could only hope that he would continue strong. 'If I knew who the man was who shared your bed last night I would see that he was executed on the Red Sands tomorrow.' The ADC's voice was thick now, his face darkly flushed and venomous, almost as if he scarcely knew the full import of what he was saying to her. 'Therefore I give you the choice of either accompanying me to His Excellency, when I will lay the truth before him – or of leaving the garrison of your own free will. Tonight.'

'I shall do neither!' Her face flamed in temper now. 'You have no right to come here and insult me – '

'Be that as it may,' Frazer retorted more calmly. 'I intend to carry out what I have said in any case. I have a file of soldiers under a corporal positioned at this moment outside your drawing room. Men of Colonel Dachenhausen's Hanoverian Brigade. They have not the chivalry of our British soldiers. Now – Admiral Darby is under orders at this moment to sail at dawn for Plymouth Sound, and a boat will be waiting at one o'clock to take you off from the Water Port to join the Fleet. The soldiers will see that you board that boat – of your own free will as I have said, Lady Kilkieran. Afterwards I shall report to His Excellency that you have decided to leave for England, that the decision was your own and that I have been instrumental in helping you. The alternative, I assure you, is disgrace and a hounding out of the garrison as a common harlot.'

'Which, surely, you would in fact wish for me, Captain Frazer? Why then offer me an alternative? Or is it the fact that you are not so sure of yourself as you would like me to believe, that indeed you know very well that His Excellency will never send me out of the fortress now against my wishes? Is that it, Captain Frazer – and also that you are frightened of the revenge of Sir Edward Grenville, who will most certainly – '

Frazer's hand came up, took her a stinging blow across the mouth. She felt blood run from her lip. He said thickly, his face suffused, 'Harlot, whore! Grenville will never hear the truth of this, for he is dead. We have word that he was lost with his ship off Finisterre seven days ago. Neither will anyone else ever hear the truth, or rather will never believe *your* story – when His Excellency of Gibraltar bears out *mine!*'

He turned on his heel and called out, using German. 'Corporal, the woman will be ready to leave in three minutes' time. You will see that she does not escape you.' He turned back to Bella. 'Three minutes,' he said. 'Three minutes to pack what you need to take with you for a sea passage. I shall wait here until you are ready, then I shall hand you over to the corporal of the escort.'

Three minutes it was.

One minute after that Bella, with a soldier on either side of her and a gigantic corporal in rear, was being marched with a small bag in her hand, along the rubble-filled streets towards the Water Port where she would embark aboard the line-of-battle ship *Royal Sovereign*, seventy-four guns, commanded by Captain Lord Erringham.

But she was not finished with Gibraltar yet.

They had gone little more than a hundred yards from her house when the corporal snapped an order and Bella found herself being propelled into a stinking side alley where dark and evil doorways leered into the moonlight. She was taken into one of these doorways and made to stand against the wall, with the men grinning at her like hairy apes. The corporal barked something at her, something which she did not understand. He kept on and on, and in the end he managed a word of English.

'Ondress,' he said.

'Please – '

'*Ondress*!' A bayonet pricked into her stomach. 'Quick.'

The men pressed close, their breath hot and foul on her face. Tremblingly, seeing that to refuse would merely invite the forcible stripping away of her garments, Bella obeyed the order, letting her clothes fall to the ground around her ankles until she stood half-naked against the wall, faintly silvered by the moon. The corporal snapped at the two men and they formed a barrier across the entrance. Then the immense corporal picked her up like a feather, grinning at her. He lifted her body across his face, drawing his lips down the cringing flesh of her stomach, then he laid her roughly on the dirty, littered ground.

What followed was horrible, utterly degrading to her. The stink of the filthy, sweat-greasy uniform, of the man's own unwashed body, filled her nostrils. His body clamped on top of her, the obscene workings of his fingers as he forced her to submit, the terrible pressure of his urgency upon her unwilling flesh, the searing pain which followed . . . all this brought her to the very verge, it seemed, of madness. She fought and struggled but to no avail; screaming was impossible, for his mouth was pressed close to her own so tightly that she could scarcely draw breath. As his movements reached their crescendo and her cringing loins felt torn apart, she swooned right away, sinking into merciful oblivion.

Hours later, as it seemed – though in fact it was scarcely ten minutes – she found herself on the march again between the soldiers, making for the Water Port to join the British Fleet for England – body bedraggled and in pain, her clothing rumpled and dusty . . . a young woman of spirit and courage who had been brought to the level of a branded, degraded harlot.

13

A pulling boat was waiting at the Water Port, manned by six seamen. The corporal of the escort handed Bella down into this boat, where rough hands took her round the waist as she descended, holding her for a little longer than necessary and rather more tightly; and then deposited her on a thwart. There was a leer from the corporal and then he turned the soldiers about and marched them away. The seaman in the sternsheets of the boat gave an order and the craft was pushed off from the jetty. Further orders were given and the oars dipped into the water. The boat moved out to sea under the low-slung stars, moving swiftly to the accompaniment of grunts and hard breathing from the sweating, pig-tailed sailors, out towards the bulky line of the British Fleet in the anchorage.

Within fifteen minutes Bella had been hoisted in a bosun's chair to the upper deck of the *Royal Sovereign*. She was politely received by a lieutenant who told her that a cabin had been prepared for her and that the Captain would want to see her in the morning after the ship was under way; it was clear from his manner that she was not being regarded as a harlot but rather as a woman naturally wishing to leave the squalor and danger of Gibraltar behind her – and for this at least she was heartily thankful. She yearned to enlist the lieutenant's support, but her confused mind stopped her lest any fuss should in some way react upon Roger Carter. The lieutenant's gaze lingered curiously but with compassion on her disarrayed, befouled clothing and this caused her the greatest confusion; but she was able to realize that her state would be put down to no more than the rigours of the siege and the condition under which all in the garrison would have been living for so long.

After a meal of soup, salt pork, moderately fresh vegetables and biscuits which she was too distraught to do more than peck at despite her hunger, she was taken below decks, deep into the ship down a succession of steep wooden ladders until she found herself on a deck so far down in the vessel and so low overhead that she had to bend almost double to pass along, a deck off which opened doors leading to minute cubby-holes – no doubt cabins and stores and ammunition-rooms, she thought. Her guide took her to the door of what she was told would be her cabin for the passage, a tiny apartment partitioned from the alleyway by thick wooden bulkheads with wire-mesh gratings let into their tops for air. A lantern, which her guide lighted for her, was swinging from a hook in the deckhead; so long as she remained in this cabin she would see no daylight. Such did not, she was told, penetrate so far down into the ship.

The cabin was almost entirely filled by a cot, which swung, like the lantern, from the deckhead; and the place gave her the most terrible feeling of claustrophobia, a feeling which was made worse by the ship-noises all around her – the constant creaking of the woodwork as the vessel rolled gently to the swell coming in from the Strait, the noises from the upper deck which she could hear faintly even down here as men moved heavy blocks and tackles and ropes and sails, or ran along as they tailed onto the sheets and tacks, hauling up to their yards the great square acres of canvas, preparing the ship for sea to the continual accompaniment of shouts, curses and blasphemy. There were cries of pain as ropes tore flesh, or as the bosun's mates laid across bare backs with canes as they drove the pressed men on in their ceaseless toil.

Bella undressed and clambered into her unaccustomed cot. She lay there sleepless, her body still painful, her mind humiliated and hurt. She thought desperately and with longing of Roger Carter, wondering if he would guess what had happened, what would be his own fate in the months that must pass before the siege could be lifted. His life would be worth little if Frazer ever found out what had been between them; for one thing, the ADC's snobbish soul would revolt at the mere thought of a colonel's widow bedding with a private soldier. Giving herself up to complete and utter misery, she cried bitterly, the sobs racking her body. It seemed years later when, as dawn must have broken over the Rock, she heard the tread of many feet as the capstan hove the anchor home; and then she felt the vessel moving, heeling a very little as the sails were shaken out and filled away. Soon she could hear the hiss of water along the vessel's side. She knew then that she was leaving the fortress finally, that they were hauling out of Algeciras Bay towards Europa, passing no doubt along the Line Wall where she had so often walked. Then, a little after, she heard the roar of cannon from the gun-decks above her, the shock as the guns recoiled, careering across the deck until the grab-ropes hauled them up short. They were coming up to the line of the Spanish cruisers, and battering their way through the small ships. Bosun's pipes shrilled and she heard the cries of wounded men and the judder of the ship as the enemy's fire briefly raked the decks, and then they were apparently through and sailing faster as the wind out in the Strait took them and billowed out topgallantsails and royals.

Bella had not been able to face seeing Gibraltar slide past, and with it Roger Carter; so she had remained in that stuffy, stifling cabin. Later she came out onto the upper deck to meet a gusty wind out of the west, blowing fleecy clouds along a blue sky; the sea itself was also of the deepest blue. She saw that the Rock was already some way astern, and dwindling . . . *but it was to the westward*. And she could see no other sail in any quarter of the compass. Frazer had told her that she was sailing with the Fleet – but the *Royal Sovereign* was alone, had not sailed in company with Admiral Darby's ships at all – and she appeared to be heading into the Mediterranean!

Bella was about to speak to one of the seamen and ask what this meant when a tall, dandified young lieutenant came up. He said in a high voice, 'Lady Kilkieran, I presume?' as though the ship were full of women.

She nodded.

'Ah – then His Lordship wishes to speak to you at once, ma'am.'

She looked at him blankly. 'His Lordship?'

'Lord Erringham, ma'am. The Captain, ma'am.'

'I see. Then will you please tell him where I am?'

The lieutenant hid a smile, cleared his throat. 'Aboard a ship, ma'am, one goes to the Captain when bid. The Captain does not come to oneself. If you look aft, you will see His Lordship on the quarterdeck.'

Bella looked, and saw a large gentleman pacing the quarterdeck with short, rapid strides, his bluff red face beneath the cocked hat turned upward as he kept an eye lifting on the set of the sails. His hands were clasped behind his back, a sword dangled at his left side, its point scraping the deck as he moved, and he wore a cloak over his uniform, a dark blue cloak with a crimson lining, a cloak which flowed out along the wind. The lieutenant said, 'If you will please come with me, Lady Kilkieran?'

Bella nodded and followed the young man aft and up an ornate companion-way onto the quarterdeck. The lieutenant waited until the Captain, who was now walking towards the stern, had turned again and was coming back for'ard and had seen him; it not being done, as he whispered to Bella, to approach one's Captain from behind. Then he went forward smartly and saluted.

'The Lady Kilkieran, my lord,' he said formally. 'You wished to see her.'

The bluff, honest face creased into an irascible frown. 'God damn and blast you to hell, Mr Pettigrew,' His Lordship said boomingly. 'I know quite well I wished to see her.'

'Aye, aye, my lord.'

'Then don't waste words.'

'No, my lord – '

'Verbosity is an abomination unto the Lord.'

'Yes, my lord.'

'Very well, Mr Pettigrew. Thank you. Off with you.'

'Aye, aye, my lord.' Mr Pettigrew turned about and disappeared thankfully, and Lord Erringham looked down at Bella with a benevolent smile.

'Well, well, ma'am,' he boomed. 'No doubt this is all very strange to you – what?'

'Yes, my lord,' she answered tartly. 'Very. It is even stranger that we seem to be to the eastward of Gibraltar, rather than to the westward.'

'Why so, ma'am, why so?' Erringham raised bushy white eyebrows in surprise.

She said, 'Why, because I understood the Fleet was under orders for home.'

Erringham pulled his cloak around his body and laughed boisterously. 'So it is, ma'am, so it is – all except the *Royal Sovereign*! My ship is under orders for Minorca.'

'Minorca?' Bella's eyes flashed. 'Lord Erringham, I was told that I was being accorded a passage home to Plymouth Sound!'

The sailor shrugged, glanced aloft again, eyes narrowed into the climbing sun. He said, 'Then, ma'am, you were misinformed, that's all I can say. I have orders to land you at Port Mahon in Minorca, where you will await another ship to England – if such there be.'

'If such there be!' Bella, in a rage, stamped her foot, her misery submerged now in her anger. 'Lord Erringham, may I ask who gave you these instructions?'

'Certainly, ma'am. His Excellency's aide-de-camp, acting on behalf of His Excellency, who was himself acting upon your own wishes, as I understood the matter.'

'Then you understood entirely wrong!' she stormed, her cheeks flushed attractively. 'Will you have the goodness to put your ship about, and return to Gibraltar, so that I can make representations to His Excellency?'

Lord Erringham stared at her, almost speechless. Then he said coldly, 'No, ma'am, I shall not. You must be out of your mind. Good-day to you.' He added, appearing to relent a little before such a pretty face and figure, 'I wish you a pleasant voyage . . . and a filled belly.'

He turned away then and moved on majestically, his cloak once again streaming out along the breeze, and Bella swung round on her heel, her cheeks flaming, and went down from the quarterdeck into the waist of the ship. She clenched her fists impotently. Captain Frazer must have known very well that her chances of getting away from Minorca would be very slim indeed, for it had been strongly rumoured that a combined French and Spanish fleet was already assembling to attack the island and thus, in taking it, effectively cut out an area of supply for the Gibraltar garrison.

★

The *Royal Sovereign* sailed on, rolling to a slight swell, her sails filling and then slatting against the masts as now and again the fitful wind failed her. Erringham was continually on deck, watching the canvas and harassing the officers-of-the-watch as his command made slow progress towards her destination. He seemed to be in a hurry to get there – no doubt he was anxious, Bella thought, to add the weight of his broadside to the defence of Minorca should the French and Spanish ships be sailing already to the attack. Bella was feeling more philosophical as to her lot now; that filled belly of which Erringham had spoken had worked wonders after the terrible short commons in Gibraltar, even though it was filled only with salt-horse and weevily ship's biscuits.

That afternoon there was great activity throughout the ship, the bosun's mates and the ship's police patrolling throughout the lower decks, busy with their canes and rope's-ends, sending all hands to the upper deck. Bella, happening to run into the dandified Mr Pettigrew, asked the reason for all this activity.

He said squeakily, 'There is to be a flogging, ma'am, that's what. One of the seamen was insubordinate towards the sailing-master while we were preparing for sea during the night. This afternoon he takes his punishment.'

'And that is?'

'One hundred lashes, ma'am.' Mr Pettigrew rubbed his hands together. 'One hundred lashes from the cat o'nine tails while made fast to the gratings. A good taste of the cat, and I'll warrant he won't be impertinent again in a hurry!'

Bella felt a shudder run through her body as Pettigrew walked off. Later that bluff sailor Lord Erringham enquired – whether or not with his tongue in his cheek she didn't know – if she would care to watch from the quarterdeck, but she begged to be excused such a spectacle. She had not, however, cleared the crowded decks towards her cabin before the unfortunate man was brought up under escort, his hands tied in front of his body. He was a young man, fair and clean-looking; stripped to the waist, he showed a fine torso rippling with muscle. There was a nervous twitch in his face as he was roped to the gratings. A bosun's mate stood by, idly running his fingers along the thongs of the cat, the cat which the prisoner had, in accordance with custom, made that morning for his own scourging. There were few sounds as Bella made her way as quickly as possible below; only a few barked orders, and the movement of the sails and the running gear. All the men were silent, watchful, tense – and expectant. It was a nauseating scene.

Bella had not got very far when the sounds became very different: There was the terrible whistle of the weighted lash itself, the nerve-racking sound as the tails bit into the young seaman's flesh and curled round his ribs, the grunt of pain that was forced from him after three or four lashes had laid that flesh open. Bella stuffed her fingers into her ears as she hurried, stumbling, falling over obstacles along the unaccustomed gundecks, but she could not, a little later, keep out the terrible screams, the screams which rose and fell at regular intervals, screams which held on a high note and faded away into incoherent sobs and gasps until the next cruel lash, delivered with all the strength of a bosun's mate, came down upon the helpless back and brought that trembling cry back to the otherwise still air. The hundredth lash was laid on as vigorously as the first, for the man wielding the cat was changed after each ten lashes so as to ensure that there was no loss of strength from start to finish.

When it was all over Bella heard screaming coming closer and then the tramp of feet as a group of men came down from the upper deck and something made her leave the cabin – some instinct, perhaps, to help and succour. She went quickly for'ard towards the little group and saw the man being brought down by his messmates. He was no longer a young, well-set-up fellow but a moaning and quivering lump of lacerated, bloody flesh quite unable to stagger along the deck on his own. Bella stopped dead, every part of her being revolted, and crying out in pity. She stumbled back against a bulkhead, unable to go on, and soon after that the awful screams rang out again all along the gun-deck as the man was laid on a mess table and cleansing salt was rubbed into the raw wounds of back, sides and ribs by his mates.

He was still screaming and sobbing when there came a sudden increase in the activity on deck. Men rushed here and there and below decks it sounded as if a series of heavy weights had been dropped. A moment later the drums of the Marines began to beat to arms and a rush of men swarmed down into the gun-decks and began manhandling the great rows of cannon that stood behind the closed gun-ports. They were run out ready for action, their snouts pointing wickedly through the ports as each was opened up.

A brutal-looking bosun's mate made his way towards the group of men round the bleeding form on the mess table. He roared out, 'All right, leave him! All hands to general quarters.' As the members of the group dispersed quickly before they too became the victims of a later flogging, the bosun's mate reached out and dragged the cringing seaman off the table and held him upright with a thick, hairy arm. He growled, 'Never mind your wounds. The Dons are bearing down from the nor'westward. We'll need every man-jack. If you don't do your share, you lubber, I'll promise you four hundred lashes next time . . . till your entrails are whipped out of you.'

He gave the man a push and he went reeling into a stanchion.

14

Erringham's face was red and angry as he lowered his telescope. On the horizon Bella, who had come up to the quarterdeck now, could see a long line of white sails. There must have been twenty or thirty ships there, as yet hull-down. And the British ship would certainly have been sighted from the enemy line in the same way as the Dons had been sighted from the *Royal Sovereign*'s main topgallant masthead.

'By God!' Erringham snapped suddenly at his First Lieutenant, a short, barrel-like man with a brisk and confident manner. 'I've never had to run yet – never! I don't like it, Mr Fanshawe.'

'No more do I, my lord, but if I may say so, it's the only possible course. Our first objective is to strengthen the Minorca defence in accordance with our orders. Here, alone, we can only weaken that defence by being shot to fragments before we even sight Port Mahon, my lord. We have a chance of keeping our distance until we join the Mediterranean Squadron, and in my opinion we would do better to take it.'

'Ah, but they can yet outsail us, Fanshawe.' Erringham wrapped his cloak tightly about his vast body, and glowered towards the line of the Spanish Fleet. 'They can yet outsail us . . . and I would rather stand and fight than be brought to a running action in the end.'

'Yes, my lord.' The First Lieutenant glanced aloft, transferring his attention to the sails. He had gone as far as was prudent in indicating his own opinion, and he would say no more now. Erringham took a few turns up and down the deck, then stopped and, screwing up his face, also looked anxiously aloft at the billowing canvas; and then once more at the distant line of ships.

There was a dead silence as his officers waited for his decision.

After a few minutes he boomed, 'Very well, First Lieutenant. We run for Minorca, with always the possibility of leading the Dons into the cannon of the Mediterranean Squadron. Fall out the guns' crews for the time being to assist in trimming the sails when required . . . we must take fullest advantage of every capful of wind now.'

'Aye, aye, my lord.'

The sailing-master, who was standing by the First Lieutenant, passed the orders to the bosun and at once the calls began their shrilling. Men went at the double to stand by the ropes or made their way aloft to lie out along the yards and begin shaking out the few extra small sails that the vessel was not already carrying. The *Royal Sovereign* ploughed onward but as the hours passed it became increasingly obvious that the lighter vessels of the enemy fleet, at any rate, had the legs of them.

It was nightfall on the following day, a fine clear night with a light wind and a bright moon which silvered the ghostly water, when Lord Erringham's worst fears were realized and he knew that he could not hope to outsail the Dons all the way to Minorca. He was now to be brought to a running action, and when he turned to fight he would turn into the guns of a closing enemy.

He stopped his restless pacing of his quarterdeck at nine thirty-three precisely and called to the sailing-master. 'Mr Amherst,' he said in a strangely subdued voice, 'kindly wear ship to starboard. I'll turn across and give 'em as many broadsides as I can before they blow us out of the water. Mr Fanshawe?'

'My lord?'

'Beat to general quarters. Inform the men that we fight to the last ball and cutlass and we shall never strike our colours.'

'Aye, aye, my lord.'

'Now, ma'am.' Erringham swung round on Bella, who had kept on deck whenever possible, feeling too claustrophic in her tiny cabin. 'I suggest you take yourself off the decks and go to my own day-cabin. I fear you will be safe nowhere in the ship ultimately, but in there you will at least be spared flying metal and shot – and many bloody scenes.' He put a hand on her shoulder. 'I am much distressed at having a woman aboard. I would not have had this happen to you for all the world, ma'am.'

' 'Tis not your fault,' Bella said stoutly. 'My lord, if I am to die, I may as well die witnessing a battle. I am not afraid, my lord. I have little to lose. With your permission, I shall remain here on deck.'

'As you like, then,' Erringham answered kindly but shortly, his attention once again on the handling of his ship and the forthcoming battle as the drums beat to quarters. 'Only keep over by the shrouds and out of the way of my ship's company – and of myself, ma'am, if you please.'

She nodded and, gathering her skirts, ran across the deck towards the mizzen shrouds on the starboard side. The moon lit up the encroaching Spanish sails so that they looked like sheeted silver on the dark sea. Three frigates of the vanguard were now within cannon shot and were racing across so as to fire their slender broadsides into the *Royal Sovereign*'s fore-castle and fore rigging, while astern of them two ships of the line were now coming up close as way came off the British ship on the turn. Those two heavy vessels looked like seventy-fours, and the mere fact of their presence must now swing the outcome of the battle heavily, indeed finally, against Erringham.

The moment his ship was round on a firing course, Erringham backed topsails and passed the word to open on the enemy; and on the instant a full broadside of some thirty-five cannon crashed out from under Bella's feet and the entire ship seemed to jerk, to jump in the very water, while the acrid smoke from the burnt powder swept up from the gun-ports below to choke and blind her. At almost the same instant a thin line of red light flickered from the nearest of the enemy frigates. As the smoke continued to drift up from the *Royal Sovereign*'s own guns, the enemy balls whistled through the rigging, cutting ropes but, so far, miraculously missing the masts and yards themselves. One ball took away a section of the bulwarks in the starboard side of the waist. When the cannon smoke drifted clear, a ragged cheer came from the

British sailors, for the frigate's mainmast was seen to have been hit and was lying across her deck in a tangle of rigging; and then, as Bella watched, a flicker of flame licked up from her after deck.

Erringham ordered the next broadside to be fired into the second of the frigates, which had by this time also opened upon the British ship; but all the balls of this vessel's salvo had fallen slightly short, sending up great spouts of water which broke over the *Royal Sovereign*'s decks and did no other harm. However, before Erringham was ready the second frigate had fired again and this time her range was true. The line of cannon fired full into the vast, towering side of the British ship, splitting cannon and igniting powder-cases and causing a most bloody carnage along all the gun-decks. The *Royal Sovereign*'s next broadside flew low through the Spaniard's rigging, raking her deck with metal, and then the frigate fired once more, point-blank now into the British vessel – and was then joined by the third frigate who fired into the great ship's other side.

The slaughter along the gun-decks must have been terrible, Bella knew, but the cannon were firing still, with no perceptible slackening of effort or rate of fire as more men were sent forward to take over the stations of the dead and dying.

Then, through the smoke and flame of the battle, Bella saw the tall masts, the great sheer sides of the enemy line-of-battle ships – the seventy-fours coming in with their devastating hammer-blows, rearing high above the little frigates, swinging round so that their full broadsides could rake the *Royal Sovereign* above and below.

In a high voice she called out, 'My lord, the line-of-battle ships are coming in . . .'

'That we have seen, ma'am.' Erringham came up briefly beside her, his face black with smoke, his cloak gone and his uniform awry. 'We shall give them a good fight, never fear.'

'I am quite sure of that!' she answered stoutly.

Erringham put a hand on her shoulder for a moment and murmured something which she didn't catch; then he turned away as the enemy cannon crashed out amid a belching of smoke and flame which lit the sea like a red and bloody dawn. The British gunners scarcely had time to bear before the Spaniards had opened together, their decks, tier on tier, seeming to blaze to heaven. A hail of balls took the *Royal Sovereign* fair and square along her starboard beam. Her sides stove in, her fore and main masts crashed down as if pushed aside by some giant's hand, smashed off some six feet above deck level to leave two useless, splintered stumps. Those great masts, each well over a hundred and fifty feet in length, fell across backs and legs and arms, and the air was filled with the piteous cry of the wounded and trapped. Pale with sheer terror now, Bella, who had felt the wind of the passing cannon-balls, looked round to see Erringham and his First Lieutenant lying dead on the deck and the great wheel smashed to fragments. The sailing-master had been decapitated, was lying in a neat heap without his head, which had rolled to the bulwarks. The ship was swinging in circles now, canvas flapping uselessly around her decks and even the sails on the mizzen torn and filled with holes where the Spanish balls had passed. Licks of flame from the upper gun-deck were curling out from the gun-ports just below where Bella stood, and indeed right along her length the ship seemed to be on fire. She would soon be a blazing inferno. Bella heard the master's mates yelling for the hands to trim what was left of the sails on the mizzen, to send fresh canvas up there in a gallant attempt to turn the great vessel round so that she could bear with the larboard-side guns. For once, but too late, luck smiled and a shift of wind carried her round; and the moment she was in position to fire, another broadside crashed out, only to be immediately answered by both the Spanish line-of-battle ships. And then, closing their prey, the Dons came up to rake the *Royal Sovereign* with musket fire from all their fighting tops and along their bulwarks while their cannon still sent the flying death across the narrowing gap.

Now the *Royal Sovereign* seemed to be filled, choked with the dead and dying. Blood was everywhere and the flames were already scorching the planks of the quarterdeck from below; the waist itself was impassable. The Spaniards, whose intentions at one time seemed to have been to board and end it with the cutlass, now discreetly sheered away to leave the British ship to burn to her destruction.

Bella saw that there was only one thing left to do, and that was what many of the sailors were doing already, though the word had not yet been passed to abandon ship: jump into the sea and hope to grab a piece of drifting timber. If she drowned, at least it would be preferable to being cindered.

Shaking with fear of what was going to happen to her, Bella climbed up onto the bulwarks and stood there looking downwards into the dark sea lit by the demoniac fires beneath and behind her. If only Roger Carter were by her side! Convinced now that she was going to die, her thoughts were wholly of him.

15

She was in the sea now.

She had taken her courage in both hands and she had jumped from the bulwarks, as the flames encroached behind her, into the dark waters reflecting back the fiery glow from above. She was gasping and fighting for life, only the air trapped in her clothing keeping her afloat, and she didn't know how long she would remain so . . . but anything would be better than remaining aboard that floating hell which had so lately been a proud ship of the line; and she had heard that the Spaniards were always chivalrous towards women.

If she lasted long enough, and if they recognized her for a woman amid the wreckage and the floating corpses, they would surely not let her drown.

Her ears were filled with the fierce sound of the crackling as timber, tarred rope and canvas burned, the flames roaring to heaven, climbing the tall mizzen-mast and what was left of the rigging, leaping out along the yards and shooting upwards from all that remained of the great sails. There were muffled explosions as powder-cases ignited, and sparks and pieces of timber flew afresh, sizzling into the sea. Heads bobbed around her; men – wounded, burnt, shocked men – screamed continuously and uselessly, a terrifying orchestra in that flame-filled night. They went on screaming until their mates mercifully pushed them under and they drowned. The corpses drifted past. Then, in that ferocious glare, Bella saw a great baulk of timber floating not far away – it had the appearance of a section of one of the shattered masts – and, kicking and scrabbling at the encroaching water, she propelled herself towards it, inexpertly but as best she could, gasping and spitting and clawing the sea-plastered hair from her eyes.

Thankfully she reached it, grasped at it with urgent fingers which merely slipped off. Close to panic, she grabbed for the timber again, sobbing in her deperation.

Then she heard the voice in her ear – a deep, reassuring, strong voice. 'All right, milady. It's all right. Just you leave it to me.'

Steely strong hands slid under her arms and tightened about her body and the rough voice went on, 'I got you safe now, milady, I'm 'oldin' you. Reach out now, and take the timber. Easy does it. Don't be frightened now.'

She reached out, felt a heave from behind and found herself almost thrown across the thick timber so that her body was clear of the water. Looking round when she had recovered herself, she saw gleaming black hair streaked across a mahogany face, thick, hairy arms holding securely onto the driftwood. The man smiled at her, showing broken, tobacco-stained teeth; she smiled back.

'I am indeed grateful,' she said breathlessly. 'Do you think the Dons will see us?'

The man nodded. 'I reckon so, milady. An' if they does, then I'm all for rescue. I don't like to think o' being a prisoner any more'n anyone else, but I reckon 'tis better'n Davy Jones's locker when all's said an' done . . . an' that way, we'll live to fight another day!'

'Will they take us from the water, then?'

''Tis very likely they will . . . when they see a woman, leastways.' He twisted round, looked back at the blazing hulk of the *Royal Sovereign*. He shook his head regretfully, then drew Bella's attention to the big Spanish vessels lying off. He said, 'They're making ready to go about, milady. But mebbe they'll be back. They'll sail clear for a while in case she blows up.'

'The *Royal Sovereign*? That may happen?'

''Tis always a chance, milady.' The sailor spat vigorously into the water. 'She'll blow all right, if the flames reach downwards inside of her and touch the powder-magazines afore 'er sides are broached to let the sea in.' He paused, then added on a note of sudden hope, 'Look, now, the Spaniard's alterin' for us after all, I do reckon! That nearer one, see . . . now, milady, just you shout out loud as you can, see. A good loud cry, milady, just as if I was runnin' me 'ands up those lovely legs o' yours . . .' He grinned. ''Tis little use bein' a dead 'ero.'

He yelled himself, in a carrying voice. Bella called out as loudly as she could, and others joined in all around them. After a while it became obvious that the Spaniard was indeed moving slowly towards them. Bella's companion said in her ear, 'See that flag, milady – flying from 'er main t'gallant masthead?'

Bella looked. 'The big one?'

'Aye, the big 'un – 'tis the admiral's flag. 'Tis the flagship that's coming for us. You'll have the pleasure o' meeting the Marquis o' Villena, milady. They say 'e's a real gentleman – even if 'e is a dago.'

Bella watched in hope as the great flagship bore down on the groups of men, dazed and half-drowned as they swam or floated or clung to pieces of wreckage as she herself was doing, clung to the broken fragments of their blazing ship. Bella saw the Spaniard's big sails being hauled round, heard the slight hiss of water past the sheer-sided hull as it approached, heard the orders being passed along the decks . . . and then, with thankfulness, she saw men along her bulwarks lowering vast nets over the sides on ropes, nets which her companion had told her were the boarding-nets. Slowly the line-of-battle ship sailed through the groups of British tars, most of whom grabbed for the nets trailing in the water as she passed. Others yelled derisively, preferring to die than be taken. Bella's companion got her safely onto the net and called at her to climb for her life, then he got a handhold himself; the men, like so many flies clinging to a wall, swarmed up as the nets themselves, loaded now, were hoisted to assist them. Within a few moments Bella found herself being lifted, none too gently, over the side as her weary body reached the bulwarks. She was left, gasping like a landed fish, on the deck while the rest of the survivors were brought inboard. She appeared to be an object of some curiosity and, so far as she could gather from the sudden bursts of laughter, crude ribaldry on the part of the victorious Spanish sailors, who would not perhaps have expected to find a woman on board the British ship. The word of this spread quickly, and soon an officer appeared and tried to make her understand that preparations would shortly be made for her comfort.

The moment the rescue operation was complete the remaining canvas was shaken out and the Spaniard gathered way, the sails filling and the water beginning to sigh strongly past her hull; and soon the blazing wreck of the *Royal Sovereign* had been left well to the south-eastward as the breeze freshened. As the captured sailors were taken below under guard, Bella was led, dishevelled and wet, below decks to a cabin where she was told to strip; and was then provided with a man's nightshirt to wear until her own clothing had been dried out. After that she was taken aft to the great stern cabin in the Admiral's magnificent quarters, where she had a long wait before the Marques de Villena came down from the quarterdeck.

He was a tall man, sallow and black haired and, as Bella had already been led to assume by the sailor in the water, not unkindly. Standing himself before the wide stern-windows which looked onto the after gallery he told Bella to sit, had brandy brought for her, and when she was somewhat recovered he elicited her identity and then began questioning her about conditions in the garrison at Gibraltar.

Bella said, 'I have nothing to tell you about that, sir.'

Villena fingered his moustaches. 'Until we reach port, the matter is of little importance . . . but thereafter – there may be ways known to my compatriots of making a pretty woman talk. I would advise you to avoid any indignities by talking to me, Lady Kilkieran.'

Her colour rose. 'I care nothing for what your compatriots may do to me. I shall never speak of any matter which it may profit England's enemies to know!'

The Admiral laughed. 'A fine sentiment, a fine sentiment! You are a brave young woman – but we shall see! Meanwhile, my Lady Kilkieran, you will be well enough treated aboard my flagship, I promise you . . . but I regret that once we reach port it will not be possible to allow you your liberty until the end of hostilities. In short, for the remainder of the passage you will have the run of my flagship, but when we reach port, why, then you will be held as a prisoner-of-war unless His Most Catholic Majesty should decide otherwise.'

Bella shrugged, saw Villena's gaze obliquely on her figure as she did so. She said, 'I expect no less and no more. Where are you making for, sir?'

'For Malaga. Not Minorca as yet.' He smiled. 'Your ships will find this confusing!'

'And Malaga is where I shall be held?'

The Admiral said indifferently as he sipped brandy, 'I cannot say. I shall hand you over to the military authorities, and it will be up to them what happens to you thereafter . . . or even,' he added with a faint smile, 'His Majesty himself might very well be interested in so . . . well-endowed a young woman! Failing that, it is possible that you will be held in a military prison.'

It did not, however, turn out quite like that.

The Spanish flagship – she was the one hundred and ten gun *Reina Isabella* – entered the port of Malaga, which was some seventy kilometres north-east of Gibraltar, amid scenes of the most tumultuous enthusiasm. News of the victory had reached the port some hours earlier by means of a despatch-vessel which Villena had detached and sent ahead of the main fleet. The dead British commander, Lord Erringham, had been a famed seaman, skilful and vigorous in the prosecution of his duty and he had been a scourge to Spanish shipping; and this victory over him had been most welcome, the more so since whatever the force of the Spanish arms before Gibraltar they had so far been quite unable to subdue the fortress or indeed to bring about any substantial gains at all, and this sea-victory could therefore be considered a fillip to the sagging spirits of the Dons. Indeed so much was being made of it that a certain gentleman of France, a General who, it was rumoured, was about to take command of the joint French and Spanish armies to end the siege of Gibraltar by force of arms, himself boarded the *Reina Isabella* to offer his congratulations to the Marques de Villena. This gentleman, the Duc de Crillon, arrived shortly after the flagship had anchored; he arrived with other dignitaries and it so happened that Bella, who had made herself as tidy and presentable as possible once her clothing was dry, was taking her exercise upon the deck at the time; and after the polite formalities were over one of these high personages took the Admiral on one side.

'The girl,' he murmured in Villena's ear, bending a frame even taller and thinner than the Admiral's, 'the young girl whom I espied upon your decks . . . she is the Lady Kilkieran, late of the Gibraltar fortress, whom your despatches mentioned?'

Villena nodded, politely but with a degree of coldness, for he had recognized the other's intent.

The tall man's eyes gleamed, and he ran his tongue over full red lips, lips which looked salacious and even indecent in the unpleasant, dead-white face. He extended a hand with long, tapering fingers and pointed nails, which he examined. He went on delicately and obliquely, 'If such could be arranged, Admiral . . . I would much appreciate a meeting with her.'

Villena said, 'So far as I know . . . she is to be treated as a prisoner-of-war. I doubt if there will be much opportunity of social intercourse, Your – '

The tall man gave a bleak smile. 'These matters are trifles, Admiral, the merest trifles. You will appreciate that I am a person of some influence in your country at present . . . you will send for the girl, Admiral. At once.'

The Marques sighed. Any girl would be in poor company with this sadistic-looking Frenchman . . . but there was nothing he could do. He snapped a request to his Flag Captain to send for Lady Kilkieran, who a few minutes later came haughtily to the quarterdeck, wild and beautiful despite her torn, washed-out clothing. The Admiral said, 'Your Royal Highness, the Lady Kilkieran . . . Lady Kilkieran, His Royal Highness the Comte d'Artois, brother of His Majesty of France.'

Bella, keeping her back ramrod-straight, looked into the cold, fish-like eyes of the French aristocrat, felt, as she did so, her clothing peeling from her body in his gaze, that gaze that seemed to peer and probe indecently into every secret part of her. Involuntarily, she shivered. In some curious way, the day had grown suddenly cold, notwithstanding the high sun of noon.

16

Brother of His Majesty of France . . . one of England's bitterest enemies! Bella returned the French nobleman's lascivious look coldly and scornfully. D'Artois went on looking her up and down, those dangerous eyes of his still stripping her and exposing in his mind the subtle and private curves of her body. Finally, a sadistic smile twisting his full lips, he turned to the Marques de Villena.

He said distantly, 'A desirable wench, my dear Admiral. Tell me . . . what is to become of her now?'

'That is for the military authorities to decide, Your Royal Highness.'

'Ah?' The eyebrows went up disdainfully. 'Admiral, if you would spare me a moment, just one moment, of your doubtless valuable time – and de Crillon as well?'

The Admiral bowed stiffly, his eyes remaining hard. He said, 'But certainly, Your Royal Highness.'

'Privately, if you please.'

Villena seemed about to speak but thought better of it. He bowed again, and then led the way aft along the quarterdeck. D'Artois and de Crillon followed him. Once out of earshot, the Admiral stopped. Bella watched as they began talking together, her heart fluttering curiously. D'Artois' moment seemed to be a somewhat lengthy one, and the Admiral was looking hot under the collar, his face stiff and haughtily withdrawn, the black brows frowning. When the three men came back towards her, Bella realized that Villena was furiously angry; his lips were tightly compressed and his face was white. He said, 'Lady Kilkieran, I have no option but to land you forthwith into the personal custody of His Royal Highness the Comte d'Artois, who is to be responsible for your safe custody. Rest assured, however, that I shall represent this matter to my superiors at the first opportunity.'

'Which,' the Frenchman said, smiling venomously, 'will make no difference whatsoever. The moment one of my postillions can reach the court at Madrid, I shall have the personal approval of His Most Catholic Majesty.' He tapped Villena on the arm, his eyes glittering, 'Your country and your king are most grateful for the armed support of His Majesty my brother, my dear Admiral! What can a mere sailor do against that?'

An hour later Bella, dressed again in fine clothes which d'Artois had bought her from a dressmaker in the town, was sitting well back inside a great gilded coach, alone with the Comte, and lumbering out of Malaga, through sleepy, dirt-littered streets beneath a hot sun, heading for the dusty track – it was no more than that – which ran to the southward through the few mean dwellings which made up the little village of Torremolinos. In the intervals between a lecherous pawing, d'Artois informed Bella that, together with the Duc de Crillon, who was in a following coach, they were in fact proceeding to the Spanish lines opposite Gibraltar – that, by the time the long road journey was completed, only a mile or so would separate Bella from the fortress which she had so lately left.

The Frenchman said cynically. 'But do not imagine that this proximity will help you in any way, my Lady Kilkieran. Your British soldiers will be quite powerless, indeed before very much longer the garrison will assuredly be overrun.'

'An attack is being prepared?'

D'Artois laughed. 'That you will see for yourself, quite soon. However, before then . . . we stop the night en route. After that, we shall be better acquainted, you and I.'

She said tartly, 'Better, monsieur? I had thought you had gone some way already.'

D'Artois laughed again, and slid his hand silkily along her thigh. He said in a soft voice, 'Dear innocent, you will not speak in that fashion after tonight . . .'

She tried to close her ears to what he was saying, not to

listen to this baring of a lascivious mind as d'Artois whipped his passions with salacious promises: but always the soft voice went on, penetrating her consciousness, giving her a foretaste of what was to come. It was a nightmare journey of heat and dust and swarming flies, through desiccated brown country with scarce a dwelling or even a human being in sight, and the discomfort was intense as the coach bumped and jolted over the shocking roughness of the track.

They spent that night at a hostelry, a small and seedy place in the little wayside hamlet of Estepona. For Bella, it was a relief to get out of the stuffy, swaying coach and the enveloping dust into a cool, dark room; but, once they had eaten – they dined with the Duc de Crillon, in such state as the little inn could manage – and had retired to their bedroom, the rest of that night was sheer horror. It was a horror during which she lay, racked with pain and indignity, dry eyed but with a sob in her throat, as the Frenchman's hands roamed her body, searching, probing, delving, his loose wet mouth pressed to her flesh and the breath rasping through his teeth. When at last he was ready for the final act the hard pressure, the thrust of his body, left her gasping but rigid. The drink d'Artois had taken had dimmed his senses more than he had suspected, and by the time he was spent Bella had long since reached her climax . . . a climax which, oddly, she had found gave her intense but swift pleasure. Her body had momentarily tautened like a bow and her legs had bent as though by a reflex, had bent and gripped him, and then the climax had passed for her and his passion was still unsatisfied. When the mounting sun stole through the small window into the stuffy bedroom and that dreadful night ended at last, Bella knew that she would never feel clean or wholesome again while she was forced to remain with d'Artois as his mistress.

She sat up in the bed, trembling and shaken, as d'Artois' valet came in and sponged down his master's naked, sweating body and assisted him in his dressing. The servant's face held a leer as he glanced at Bella holding the bedclothes over her breasts, as if he knew in detail – as indeed he must know – what his master's habits were.

D'Artois said suddenly, 'It is time you were dressing, my

pretty. We must be upon the road shortly, to reach San Roque by nightfall.' When she remained silent he added sharply, 'You heard what I said, Bella? Dress, if you please.'

'I do not please. Your man – '

'André?' D'Artois laughed. 'Do not concern yourself about him – he is a servant. Come, my pretty – get dressed. At once!'

Still she sat there, gazing at him dumbly now, a hot flush stealing over her cheeks. D'Artois gave a short exclamation and strode across the room. As the valet watched, he tugged at the bedclothes, ripping them from her grasp, and she cringed, hiding her nakedness as best she could with her hands. D'Artois bent and dragged her upright, and she felt both men's gaze upon her flesh; it seemed as though it was another manifestation of d'Artois' abnormality, that he should get pleasure from exposing his mistress to his valet. Then suddenly, and to her own amazement, she did a surprising thing: Biting back her feelings, determined only to show this lewd Frenchman that British women were not to be brow-beaten, that she could carry off any situation as she wished, she squared her shoulders, feeling the upthrust of her rounded breasts as she did so; then, swinging her hips, thrusting forward the lower part of her abdomen provocatively, she walked across the room. She did it like a queen, and she passed as tantalizingly close to the valet as she was able, catching his eye and smiling at him.

That angered the Comte – shook him, as she had intended, out of his complaisant calm. He shouted at the valet, 'All right, André, what are you standing there for – have you never seen what a woman has to offer? Find yourself some Spanish wench for a good night's rutting when we reach the coast – and in the meantime, clear out of here!'

After a plain but solid early breakfast the coaches were brought to the door of the inn; and in clear crystal air they rolled away for what would soon become another day of heat and dust and aching thirst, along the road to San Roque and the cork woods where the besieging might of France and Spain, the guns and the armies, were encamped. Bella spoke little during that journey; she answered d'Artois in mono-syllables when he spoke to her, which was not often. As the coaches neared the southern part of Andalusia, the Frenchman seemed to be possessed by some curious excitement. His cruel face became dark, more sadistic than ever. Bella kept frigidly in her corner of the rocking, swaying vehicle as the driven horses made what speed they could over the bumps and potholes. It was, for much of the way, a beautiful drive, with the deep blue of the Mediterranean fringing wide beaches of golden sand and stretching into the far distance below the high, precipitous coast road, and the great dominance of the mountain ranges, purple and misty blue and silver in the west and north as they shimmered beneath the sun; but Bella scarcely noticed any of it, scarcely noticed the changing colours as the day wore on towards a glorious sunset. From now on, all her days were to be overshadowed by what she knew would take place at night in the privacy of d'Artois' bedroom.

It was late when they rolled wearily into San Roque, past a cluster of little white-washed hovels, and made for the Duc de Crillon's newly established headquarters, an encampment under the shade of the cork trees where the whole area was redolent with the smell from the charcoal-burners' fires. The Duc's staff had arrived ahead of him and were already quartered in an impressive array of vast and stately marquees, above the central one of which hung, limply in that still air, the Royal Standard of Spain, the King's personal standard under which the operation of the siege-armies was being conducted. It was late, but not too late, after they had refreshed with a wash in clear cool water, for a glittering repast. Long tables groaned under the weight of food enough, it seemed to Bella, to maintain the whole Gibraltar garrison for a year; many white-gloved servants waited upon the high-ranking officers of France and Spain; much wine was drunk and there were many toasts. Bella had a strong feeling that something tremendous was in the air. A final assault, perhaps, against the beleaguered garrison, the great Rock which she could see in the near distance, silhouetted against the star-hung sky?

Did the Dons feel that final victory was near?

That night she lay awake for hours, thinking and thinking, unmolested by the Comte, who had flopped into his bed in a drunken stupor which had utterly destroyed even his physical capacity to make love. He was snoring like a pig alongside her, one hand flung across her thighs, the fingers, even in sleep, enmeshing in her body. And all night there came the sound of bugles, and of marching men, and, over all, the ceaseless clamour of the guns as they rained their shells upon the near-helpless garrison – and upon Roger Carter, if indeed he was still alive.

Her heart ached for him.

17

As the days passed Bella became more and more apprehensive, more and more certain that Gibraltar's days were numbered, that the heroic defence was about to be cruelly smashed. More men were being moved into the Spanish lines daily, they came in a never-ending stream of uniforms; more batteries were constructed until the coast bristled with their cannon, and the damage caused by the shot from Gibraltar was always quickly repaired. Indeed Bella could no longer be in any doubt at all as to the Dons' intentions, for she heard much of the high-level discussion which took place between de Crillon and d'Artois. She learned with anguish that all the information suggested that the garrison of Gibraltar was weakening fast, coming to the very end of its pitiful resources. Scarcely a ship had entered for weeks past, and none since she herself had left the Rock.

And now everything seemed set for the final act of the tragedy.

There was one slender consolation for her: The Comte d'Artois was being called into private conference from time to time and had lengthy talks with the Duc de Crillon and the subordinate commanders. This left Bella free of his detested company, gave her a few precious hours of freedom from his lecherous glances and attentions. No restraint was being placed upon her movements now – none, that was, apart from the inescapable and basic fact that she was in a military encampment and that wherever she went there were soldiers, always soldiers . . . From the Dons' point of view she could scarcely be in a safer place, and they had no reason in any case to fear her escape. She would never get far; almost everyone in the great series of camps had heard about her by now, if they had not seen her. Militarily she was of no account; she had been closely questioned the day after her arrival by the Duc de

Crillon's staff officers and by the Duc himself, but she had given nothing away as to conditions inside the fortress except to say what the Dons must already know – that the soldiers were hungry! And so she was able, during that blessed freedom, to wander through the cork woods, with the fresh wild flowers springing around her and the smell of the charcoal-burning, or sometimes along the banks of the Guadacorte River or – which she much preferred since she could walk in greater solitude there – along by the sea to the westward, outside the range of the Gibraltar guns which were still sending across their shells. Here she could look clear across the bay to the Rock of Gibraltar, rising grand and grey in the middle distance. She stared with longing, her eyes filling with tears as she thought of what the indomitable defenders were undergoing . . . the privations, the terrible suffering of mind and body, the damage to the buildings, the dead and wounded who must surely be mounting most pitifully. Most of all she found herself thinking, as indeed she had done for the greater part of the time since she had been put aboard the *Royal Sovereign*, of Private Roger Carter. She recalled his slender, youthful body, his wonderfully tender caresses, so different from the gross gropings of d'Artois. She longed with all her heart and soul to feel his hands upon her again, to submit, to surrender to the sublime sweetness of bodily contact which carried her away at the moment of climax into realms of joy and wonderment, and, above all, content . . . even as she thought of the warm, hard contact of his firm limbs tears sprang to her eyes.

At times, when self-pity was momentarily uppermost, she thought of her own fervent but vain wish to remain in garrison until the siege was lifted – that, now, was nothing but a dream, a fond memory of the utter certainty which once she had felt that Gibraltar would be relieved and would fight back. The siege of Gibraltar was never going to be lifted except after a Spanish victory, she knew that now. Too much was ranged against the Rock. The cruiser-cordon seemed to have been strengthened recently, was far too strong now, she fancied, to admit ever again the passage of any British ships – short of some great commander like Lord Rodney attempting to force the entry with the whole of the King's Navy behind him and all guns bearing. For the land assault, the Spanish lines teemed with men, the camps and fortifications were strained to their seams; though the supply and commissariat was equal to the occasion, as was the ammunition-train. There were great stacks of roundshot and shells and dumps of powder practically all the way from San Roque to La Linea, and the very air seemed to be filled with the shouted commands of officers and NCOs, the neighing of cavalry horses and the rumble of transport wheels.

D'Artois said, 'Bella my sweet, we move on today.'

'Oh?' She was startled, sat up suddenly in the bed. 'Where to?'

'Not far away,' he murmured softly. Everything about d'Artois except his eyes was soft – soft, fleshy, puffy. His white hand caressed her horribly, sliding down her quivering stomach. 'As far as La Linea – the nearest point, barring only Fort St Philip itself, to the Rock. You see, de Crillon is moving his command post.' He stopped his fumbling and looked at her intently. 'You realize, of course, what that means?'

She said shortly, 'I am not a fool, d'Artois.'

He laughed. 'Quite . . . quite! I see that you understand that it means the end for Gibraltar. Within a few days, little more, the Royal Standard of Spain will fly over the British Governor's residence, and your batteries will be silent . . . and it will have been brought about by force of French arms, my dear one – the Spaniards have no real stomach for fighting, I regret to say.'

She answered hotly, her face flushed now with more than his hand's explorations of her body, 'It is a cowardly war! What hope have the men in the fortress, hungry as they are, and after so many months of battering?'

'They can always surrender.'

'They will never do that, and you know it. But – where is the honour in such a victory?'

He shrugged, rubbed a hand over the stubble on his chin. 'They were not forced to go to Gibraltar, the British. His Most Catholic Majesty did not ask them to. Gibraltar, my dear girl, is Spanish – by geography, by association, by language and by logic. It is past time you arrogant British were taught a lesson. A lesson that you are not, as you think you are, beloved by the whole world.'

And that morning the headquarters of the assault force moved. The horses and transport were assembled and the Staff moved the few miles along the dusty, fly-ridden track into the sleazy township of La Linea, immediately before the great face of Gibraltar's North Front which stared across the neutral ground into Spain. Not far off Bella could see Fort St Philip, with its guns facing always towards the advanced British outposts, towards the lines where Kilkieran had been killed – so long ago that seemed! – and its sentries on watch day and night, looking across into the fortress.

So short a distance! So short and yet so utterly impossible to cross!

At dinner that night de Crillon boasted a great deal of the action to come, of the fate which lay in store for the English troops. As he spoke, a little the worse for drink, he kept glancing towards Bella; she had, indeed, noticed that the army commander had been eyeing her speculatively ever since they had met in Malaga and she had the idea that if d'Artois had not staked his claim first, de Crillon would by now have been her lover. Tonight, for reasons of her own, she decided to play up to him. If it could in the present circumstances do little good, at least it could do no harm for her to find out all she was able about the Spanish designs. And, from her observation of de Crillon, she had an idea that this man would best be approached as it were by means of attack.

So, speaking during a lull in the conversation, she said loudly, 'Tush, sir! The garrison will be well able to repulse any armies which you can send against them!'

The lull became a tense silence at that. All the way down the long table, gilded uniforms stirred and heads craned to look at this slip of a girl who had answered the great Duc de Crillon. There was, however, a distinct glint of humour in de Crillon's eye as he asked, 'And what, my Lady Kilkieran, do you know, beyond what you have already told my staff, of the state of your gallant but impotent garrison?'

She said stoutly, 'I know nothing of military importance and if I did I would not say – as you well know, sir. But,' she went on passionately, her lips trembling on her words, 'I feel in my bones that our British regiments will prove more than a match for you. We have never retreated, we have never surrendered – and we never will! The men of the fortress will break your hired mercenaries and the lackadaisical soldiery of Spain!'

'Inaccurate, but spirited . . . indeed, I should have expected no less from a woman of courage, such as you are,' de Crillon responded, in no way put out despite the rising murmurs of anger and astonishment that came from the rest of the diners. 'But what you say is a mere expression of patriotism, such as anyone would make unless they were cowardly slaves. It has no basis in fact.' He leaned forward and stared at her penetratingly. 'Lady Kilkieran, we have heard quite enough from the men who have successfully deserted the fortress of Gibraltar to convince us beyond all possible doubt that a garrison such as is at present on the Rock can never hope to withstand a determined assault.' He waved an elegant, lace-cuffed hand. 'Why, more than half of them are sick of the scurvy, and the rest scarce able to drag themselves to their palliasses or to the surgeons to report themselves sick! There is not a man in the garrison who would be capable of laying a strong woman – or whose body would respond even if all my soldiers were women, and advanced naked across the neutral ground!'

There was a general and sycophantic laugh at this sally. De Crillon, smirking, went on, 'Why, Fort St Philip alone is enough to decimate what is left of them.'

'Then why,' Bella asked tartly, 'do you mount such a tremendous offensive? Why do you not leave it all to the brave men at Fort St Philip, to end the siege on their own?'

De Crillon shrugged and said lightly, 'Simply because His Most Catholic Majesty wishes to bring this wretched affair to as speedy a conclusion as possible – out of his kindly consideration for the British! No other reason.'

Bella stared at him speculatively. She was now the centre of attention of the whole table; men neglected their glasses, wondering what this woman was going to say next. 'This Fort

St Philip of which you boast so much,' she said after a pause. 'Has it not been damaged by our fire?'

'A little,' de Crillon admitted generously, 'but always we make good the breeches. We lose men, but' – he shrugged again – 'there are many more to fill the gaps.'

'I am glad to have your confirmation that it has been damaged – and that men have died in its defence.'

De Crillon stiffened at that. He said coldly, 'Have a care, Lady Kilkieran. Remember that you are in Spain . . .'

'Yet I say that, and I say it again!' Bella's face flamed with sudden fury and she rapped the table with a small, clenched fist. Then, as suddenly, her angry colour left her and she said quietly and simply, 'Your Grace, I have told you that my husband, Lord Kilkieran, Colonel of the 74th Regiment of Foot, was killed before the neutral ground. What perhaps I did not say was that it was a shot from your Fort St Philip that killed him . . . you cannot expect me to say other than that I am glad to hear that some direct vengeance for that death has been exacted. As a soldier, you will understand . . . my words were intended as no personal affront to your soldiers, amongst whom there must clearly be many brave and honest men – and, if I may remind Your Grace, men who possess that chivalry for which Spain has always been noted insofar as women are concerned.'

She hesitated, looking down at her lap, and de Crillon bowed his head slightly. Regarding Bella with close attention he said, 'Pray go on, Lady Kilkieran. I believe you wish to say something further.'

'Yes, I do.' She was looking straight into his eyes now. 'I have a request to make, no doubt a rather strange request and one which it is difficult to put properly into words . . . I do not wish anyone present to misunderstand me, but . . . I have an urgent feeling that – that I would like to see the place whence that shot was fired at my beloved husband . . . to see the damage, I must in all honesty confess, that British arms have caused to Fort St Philip. Is this possible?'

De Crillon's eyes narrowed and he frowned, seemingly puzzled. 'A curious request certainly,' he murmured, 'yet in a way I can understand it.' He glanced briefly at the brother of the King of France and then went on slowly, 'It would indeed be possible, Lady Kilkieran, if you so wish it. I shall myself be visiting Fort St Philip tonight, as it happens. I would arrange for you to accompany me, if the Comte d'Artois has no objection. . . ?'

The Frenchman's loose mouth tightened; his bloodshot eyes tried to focus and failed. He said thickly, 'No objection in the world since I myself shall accompany you as well, de Crillon.'

'But of course, sir, of course!' De Crillon laughed genially, but there was a curious edge, an undercurrent in his laughter. He pushed a bottle of brandy across the table towards d'Artois. 'First, another drink – and a further toast to the resounding success of our arms against Gibraltar!'

There was a clatter of swords as the officers rose to the toast, a harsh cacophony of many voices as the toast was drunk. D'Artois seemed mightily unsteady on his feet – a fact which appeared to please the Duc de Crillon, who thereafter seemed in no hurry to finish dinner. He saw to it personally that the Comte's glass was kept replenished; and it was a little under an hour later that the Comte d'Artois gave a loud hiccough and slumped in his seat, sliding down until he was half beneath the table.

De Crillon signed to the attendant orderlies. 'His Royal Highness to his tent!' he ordered sharply, and then rose, and bowed to Bella, holding out his arm. 'And now, my Lady Kilkieran – Fort St Philip awaits us!'

On the arm of the Commander-in-Chief, Bella swept magnificently out of the marquee.

18

The night was moon-filled, brilliant.

The Rock stood out sharply beneath that bright high moon – crouched like a great replica of the British Lion, Bella thought as, her heart beating rapidly, she sat beside de Crillon in the great coach as it lumbered heavily across the rough ground towards Fort St Philip, leaving behind it the protection of the main Spanish lines fronting the neutral ground.

It was an eerie feeling, to be approaching so closely to the British advanced guard in company with the enemy commander. Bella had an uneasy thought that at any moment the coach might well be smashed to smithereens by a shot out of the garrison, but no such thought appeared to trouble the Duc who was in excellent spirits. He sat back in his corner, humming to himself and casting an occasional glance from the window. There seemed to be little activity tonight; the Spanish batteries themselves were silent, and only an occasional shot was being sent across from the Rock. It was as if Gibraltar knew already that something was in the air, as if the garrison were conserving their ebbing energy and their remaining ammunition for the grand assault.

The coach rattled onward with a jingle of harness. Neither of the occupants spoke until the horses stopped at Fort St Philip; each, since leaving the lines, had been occupied with private thoughts. For her part, Bella knew very well that de Crillon had consented to her coming out to the extended post for one reason only – and she had her own reasons for coming, anyway. She had a strong feeling that it was now or never, that tonight had brought the moment of action.

As they stopped, an officer came forward to open the door of the coach which had pulled in beneath a guarded gateway into a small central courtyard. De Crillon got down, followed by Bella, to whom he gave his hand. Turning to the officer he said, 'A quiet night, Colonel.'

'Very quiet, Your Grace. The activity has been trifling. I suspect that the garrison's strength is now at a very low ebb.' He glanced with interest at Bella, and de Crillon, catching the look, made the introductions.

'Lady Kilkieran . . . Colonel Sanchez, commanding at this fort,' he said. 'Lady Kilkieran is lately from the Gibraltar garrison,' he added to the soldier. 'She wished to see some of our strength, and so I brought her with me.'

Colonel Sanchez bowed. He looked as though he wished to kiss her hand, but Bella kept both hands pointedly folded. This man, perhaps, had been in command at Fort St Philip when her husband had been killed, and she had no wish to have any contact with him except insofar as it might be necessary for the furtherance of the plan which she had conceived during dinner. Sanchez fell back when he saw that he was being rebuffed, making way deferentially for de Crillon, who went towards a flight of stone steps leading upwards to the parapet. Bella looked about her; this was a gloomy place, filled with fearful moon-shadows cast by the grim, historic walls. Soldiers were outlined on the battlements above as they stood their watch over the great guns facing towards Gibraltar and the close outpost of the Devil's Tower.

Reaching the gun-platform, Bella found herself behind a breast-high parapet, with the muzzles of the guns pointing wickedly through the embrasures. Beyond, she could see the advanced British sentries at their posts by the Devil's Tower; under that bright moon – that moon which could prove so dangerous for this night's work – she could even make out the patch of ground where Kilkieran had died. Suddenly she felt a renewed surge of anger, a hatred in her breast, a loathing, a detestation of all things Spanish. It was a desperate thing she intended to do that night, but she knew now that she would have the courage and the strength to go through with it whatever the difficulties and dangers. Just that one sight of the Devil's Tower had finished what her mind and her will had begun . . . that sight of those few, half-starved British soldiers, those ragged redcoats, carrying on with their duty, manning their dangerous post as nonchalantly as if they had been parading with full stomachs on the Horse Guards at home in Westminster. If those men, with no food in their bellies, could carry on with their duty, then so could she.

She walked on behind the Duc de Crillon as he paced the platform in a leisurely manner, speaking now and then to the gunners, telling them that their long vigil would very soon end in victory for Spanish arms. As they circled the parapet and came back towards the steps leading down to the dark courtyard, Bella realized that the moment had come. She hesitated in her stride, staggered a little against the stonework, and gave a sudden gasp.

De Crillon swung round, saw her sliding slowly to the floor of the platform. He went towards her quickly and reached out an arm, lifting her against his body. She felt the instant reaction in him, the passion making his limbs tremble as he said, 'My poor child, you are sick!'

He understood what was in her mind, she felt certain of that, or rather, he understood what she wanted him to understand; she had not misinterpreted his looks earlier. She said faintly, 'Not sick, Your Grace. Only – tired. So tired . . .' She smiled up meaningfully into his eyes and murmured so that only he could catch it, 'The Comte d'Artois is a virile man!'

The Duc's face seemed to suffuse; it had been obvious all along that he and d'Artois were not the best of friends; now, the mere mention of the Frenchman's name seemed to set the blood racing in de Crillon's veins. Over his shoulder he said abruptly, 'Colonel Sanchez, I wish to take Lady Kilkieran below for a few minutes until she has recovered. Will you be so good as to put a private apartment at her disposal?'

'But of course, Your Grace. Your Grace realizes that such rooms as we have, are scarcely fitted for a lady, but –'

'Go, Sanchez,' de Crillon interrupted. 'We will follow you down.'

Sanchez bowed, clicked his heels and turned away for the steps. De Crillon followed, carrying Bella in his arms. As they reached the bottom Sanchez called out and a sergeant approached, carrying a lantern. Sanchez gave him an order and he turned away, swinging the lantern high, and headed for a dark passage-way which seemed to burrow the very walls of the fort. They went along this for some twelve yards and then the sergeant halted in front of an iron-studded door, took a key off a chain attached to a belt around his waist and turned it in the lock. Swinging the door open, the man stood aside for the others to enter. Bella saw a bare room with a single table, a table on which the sergeant now set the lantern, and a ready made-up bed.

Sanchez, who had a knowing glint in his eye now, said, 'This room is kept constantly ready for the use of visiting officers, Your Grace. Her ladyship is very welcome to use it. She will be able to rest here, and if there is anything she wants she has only to ring this bell.' He indicated a bell-pull, its tassel hanging over the head of the bed.

The Duc nodded. 'Her ladyship will require nothing beyond rest and quiet,' he said curtly. 'Thank you, Colonel Sanchez.'

Sanchez understood perfectly – so much was obvious in the man's half-smile as he bowed himself out. When the door had closed behind him de Crillon waited to hear the footsteps die away along the tunnel and then softly he opened the door, removed the key, fitted it into the inside lock, and turned it. Then, smiling at Bella, he walked across the room towards her. He said, 'Two minds with but a single thought! You did that very well.' Then his face hardened. 'D'Artois is a drink-sodden lecher, yet even I dare not offend the brother of the King of France. Had it not been for that, my Bella, I would have removed you from his household before now, let me assure you of that.' He reached out to her, taking her shoulders in his hands; her body was quite unresistant to him. She let herself go slack in his arms, but her mind was as crystal clear and determined as ever now that the decisive moment, the moment of action, was approaching. De Crillon murmured, 'Anywhere else, it is not wise that we should be alone together. Here . . . Sanchez knows better than to open his mouth. You understand?'

She nodded. 'That is why you agreed to let me come out to the fort?'

'Of course!' The dark face broke into a smile again; he was a handsome, attractive man, tall and dark, still slim, swash-buckling . . . she felt almost sorry for what she planned to do. 'And – you? That is the whole reason why you asked to come, is it not?'

Again she nodded. She said simply, 'I wished to be laid by a man instead of a brandy-cask. You attracted me. I, too, realized only too well that d'Artois must be treated with the greatest discretion . . .'

Her voice shook a little; already de Crillon had begun to unfasten her dress. Now she helped him, with swift fingers, let the garment fall to her ankles. She stood there before him, every secret of her body revealed to him now. De Crillon, his face flushed, fell on his knees, kissed her until her loins felt weak with desire, as though such a fire burnt within her body that it could be quenched only by this man's offerings. After a few moments de Crillon stood up, lifted her effortlessly, laid her naked on the bed. Quickly he began to strip off his own clothing, laying his unbuckled sword-belt across the back of a chair near the head of the bed. Bella reached out for the sword itself and stroked it, caressing the hilt . . . she caught de Crillon's eyes and they smiled at each other, as if there had been something symbolic in her act, the touching of so masculine an article as a sword.

She said softly, 'It is a beautiful sword, Your Grace.'

'The best of Toledo. Fine steel, straight and true.'

She felt the blood pumping in her veins, the thud of her heart. 'Let us – unsheathe it,' she whispered.

He laughed. 'In God's name – what for?' He saw her flush and, perhaps following out the symbolism, seemed to under-stand. He touched her lightly on the cheek with his hand and smiled. 'As you wish, Bella, as you wish. There.' He withdrew the shining blade, laid it in her hands. The light from the lantern sparked off it, brought fire from the jewels in the hilt, red and green and blue. 'Straight and true, as I said. Toledo makes the only good swords in all the world.'

She nodded, laid the sword against the chair, still free of its sheath. She whispered, 'Oh, my dearest . . .'

His own clothing was stripped off now. She could smell his sweat as he stood above her for a moment, his strong body

tufted with dark hair; he was exulting in his obvious man-
hood. She felt a genuine thrill deep inside her, a thrill which
told her unmistakably that she was going to enjoy this
experience. De Crillon now sat on the bed beside her; she
could almost hear the beat of his heart as his hands traversed
her thighs, went on to coax her into a vital and urgent
awareness. Slowly at first, and then with a convulsive jerk, her
legs moved for him. Panting, she found speech.

'Now!' she gasped. 'Now, quickly . . .'

She closed her eyes ecstatically as she felt his body stealing
over hers and then came the moment, the magic moment, of
his entry, an inexorable thrust yet a gentle one. When some
time later he reached his climax in time with herself she gave
one muffled cry of bitter-sweet joy, arched her back, moved
violently for a moment of time out of this world, and then lay
still, hearing de Crillon's heavy breathing loud in her ears and
feeling the rapid beating of his heart. When he quietened he lay
with his eyes closed, his mouth caressing her ear, his body still
as one with hers. For a long time, it seemed, they lay like that;
and then Bella moved a little until the close contact of flesh was
broken. De Crillon gave a low sigh of content and rolled over
to lie by her side.

Gently, scarcely moving her body at all now, Bella reached
out sideways until her fingers closed over the jewelled hilt of
de Crillon's unsheathed Toledo sword.

19

Slowly, very slowly, Bella drew the sword towards her, scarcely breathing in case she disturbed de Crillon, whose hand, aimlessly now, was still laid between her thighs. Everything depended on how swiftly she could move once she was ready to get off the bed, and on how somnolent de Crillon would in fact prove to be.

Her fingers were firmly around the hilt now. She swung the sword clear of the chair, let the point drop below the level of the bedclothes. She remained still for several moments after that and then, giving a little sigh, she shifted her body until it was away from de Crillon's. He mumbled something as his hand slid limply across the base of her stomach and then reached out to her again and began to caress her breasts, feeling drowsily for the nipples

She gave an indistinct murmur as of sleepy contentment.

Then, with a speed which amazed even herself, she was twisting sideways and was off the bed, standing by the side of it, her breasts heaving, the sword-point directed at de Crillon's chest and pricking into the flesh. Opening his eyes, he gave a start, looked up at her in sheer disbelief, seeming not fully to comprehend what was happening. Drawing upon her last reserves of courage, even as he started to lever himself up in the bed and grab for the sword, she pressed the point home with all her strength, putting the whole weight of her body behind the thrust. The shining blade, razor-sharp, slid in quite easily until it jammed between the ribs; blood welled from the wound and de Crillon, still looking sheerly surprised, gave a low moan. Bloody flecks appeared in foam at his lips, his face was chalk-white, ghastly in the flickering beams of the lantern. His voice when it came was hoarse and slurred but still strong.

'You bitch . . . you filthy English whore.'

She said shakily, 'A fine one you are to talk . . . you intended murdering our poor starving garrison, did you not? You meant to attack sick men with your fine war machines . . .'

He was heaving himself up on the bed now, his face haggard and drawn with pain. Bella realized that she had missed the heart, but it was more than she could bear to withdraw that bloodied blade and plunge it in a second time – but de Crillon had to be silenced or her plan would be still-born. Desperately she looked around, saw the Duc's two pistols lying with his clothing on the floor. Bending swiftly, she seized one. There was no time to load and in any case a shot would bring the soldiers running. Reversing the pistol, she lashed out at de Crillon's temples. His head weaving, the grey-faced man on the bed was able to evade several wild blows, but he was weakening fast and fighting a losing battle now. Bella caught him twice, both blows hard ones with all the strength of her arm behind them, and he sank back on the pillow, blood spreading now from his head to join that from his punctured lung.

Then, suddenly, she had an idea. De Crillon had been wearing a white shirt . . . she could make good use of that! Breathing fast she took the sword-hilt in both hands and pulled. It was some moments before she could bring the blade out, and when she had done so she was shaking violently as though with a high fever. With repugnance she wiped the blade on the bedclothes and, desperately now, began to dress. When she was fully clad she seized de Crillon's white shirt from the pile of clothing, hurriedly tied the arms of it to the sword blade, wrapped the body of it round the blade and thrust the whole thing down the front of her dress. The hilt rested in the cleft between her breasts where she could only hope the dress would keep it hidden for long enough. After that she took up one of the pistols, loaded it, and pushed it into a fold of her dress.

Then, her heart beating fast enough, it seemed, to choke her, she made for the door and unlocked it. There she hesitated; should she lock it from the outside, throw away the key – or not? De Crillon lived yet; he could perhaps be saved if he received attention soon – and five minutes or so would be ample for her purpose. After that time, she would be spotted from the parapet whatever happened or did not happen to de Crillon – so he might as well have his chance to live even though his death might serve largely to disrupt the Dons' plans. Somehow she felt that she owed him that much. He was not a bad man; he was merely carrying out his duty to attack Gibraltar, and her own action had been a treacherous one. Besides, she had enjoyed that night's experience in his arms. He had been gentle and understanding as he had guided her to her climax . . .

Coming to a decision, Bella left the door closed but unlocked and went quickly along the passage into the courtyard.

The coach was waiting where they had left it, but turned now to face the gateway ready for His Grace's departure. Bella called up to de Crillon's coachman, who was waiting patiently on his box for his master. The man clambered down when he heard her voice. She said steadily in such Spanish as she had, 'His Grace commands you to take me back to the lines. He will remain here himself for the time being, and you are to return for him as dawn breaks.'

'*Si, senora.*' The man inclined his head and opened the door for her. When she was inside he scrambled up to the box, released the brake and shook the reins. The horses went forward at a walk towards the gateway. Inside, Bella was shaking like a leaf, consumed with fear and impatience as the horses were pulled up at the gate. The coachman repeated Bella's words to the sentry, who came across and peered in the window.

Bella wound the window down. She said imperiously, 'His Grace wishes for a bottle of brandy in five minutes' time. I could find no one to tell. You will perhaps see that his wish is carried out?'

'*Si senora* – ' Bella didn't wait for him to finish; she raised the window with a bang and the sentry stepped back and waved the coach onward through the gateway.

They rolled out of Fort St Philip, turning under the lee of its northern wall for the track which led to the Spanish lines. Just before they reached this track, Bella put her head out of the window.

'Stop!' she called. 'Stop, there!' The motion checked; she heard the horses being pulled up. She opened the door and got down. She said, 'It is such a beautiful night . . . I wish to ride on the box. It is stuffy inside the coach.'

A muffled sound like an oath came down to her above the stamping of the impatient horses, and the coachman spoke nervously. 'Make haste, *senora*, if you please! We are within range of the English guns, and they will have no means of knowing that you are one of their own – '

'They soon will have!' Bella had already reached the box. Now, from a fold in her gown, she brought out de Crillon's pistol. She held it at the astonished coachman's head and said levelly, 'Drive on. When you reach the track, turn to the southward – not the northward. Drive, and drive fast, for the Devil's Tower.'

'You – '

'Do as I say,' she told him with harsh determination, 'or I shall blow your brains out, assuming you have any, Spaniard! Just one false move and I shall at once pull the trigger. It will not then matter to you who survives this siege.'

Her tone was hard, not to be denied.

In the moonlight she could see the sweat beading the man's face. He was clearly terrified . . . looking sideways at her set expression, he grasped the reins, jerked them, urged the horses on for the track ahead. Reaching it, he pulled the animals reluctantly round to the southward. They went forward at a trot, amid the coachman's voluble protestations and appeals for the English milady not to endanger his life.

'Silence!' Bella said curtly. 'And drive faster – as fast as you can. Flog the horses into a gallop. Quickly – or by God I fire!'

The man obeyed.

The horses strained ahead, their great shoulders heaving, and in a moment the coach was going hell-for-leather towards the Devil's Tower and the British lines beyond. As they rattled away past Fort St Philip Bella drew de Crillon's sword clear of her dress, held it, with the white shirt flapping, high above her head with her left hand. The moon shone down upon it, bringing it up like a streaming banner, a big silvered banner, the wind of their passage billowing it out. She cried in savage triumph, 'See, we go in under a flag of truce! The British will not open fire!'

She held the pistol very steady, though a wild exultation filled her heart now. At that moment, the firing broke out behind them from Fort St Philip. Musket balls peppered the coach, flew past her head. She shouted above the din at the coachman, telling him to urge the horses on faster. Then the heavy guns opened and after that, as at a signal, the British northward batteries broke their silence, opening on Fort St Philip with everything they had. It was a tremendous, an inspiring barrage. Flashes filled the night sky, the shot fell like rain on Fort St Philip and the Spanish lines. But none of the guns fired short as the coach rocketed towards the Devil's Tower; that strange, blood-stained flag of truce had been seen in time. Bella wondered if she herself had been recognized . . . but she had no more time for idle supposition when the enemy shot began to fall closer and then, long before they had closed the gap of the neutral ground, the coachman gave a sudden cough, clutched at the back of his neck, lurched sideways, and then plummeted from the box.

Neighing in terror as the reins fell slack, the horses tore on with the coach rocking and swaying murderously behind them.

20

The firing was wild, very wild from Fort St Philip, as if the Dons, on discovering their Commander-in-Chief bleeding and unconscious, had panicked. It had been a mere lucky shot which had taken off the coachman. No more metal came really near, but Bella was quite unable to control the maddened onrush of the rocking vehicle. The reins, dragging now along the ground and being torn to shreds by the racing iron-bound wheels and flying hooves, were uselessly out of her reach. The coach plunged on, the horses fortunately keeping to their general direction and making at breakneck speed towards the Devil's Tower.

Bella felt that any moment must be her last. The coach couldn't fail to overturn soon, she would be crushed; or the horses would career full into the barriers erected against the enemy, or even, by some lucky chance passing through, then into the sheer rock side of the North Front itself . . .

Then, as she rocketed up for the Devil's Tower, Bella saw two men running out to cross her path. Clinging to the box, feeling that she was ever about to plunge over the side as the coach bumped and jerked, she saw the soldiers leap for the horses' heads, one on either side. There was a wild shout, one of the men seemed to disappear for a moment beneath the off-lead horse. But the pace began to slow, and then a couple of hundred yards farther on, and inside the British lines now, the horses were pulled up, sweating and trembling and foaming, heads up, ears hard back and eyes gleaming like devils out of hell in the fitful light of the flares – flares which, as the firing commenced again from Fort St Philip, were hastily doused.

Hands reached up and Bella slumped into the arms of a private of foot . . . and just before she lapsed into un-consciousness she recognized Roger Carter and saw the unbelieving joy in his face. Safe in his arms, those arms which had caressed her so intimately in the past and in which she felt security, she simply let go.

She had come home to the 74th.

Eliott, woken from sleep, asked, 'She has been seen by a surgeon, of course?'

'Yes, Your Excellency.' The aide-de-camp's dour face was long and dark and evil with displeasure – and discomfiture. It seemed as though his subterfuge had rebounded nicely on himself; the Lady Kilkieran was likely to become the heroine of the hour now.

'And his report?' Eliott went on.

'She is physically unhurt, Your Excellency, except for a number of bruises and abrasions. She has, however, been under great strain – '

'A child could have told me that, Captain Frazer.'

The ADC bowed. 'Quite so, Your Excellency. I merely repeat what the surgeon reported. He also said that Lady Kilkieran will be quite fit after she comes out of the fainting state. All she needs is rest in bed.'

'Very well. She is to be brought here at once, Captain Frazer. See that a room is made ready for her.'

Frazer frowned. 'Does Your Excellency think that is wise? I mean – '

'I know very well what you mean, my dear fellow. Had I not thought it wise I would scarcely have given you the order . . . and in any case I care nothing for the "wisdom" of it in your sense. Lady Kilkieran very likely has information for us, and it is merely prudent that she be in a safe place where she can readily speak to me when she is fit – to say nothing of the fact that there is nowhere else in the garrison for a sick woman to be taken.' Eliott dusted snuff lightly across his nostrils. 'You have my orders, Captain Frazer. That is all.'

'Very good, Your Excellency.'

Frazer bowed himself out of the room. He was, in truth, seething with fury by this time and shaking with something like fear as well. It was the most damnable luck that the woman had so unexpectedly returned to the garrison –

especially under such circumstances! It would be more than he could bear, to watch the adulation that she would be sure to receive. He would, naturally, in due course take an opportunity of himself praising her courage to His Excellency so as to show his own impartiality, while at the same time hinting that a woman of whom the garrison had had the good fortune to be rid, could bring nothing but trouble by her return; and that the first chance should be taken of despatching her once again to England – and more permanently this time. Meanwhile, he could only do his best not to allow His Excellency to guess his true feelings.

It was the following evening before Bella had recovered enough from her experiences to speak. She had regained consciousness fairly quickly but had been very weak, so weak that she could do nothing but lie in her bed and sob, her whole body shaking with the memory of what she had had to do to the Duc de Crillon. She would never, never forget that terrible sword-thrust, or what she couldn't help but regard as her own treachery, however worthy the motive for that treachery might have been. But when after a refreshing sleep she had collected herself, she knew that she had to speak urgently to His Excellency.

There was a bell-pull by her bed and she tugged this until an orderly, thin and haggard, his eyes large in a gaunt face, came into the bedroom.

She said, 'I must speak with His Excellency. Pray see that he is informed that I am able to receive him, and that the matter will not wait.'

'Very good, milady. His Excellency has been anxious to speak to you, that I know.'

The man seemed scarcely to have the strength to turn his body, he was so wan and sick-looking. Bella's heart contracted in pity; de Crillon had been right – this poor garrison could not hope to withstand any attack in force, the defences would crumple like paper before the first onslaught.

Eliott came to her at once; he looked in no better shape than the orderly. His face was more lined, greyer than she had remembered it to be when last they had met, his shoulders quite bowed beneath the weight of his terrible responsibilities and what she was convinced was his own gnawing sickness. His hands shook as though he had an ague, his uniform, tattered now, hung about him as if on a clothes-peg – than which, indeed, his shrivelled body seemed scarcely thicker.

He said, 'Lady Bella, you have done a most courageous thing. I welcome you back to the garrison . . .'

'Thank you, Your Excellency.' She smiled up at him, weakly. 'You know, perhaps, how I came to leave it in the first place?'

'By your own wish, or so I was informed at all events.'

She hesitated. Now was her chance to tell His Excellency, in private, of the vendetta which his aide-de-camp had waged against her so consistently. Yet if she did speak, he would never believe her. This man would never believe her for one moment if she said that his own aide, having had his advances spurned, had allowed his brooding mind so to fill with hatred for her that ultimately he had arranged for her to be put aboard a ship-of-war proceeding into a danger zone – and had moreover delivered her helpless into the hands of soldiery who had taken their outrageous pleasures upon her body before she had been permitted to embark. She would simply play into Captain Frazer's hands, show herself as a trouble-maker of whom the garrison was infinitely better rid; and besides all this, she was genuinely reluctant to worry this tired man any further than need be. So she merely gave, in answer to Eliott's question, a non-committal movement of her head and said, 'Whatever the circumstances of my leaving, Your Excellency, I am delighted to be back on the strength. My place is here, as my husband's was. I shall yet,' she added stoutly, 'be in garrison with the 74th of Foot to see the lifting of the siege!'

'That is your wish – still?'

'My dearest wish still, Your Excellency. And now – you will forgive me – I have many things to tell you.'

Eliott nodded, sat down tiredly in a bedside chair. 'I hoped as much. Take your time, Lady Bella. Tell me everything as it happened, from the time you left Gibraltar.'

She did so, leaving out nothing of any importance. Eliott was shocked to hear of the loss of the *Royal Sovereign*, news of which had not so far reached the Rock since no vessels of any kind had entered from either east or west in the meantime. She told him something of her treatment by the Comte d'Artois, and – shamefacedly – of what she had done to the Duc de Crillon. She added that he could well be dead but she didn't fancy somehow that this would prove to be the case. She had missed his heart and he would have been found very quickly once the alarm had been given; and after that no time would have been lost in sending a surgeon to succour the army commander. So he would probably live, though naturally he would be out of the fight for some while to come. Then Bella said crisply, 'And now, Your Excellency, for what I have been able to discover, which in truth is little more than you have most probably deduced for yourself: the Dons are almost ready to march in strength against the fortress, to shatter our defences with many guns. They have brought up a consider-able number of extra men, and many stores.'

Eliott sighed. 'Yes, indeed I have suspected as much for some time, that is why we have tried to harass their lines as much as possible with our batteries.'

'They repair the breeches very quickly, Your Excellency – and always more men come up from behind. There seems to be no shortage.'

'Well, we're as ready as we can be for anything they can do.' The General's voice was heavy and weary – desperately weary. 'Nevertheless, you can help, my dear. You will have some idea of the positions of their ammunition dumps, redoubts, and supply trains – that kind of thing?'

She nodded. 'And will be pleased to direct the guns onto them if you so desire, Your Excellency!'

'Thank you. Now – when is this assault to take place?'

'That I was unable to discover for certain, but I feel it cannot be long delayed,' she said earnestly. 'The lines are filled with men and munitions and the batteries are in an instant degree of readiness to fire in support of a landward attack by the infantry–'

'No word of a fleet, a sea attack?'

'None, Your Excellency. I heard nothing as to that. But the land assault will be quite bad enough! They will pour into the fortress and the town like a flood!'

'We shall give a good account of ourselves, whatever they may do.' Eliott rose and took a turn or two up and down the room, stood for some moments at the big window which overlooked the bay. Beyond, the Spanish lines stood menacingly, in a semi-circle from La Linea to San Roque and beyond. Turning he said heavily, 'Your escape into the garrison must cause the Dons to advance their plans, my dear.'

Bella shook her head. 'If I may presume to contradict, Your Excellency, I truly believe that will not prove to be the case. They will attack the moment they are ready, not one second before that . . . you see, they are basing their intentions, and their hopes of success, solely on the weakened state of our men – and my escape cannot alter that. Indeed, with the passing of each day we become more and more an easy proposition for the Dons. The mere fact that I will be assumed to have confirmed to you that they are almost ready to attack, cannot alter or improve our defence in any way – and this they will surely know. I feel convinced that they will not upset their schedule, will not advance their plans and attack before they are completely ready.'

Eliott made a gesture of self-derogation. 'Yes, you are right, my dear,' he said, sighing. 'You would make a better Governor of this fortress than I!'

He smiled, and she smiled back, looking at him critically nevertheless. 'Your Excellency, you yourself have suffered with the rest of us . . . you are not well – '

'Well enough, Lady Bella, for what I have to do,' he retorted a little sharply. 'And there will of course be somewhat extra to do, now that we know the assault is definitely coming, and soon.'

'Cannot the Lieutenant-Governor do much of that for you, Your Excellency?' she asked persuasively.

'Indeed, you are most careful of my welfare, child!' Eliott said; then he shrugged. 'General Boyd has his own problems. Be assured that I am still perfectly capable of carrying out all my duties and bearing my overall responsibilities, Lady Bella.'

She nodded, then asked tentatively, 'Your Excellency, may I be permitted to make a suggestion?'

'As to the military situation – again?'

'Again!' she said, smiling. 'It is this: confound the enemy, Your Excellency! Do not wait for him to attack *us* – let us attack *him* across the neutral ground! He will be utterly bewildered, taken entirely by surprise – he will never in his maddest moments suspect that our hunger-weakened garrison is capable of mounting any kind of counter-attack, the more particularly in view of the tremendous superiority of the Spanish numbers which you will now be assumed to know from me. And the moral effect both upon the enemy and upon our own men will be really tremendous!'

Eliott said slowly, 'A bold scheme, and what I have learned to expect from you, Lady Bella. But alas . . . what the Dons suspect is indeed the simple truth. We *are* too weakened to attempt such an affray . . . and now will you be good enough to excuse me . . .'

She was looking at him in growing concern, when, abruptly, he turned away as if to hide something in his face. As he reached the door he seemed to stagger, his body falling heavily against the door-post and then sagging to the floor unconscious. Bella was out of bed in a flash, her own troubles forgotten; and she reached Eliott at the same time as an orderly sergeant who had been waiting outside.

Kneeling down beside the Governor she examined his skin. She said crisply, 'Sergeant, His Excellency has the scurvy. You must fetch a surgeon at once, and you must have His Excellency removed to his room in the meantime. Captain Frazer and General Boyd should be informed immediately.' When the man had gone, white and anxious, Bella lifted Eliott's head and cradled it in her lap. 'You're not going to be very pleased,' she murmured to the unconscious Governor, 'but you won't get rid of me easily now! I am going to remain here to nurse you back to health, and see that you get good food. You are going to think of yourself for once, Your Excellency – for Gibraltar has need of you at this moment, and has bad need of you! You have personally to infuse an aggressive spirit into our poor men, so that they, trusting you implicitly, will be able to mount that counter-attack of which I spoke just now.' Her face was shining, her eyes looking into far distances, and her voice was filled with a strange and glowing pride. 'We shall call it . . . the Sortie, and the day upon which we march against the might of France and Spain will be long remembered in British history . . .'

21

For most of the next two days Bella remained by Eliott's bedside, seeing to it that he was fed, whatever his own protestations, with as much fresh food as was available. She began to realize that she had some kind of influence over His Excellency, that he was at heart delighted to have an attractive woman near him during his illness

Exploiting this for all she was worth, she stuck to her point firmly that he was desperately needed, that his sickness could prove fatal to Gibraltar as a whole, that it was his plain duty to eat – and that the small amount of food diverted to the entirely honourable cause of restoring him to health could of itself make little enough difference to a garrison of six thousand men in any case; and that his was the most important single life of all, for he was a symbol of Gibraltar's will to live and remain British. She shared her vigil with the wife of one of Eliott's brigadier-generals who had also remained upon the Rock – a well-intentioned, brave but vinegary woman and unpleasing to the eye, Bella was somewhat maliciously glad to note . . . but mainly it was Bella who was there each time His Excellency awoke, Bella who was there to soothe and to comfort and to encourage – and to talk, whenever the moment seemed from all points of view propitious, about the sortie which she was still determined should be made against the Spanish lines.

At the end of those two days Eliott, much fitter now thanks to Bella's care, announced his intention, with finality, of getting up and resuming his visits to the batteries and the outposts, to bring cheer to the men and let them know that their Governor was once again up and about.

Bella said warningly, 'Your Excellency should take things easily for a few more days yet. I suspect that this is the first time you have retired to bed for a proper rest since the siege started . . . almost two and a half years ago.'

'It is!' Eliott smiled up at her, some of his lines of anxiety wonderfully smoothed away now; his rested mind, his replenished body, were removing from him some of the seeds of what had come at times dangerously close to defeatism. 'And now, you see, I have had enough of it – though I am full of gratitude for all you have done for me, Lady Bella. Besides,' he added, 'I have had time in which to consider, with a fresh mind, what you have been suggesting. I have come to the conclusion that you may well be right . . . the Dons could indeed be taken most utterly by surprise and thrown into the greatest confusion . . .'

Bella felt a great upsurge of joy, of pride. 'Yes, Your Excellency,' she whispered, her eyes alight.

'No promise yet, but I shall talk the matter over with my subordinate commanders and I shall assess the state of the regiments and corps for myself meanwhile. If necessary, may I call upon you to explain to my generals and colonels the positions of the various targets, the ones which will be the most worth attacking?'

'Better than that, Your Excellency!' Bella's blue eyes were dancing with eagerness. 'If I were to accompany the sortie . . . I could show the commanders exactly where to go!'

Eliott shook his head and laughed. 'Great heavens – that is quite out of the question!'

'But Your Excellency – '

'Enough, my dear child.' Eliott reached out and patted her arm. 'I cannot and will not consider that as a serious proposition and there is an end of the matter.'

Bella sighed; but having, as it seemed, won her main point she decided to say no more for the present.

Having spoken to his commanding officers and toured the defences exhaustively, visiting even the Royal Battery and the high Rock Gun and the Devil's Tower – which latter visit brought down a hail of shot in the vicinity so that Eliott, having compassion for his men, decided to return inside the lines – His Excellency that afternoon called a Council of War and told Bella that he would like her to be present. Shortly before the meeting he had a private conference with the Lieutenant-Governor, after which he informed Bella that he had already decided to make a sortie into Spanish territory and that he intended making it that very night.

He instructed his subordinate generals at the Council – a colourful affair, with the candelabra shining kindly towards the shabby uniforms – that a detachment was to assemble at midnight upon the Red Sands.

'They are to be supplied,' he said, 'with devils, fire-faggots and working implements . . . this detachment will consist of all the men of the 12th and Hardenburg's Regiments, the grenadiers and light infantry of all the other regiments in garrison, one hundred men of the artillery, and workmen and others who will be under the command of Brigadier-General Ross. At the same hour, the 39th and 58th Regiments will assemble on Grand Parade under Brigadier-General Picton, who will sustain the sortie as and where necessary. The main detachment will be divided into three columns. These columns will be led by Lieutenant-Colonels Trigge, Hugo and Dachenhausen.' He paused. 'Your orders, gentlemen, are these: You will leave the fortress by Forbes's Barrier in dead silence and you will march upon the Spanish lines. Upon arrival you will carry the enemy's works – their positions and defences will shortly be described to you fully by Lady Kilkieran – destroy the fortifications, blow up the magazines, and smash the batteries. In short, gentlemen, you will use every endeavour to spoil the enemy's months of preparation and leave him in no fit state to mount a landward attack on this garrison – and leave him also in no doubt as to the morale of the Gibraltar fortress!'

This news was received with great enthusiasm by the commanders. Once Lady Bella had, with the aid of maps, pinpointed the best targets as closely as possible and described to them the general lay-out of the works, they left immediately to prepare their commands and see the orders put into expeditious effect.

At about nine o'clock that night Bella slipped away from His Excellency's residence. Avoiding both Eliott and the ADC, who were closeted together in earnest discussion at this late hour, she made her way to Hargrave's Barracks, of which little was now left standing. The continual bombardment had reduced the place to a shambles in which the men lived in holes and caves which they had dug out for themselves. Bella was admitted without question and was soon surrounded by groups of cheering men, for her adventures had become known to the whole garrison by this time – and the 74th Regiment regarded her as their private property, their mascot.

Taking the arm of a sergeant she said, 'I wish to speak urgently to Private Carter. Is this possible?'

There was an eager, flushed look about her which did not escape the sergeant's notice. He said, 'Certainly it is, milady. If I might presume to make a guess . . . I dare say you'd wish to speak with him alone?' He gave her a friendly, rather conspiratorial smile, and she nodded happily. He went on in a confidential tone, 'That young man is no common soldier like us, if you ask my opinion, milady – '

'Which I did not!'

The sergeant grinned. 'No more you did – your pardon then, milady, I'm sure. But he's a handsome young fellow and you seemed anxious to see him . . . and it is rare for a lady of the regiment to enquire so feelingly for a private soldier!'

'Go on with you!' Bella said sharply, but not entirely with displeasure. 'Find Private Carter for me, that is all I ask.'

'That I will do at once, milady. I'll take you first to the Number Two Store, which is almost the only part of the barrack left undamaged. I will send for Private Carter to join you there.'

He turned and marched off, Bella following his tall, gaunt form through the shadows. Reaching the store he unlocked the door and led her into a long, high, vaulted room in which there were pitifully slender stores remaining. He lit a storm lantern. Rats scurried away from the light – long, lean, rangy brutes with angry, predatory eyes, brutes as hungry as the humans whose food they would steal.

When the sergeant had clumped away Bella gave an involuntary shiver. The very air of this place smelt of death and decay, and she sighed with relief when she saw a man approaching through the mounds of rubble of what had once been a spruce parade ground. She recognized Roger Carter instantly; his tall, slim figure was as erect and supple as ever.

When he reached the store, his thin face was beaming. Bella was trembling and pale with emotion. 'Oh, my dearest . . .' she whispered, her lips unsteady. His arms went round her tightly, his mouth came down on hers. When, minutes later, she withdrew her lips and, putting her head back, stared up into his eyes, she could scarcely see him through a mist of tears.

He said huskily, 'Bella, my Bella . . . I never expected to see you again, my dearest love. This is heaven upon earth, a heaven which came to me when I lifted you from the coach the other night . . .'

'My darling,' she said fervently, 'it is the same for me also, and my constant prayer is that it may continue so, which, if God is willing, it surely will. But – I have an urgent matter which I must talk to you about, Roger. It will not wait.'

'Yes, Bella?' His lips hovered over her hair.

She said, 'You are one of a grenadier company, Roger. This means that you will be going out of the garrison tonight – you have had your orders already, I expect?'

'Yes, indeed I have, dearest – '

'Good!" Her manner had changed, had grown incisive. 'Now, I wish to accompany the sortie – '

'*What?* Bella dearest, are you mad?'

'No,' she said impatiently, 'and it is not the slightest use your looking at me like that, dear Roger! And please do not argue – I have made up my mind and I have not the least intention in the world of changing it.' There was a stubborn, almost tempestuous note in her voice now. 'I and no one else can tell our men exactly where the biggest damage can be done to the Spaniards. I demand it as my right that I should be allowed to do my duty – '

'Your duty!' His voice was harsh with alarm for her. 'A woman – '

'A woman, yes, a woman can guide as well as any man, Roger!' She stamped her foot angrily. 'But now listen: His Excellency will not hear of my going – '

'I am most delighted – '

'– so it is up to *you* to help me. Your grenadier company is no doubt depleted and you can get me a uniform so that I can make up the numbers. I shall go with *you* – as a soldier of the line, Roger!'

He laughed, jeeringly. 'You would have no chance of getting away with that, my Bella! You of all women could never pass for a man! And there is the sergeant – '

'He will see nothing, and no one will ever notice my – my figure. The detachments assemble in the darkness, and I shall never be remarked upon, joining your company in uniform upon the Red Sands! I tell you it is perfectly possible,' she went on with hot conviction. 'All you need to do is to get me the uniform and the weapons. You will yourself be by my side – until we are out of the garrison at all events, for then I shall make myself known to the detachment commander, General Ross. It will be too late then for him to send me back, and he will have to accept me as his guide. Now – you will do this for me, Roger?'

He snapped, 'Of course I shall not!'

'Very well, then!' She was quivering with anger, her voice icy and contemptuous. 'I shall still go, Roger, without your help if you insist upon refusing it – the danger will be the greater, of course, without you beside me to protect me, but – '

'But Bella, my dearest Bella . . . I shall have my duties in any case. I'd not be able to be beside you all the time!'

'No matter,' she stormed unfairly. 'You have failed me – me, who saved your life when you were about to be tried by Court Martial for desertion – you remember? But I shall still go whatever happens, Roger Carter, even if it means that I have to *kill* one of your company to obtain his uniform! Oh, believe me, Roger, I can kill – now! And kill I shall, Roger, if it is necessary that I should kill in order to march tonight with the grenadier company of the 74th! Sure an' you're a poor, witless poltroon and no use to an Irishwoman if you're afraid to take a risk!'

She turned and walked out of the store, head and colour high. Roger, his face desperately worried and unhappy, watched her in the moonlit darkness until she was half-way across the parade ground, picking her way among the heaps of dust and rubble. Then, smothering an exclamation, he ran swiftly after her. Catching up with her, he took her shoulders and swung her round so that her head rested on his shoulder.

'All right, my love,' he said softly and tenderly. 'May God forgive me for anything that may happen this night, but I shall help you, Bella.'

22

They assembled, those near-desperate men with their faces blackened by burnt wood or cork, at midnight on the Red Sands as ordered, moving silently to their stations and without benefit of drum or fife – a seemingly decrepit gathering of sick men whom one would have thought scarcely able to hold a musket. Had the Dons been able to see them they would very likely have dismissed this pitiful force with a contemptuous shrug of the shoulders.

Bella, dressed uncomfortably and wholly incongruously in the uniform of the 74th's grenadier company, waited in the deeper shadows beyond the Red Sands. She had hurried from the Governor's residence immediately after Eliott had left himself – for His Excellency was going to accompany his soldiers on the sortie. She had left in her own clothing, with the uniform bundled under her arm, and she had flitted along the ghostly, ruined streets like a woman of the night, picking her way from shadow to shadow and not lingering in the few patches of fitful moonlight which broke through the clouds scudding across the sky. She had stripped off her dress in hiding on arrival near the assembly point and had pulled on the uniform. Now she could only hope it would pass in the darkness; any shortcomings would not be noticed anyway, with all the regiments dressed like ragamuffins these days and making do with all manner of clothing as the uniforms wore out. It could only be her voice and her figure which might give her away; all she could do would be to remain silent and keep her step as masculine as possible. So she was waiting now until the order to move off was given, when she would attach herself to the marching men and fall into step as near to Roger Carter as she could get, still in that friendly and yet fearsome darkness.

★

At last the columns received the order to move off.

Officers and sergeants had been moving up and down the lines of patiently waiting men, checking on last-minute details, repeating orders and making sure everyone fully understood what his duty was that night. There had been no possible doubt that the idea of action at last had appealed most strongly to the men, whose voices had in the last few minutes become more alive, whose movements had become more vigorous, than had been the case for many a long day past. Their morale was being restored, would spur their ailing bodies on to fight well and to the death; this was obvious even to Bella, shivering in the cool night shadows, her teeth chattering from time to time, her nerves on edge now. When the order to move had finally come, and the columns, every man in them conscious of a sense of drama and of history in the making, had begun to march away, she had been greatly relieved that the waiting period had come to an end. She slipped from her hiding place and attached herself in rear of the men at the tail of Colonel Hugo's column, in which Roger Carter was marching.

Men glanced vaguely, casually at her as she moved up the line, looking out for Roger. A strange face as such was quite unremarkable, for the companies were now mixed and fluid, with the sickness, and the replenishments from other regiments too reduced to form units of their own. There were a few hissed remarks, the jokes of men about to go into battle, jokes about what the sergeant was going to say when he found one of his company had almost missed the parade – which well suited Bella's purpose. If she was taken as a late arrival, a defaulter trying to slide into place without being seen by authority, it couldn't be better. Her heart was racing with excitement but she found the beginnings of real fear fluttering in her stomach as the columns neared the exit from the fortress into the neutral ground.

Thankfully, she saw Roger, right-hand man of the file which she was just approaching. Sliding up to him she breathed his name and he turned his head fractionally, jerked it in silent indication that she was to fill the blank file next in front of him and keep her tongue in her head.

It was three o'clock in the morning precisely when the tail of the last column moved out through Forbes's Barrier. They were moving slowly now, moving out towards Spain in the most profound silence; and then later, as the column divided into three so as to advance on a broad front, a challenge came from Fort St Philip.

At once Roger reached out a hand to Bella. 'Steady!' he whispered. 'One or other of us'll open fire now . . . keep your head, and keep by me.'

'But I've got to get to the head of the column . . . I've got to act as guide – '

'You'll do exactly as I tell you!' Roger's voice was hard, like a whiplash to her. She had never known him like this before, so determined, so sure of himself – but then, not surprisingly, she had never seen him approaching action before. 'You'll stay here, where I can keep an eye on you, or by God I'll – '

He broke off as the crackle of musket fire swept down on them. 'The Dons!' he said. 'We've no further need of secrecy or silence now.'

Immediately following upon the firing, Colonel Hugo's voice roared down the line, passing the order that his column was to form the attacking corps and press on for the Spanish lines, come what might. Sergeants and corporals moved quickly up and down the files, repeating the orders, and soon the whole column was swiftly on the move, advancing at the double and outflanking Fort St Philip, with their heavy equipment, the muskets and grenades and fire-faggots, clanking and banging at their sides as they rushed on over the rough ground baked hard by the sun. Despite the attentions of those advanced sentries, the attackers still had all the advantages of utter surprise, for the lines themselves had been totally unready, and Hugo found practically no opposition at all. Within a short time, and much to his own surprise, his column had reached the works at the extremity of the Spanish lines, and reached them almost unscathed. Hugo at once set his pioneers to dismantle the defences.

That surprise had indeed been complete.

The defenders had been caught with total unexpectedness,

though Bella, still ploughing on breathlessly with Roger Carter beside her, soon found herself in the thick of it. She and Roger had become one of an attacking force in front of the towering St Carlos Battery, one of the biggest and reputedly the most redoubtable of the groups of enemy guns. The moment this attacking force was seen, all hell was let loose as the St Carlos Battery opened right above their heads. The great guns roared out, harmlessly so far as they were concerned since the Spaniards could not depress them far enough to bear; and the surprised, astounded defenders, scarcely able yet to believe what was happening to them, now opened with muskets, sending shot down spasmodically into the British ranks. Men fell, screaming, clutching stomachs and limbs. Bella was deafened and bewildered by the appalling racket. She was sent flying as soldiers rushed the redoubt, scrambling for a foothold on the high, almost precipitous works below the belching guns.

She cried out and a moment later a sweating, smoke-blackened figure knelt down beside her. 'Bella!' he shouted hoarsely. 'I couldn't see you for the moment . . .'

'Oh, Roger . . .'

'Are you hurt, dearest heart?' He ran practised hands over her body, searching for wounds; once again she was surprised at his self-possession, the way he suddenly seemed much older, all boyishness gone.

She said, 'Only winded by your brutal soldiery, and I dare say somewhat bruised!' His presence gave her courage; she was able to smile up at him as she spoke. 'Help me up, or we shall both be crushed to death by the clumping boots of your comrades, Roger.'

He lifted her to her feet, and looked at her critically. He said, 'I must go with the others now, Bella.'

'And leave me here?' She was laughing now, laughing with a strange and almost savage exultancy, with the love of the Irish for a fight. 'A likely thing, sure! I shall come with you, Roger.'

He said hurriedly, 'All right, I cannot wait to argue now. Stay close, and keep behind me, not in front.'

He got up. Looking about him he saw that the British

soldiers were falling back from the battery now. The Spanish fire was considerably improved, the Dons leaning through the embrasures to fire down upon the attackers with good aim. A private of foot started running to the rear; Roger stuck out a boot and tripped him.

'What's the hurry, man?' he demanded savagely, his face glowing red and devilish in the glare from fires which had started up along the line. 'Get back there, and advance!'

'I'll see you dead first, matey! The officer's gone, and so's the sergeant, and I'm for getting out!'

He lifted his musket, aimed it at Roger. The young soldier side-stepped, ducked, and came in beneath the extended weapon. Seizing the man by the throat, he shook him like a rat till his teeth seemed to dance in his jaw. He snarled, 'Get back in and fight or I'll stick a bayonet in your gullet. Move!'

Dazed, the man stumbled back towards the battery. Roger cupped his hands and yelled, 'All right, men, advance – and let's take that damned battery! Follow me.'

He touched Bella lightly on the shoulder then raced ahead. Getting a grip on the earthworks, he went up as fast as he could, feeling the bullets rip through his tattered, filthy uniform, his life seemingly charmed. Bella, keeping behind him as ordered, found herself remembering what the sergeant had said earlier that evening: 'That young man is no common soldier . . .' The sergeant had been right; Roger was a leader –and he knew exactly what he was doing. This was by no means the first time he had been in action. And he seemed, in a way, to be possessed – as though his very life hung upon the way he conducted himself in action. Within minutes he and a handful of other men had reached the parapet, Bella with them, her sides splitting with her un-accustomed exertions, her breathing coming in painful gasps, her breast rising and falling rapidly. They jumped down onto the catwalk yelling fiercely, the infantrymen with bayonets fixed, the grenadiers with their grenades ready. When the Spaniards saw those men of the grenadier company, they simply dropped their own weapons and fled in utter disorder; they were completely unable to sustain hand-to-hand fight-ing. Roger shouted to his men to pursue them, and himself led that pursuit, detaching some men to remain behind and take over the great battery.

With the capture of the St Carlos Battery, the biggest and most formidable of all their works, the fight seemed to go out of the Spaniards altogether – and by the same token great heart was put into the attacking force. From now on, nothing would hold them back. The second column, under Colonel Dachenhausen, had outflanked the sector by now and had joined up with Hugo's column on the ground in rear of the St Carlos Battery. Colonel Trigge's column had gone into action independently and the enemy was giving way before it, was in fact giving way on every side despite that massive superiority in numbers and equipment, abandoning with undignified and panic-stricken haste all the works which had cost them so much and taken so many months to build up. It must indeed have come home to those bewildered defenders that they had seriously underestimated the strength and fitness of the Gibraltar garrison, and that the whole body of the besieged had suddenly descended upon them. Very soon the batteries were in a state for the fire-faggots to operate, and after that the flames spread with astonishing rapidity into every part.

It was incredible; but it was soon to be all over.

In just one hour the object of the sortie was fully effected. After powder-trains had been laid to the magazines, Brigadier-General Ross ordered the regiments to withdraw. Just as the rear column, convinced that it had taken part in nothing short of a miracle, had got within the garrison, the principal magazine blew up with a tremendous shattering explosion, and was followed by others too numerous to count. Vast pieces of blazing timber were thrown up into the air, to fall back into the flames and add to what was by now a general conflagration. The enemy, meanwhile, seemed too utterly confused to attempt to save or avenge their works but simply directed a militarily useless fire into the town. The casualties among the sortie had been ridiculously small considering what had been achieved – and they had even taken a token handful of prisoners, who later confirmed that the Duc de Crillon lived yet, was indeed recovering from his sword-thrust and was still in command, directing operations from his sick-bed. Bella felt oddly relieved and glad when she heard this news.

The sortie took place on 27th November 1781; three days later the Spanish batteries were still burning, and when they ceased to smoke the works appeared from the fortress to be completely destroyed, nothing but heaps of sand remaining. All in Gibraltar knew very well, however, that the end of the road was not yet in sight, for the French and Spanish armies were themselves still very much in being.

23

After the raid Bella, for want of any other accommodation whatsoever, was forced to remain in His Excellency's household; neither he nor she was averse to this arrangement, as it happened, though relations with the ADC were considerably strained thereby.

The morning after the sortie, however, no one was worrying particularly about such mundane matters. A tremendous enthusiasm prevailed throughout the garrison. Eliott, who seemed to have become a new man overnight, was tireless in visiting his whole command and talking to the men. He was cheered lustily wherever he went. The food shortages, the terrible deprivations, were, temporarily at any rate, forgotten in the flush of victory for their arms. The great success of the sortie had left behind it an impact on morale which was food for the soul, and they were well content. Now that they had shown the Dons what they were capable of, the siege would not, could not, last much longer . . . just let a large convoy enter to replenish them, and they would show in no mean fashion what full stomachs could do.

One of the things that most pleased Bella was that several independent reports had reached His Excellency of the courage and leadership shown by Private Roger Carter at the storming of the St Carlos Battery. Eliott told Bella about this, knowing how pleased she would be that one of the 74th had been singled out for his resource; especially a man who had once been accused, so wrongly, of desertion.

She said, 'I know him to be brave, Your Excellency.'

He glanced up from his desk. 'Kilkieran had spoken of him to you, Bella?'

She shook her head. 'Oh, no. Not that I recall, Your Excellency.' There was a devil of mischief dancing in her eyes.

'Then. . . ?'

'You see . . . I witnessed his bravery . . . last night, at the St Carlos Battery itself.'

'*You* did?' Eliott looked at her sharply, puzzled. 'I do not understand.'

She said in a small voice, 'I accompanied the troops, sir.'

His Excellency was thunderstruck. 'You, Bella? You accompanied the troops – in spite of my order that you were to do no such thing?' He shook his head. 'I cannot believe it! How did you manage such an escapade – how did you join the columns?' He repeated, 'No, I do not believe it. You make a game of me . . .'

'No, it is true, Your Excellency,' she insisted. 'Indeed I regret that I was forced to go against your wishes . . . but I felt the need to show your commanders where to mount their attacks.' She added ruefully, 'In the event, I was not needed – but I did what I felt was essential for the success of the sortie, since I had myself made the suggestion in the first place – '

'I could have you publicly whipped for this – sent out of the garrison in disgrace. You realize that?' Eliott was white with anger.

She said simply, 'Yes, I know, Your Excellency. I am sorry.'

'You knew, yet you took the risk . . . and the risk to your life as well. God help me,' he ejaculated, 'but you're a strange young woman!' The General got to his feet, took a pinch of snuff from a gold box, and went across to the big window, his face like a thundercloud. After two full minutes he turned round. He said slowly, 'Strange, yes . . . and also brave. I do not forget that you risked everything to bring information to this garrison.' He walked over to her and took her face in his hands; his own face was stern still, but kindly and understanding. 'It appears that you brought no harm to the operation or to yourself, so I shall pardon your disobedience – this time. In future, you will obey my orders as though you were a soldier in the field. You understand?'

'Yes, Your Excellency,' she said in a small voice, lowering her eyes. Then, looking him straight in the face again, she added with a sudden, mischievous smile, 'And if it be rewards and recognitions you are thinking about . . . then I would be well satisfied if some sign of approval be given to Private Carter for his part in the sortie. I am convinced that he saved my life on several occasions in the course of it . . . and had not the St Carlos Battery fallen when it did, the result might well have been different.'

Eliott gave a short laugh. 'May I remind you, my dear young lady, that I am a soldier? I am fully aware of the value of what Private Carter did . . . and now I do not wish to discuss the matter any further.'

Nevertheless, Roger Carter was summoned the very next day by the Governor and was informed personally that His Excellency had seen fit to commission him into the 74th Regiment as an Ensign, in the room of the officer who had been killed in the storming of the St Carlos Battery.

Bella was quick to realize that his promotion might well mean that she and Roger could see a great deal more of each other than had hitherto been possible or prudent. And she thrilled to this knowledge.

Her circumstances had changed a great deal now.

To be one of the personal household of His Excellency, however nebulous her position within it might be – and Eliott gave not a jot for the idle and malicious gossip of the smallminded – meant much; so did the fact that she was, as Captain Frazer had feared she might become, a veritable heroine in a rejuvenated garrison. And she did indeed see very much more of Ensign Carter as the weeks went past, those first few weeks during which the fine flush of the sortie had not yet worn off.

She had met him for the first time since his promotion from the ranks when, a few days after the sortie, she had taken a walk along the Line Wall, past the great seaward-facing batteries designed to repel a seaborne attack, listening idly to the lap of the blue water against the thick defences. Roger came along, tall, proud, so handsome she thought with a pang . . . he was accompanied by an orderly sergeant and a file of the 74th, but he halted them when he saw Bella, smiling at her with delight.

'Why, Lady Bella,' he said. 'What brings you here?'

'A mere constitutional, Mr Carter.'

He laughed at the implication of the doubly unaccustomed title. He asked, 'You have a few minutes to spare, perhaps?'

'Certainly!'

Roger beckoned up the sergeant. He said crisply, 'Carry on with the rounds, if you please, sergeant. I shall overtake you at Rosia.'

'Sir!' The sergeant saluted and barked an order at the men. The file clanked away. Roger watched them go, then turned to Bella, took her chin in his finger-tips and tilted her face upwards so that he was looking into her eyes.

'You are very charming,' he said gravely, 'if I may be allowed to say so.'

She dimpled. 'You have told me that often before now, Roger.'

'Not often enough, my dearest one. I should like to be able to say it day and night until my mouth ached with it. But now I have something else to say about you, my Bella – '

'Then, sir, kindly say it, and do not keep me in suspense!'

'Very well. Apart from being charming . . . you are kind, and generous, and good.'

'La!' she said lightly enough, though she felt a surge of pleasure and happiness. 'How so, Roger?'

He chuckled. 'You were with me at the St Carlos Battery. Who else would have interceded with His Excellency with such effect that I have been granted the right to wear this fine uniform with which I now confront you, dearest Bella?'

She shook her head, feeling a sudden rush of tears behind her lids. Roger was so obviously pleased . . . She said, 'Not I alone, at all events. Others spoke with more effect than I – your officers and comrades. And I am so very glad for you,' she added with simple pleasure in his happiness. She fingered the facings of his uniform coat – property, she guessed correctly, of the dead Ensign who had no further use for it. 'Tell me, Roger,' she went on. 'You take well to the command of men, it seems. You act as if to the manner born. What were you, Roger, before you took the King's Shilling as a mere Private of Foot?'

He looked down at her steadily, but his face had tightened, hardened. He said lamely, 'It is a long story, and one which I do not wish to bore you with.' He hesitated. 'Also it is one which it would be better for no one to know, in the circumstances.'

She touched his cuff. 'You mean because of the promotion?'

'Yes, Bella,' he said quietly. 'I mean exactly that. I should be in danger of losing it . . . if certain things were known. There was nothing dishonourable, however, I assure you – at least, not in *my* eyes.' He held her gaze magnetically. 'I can say no more than that. Let us now forget it, I beg of you. And now . . . when can we see each other again, dearest Bella?'

'Let me see,' she said, screwing up her eyes as if mentally consulting some engagement book. 'There is Lady Tittle-Tattle's tea party at Grosvenor Square . . . and Lord Eustace, of course, will be holding a reception at . . .'

'Please, Bella. There is no time to trifle. I must be on my way to Rosia – or I shall be rightly accused of dalliance with a lady during my duty!'

'All right,' she said gently. 'I am sorry, Roger.' She flushed – flushed charmingly, he thought. 'You mean – see me . . . properly?'

Their eyes interlocked. 'Yes,' he said, his throat constricting.

She asked softly, 'When will your duty be finished today, Roger?'

'At midnight.' She saw the sudden rush of blood, the eager pulse at his neck above the stock. 'I am free from then until first parade tomorrow, unless there is an alarm to arms in the meantime.'

'Then I shall see you at the midnight hour, my dearest, or shortly after, if you will tell me where to come.'

'I shall come to you.' Gently he took her hand. 'In truth there is nowhere else to go where we can be alone. I am accommodated in the barracks. May I see you in His Excellency's garden, by the wall overlooking the water? Is this possible, dearest heart?'

She nodded. 'Entirely possible and will be done, Roger.'

His face lit up and then he swung about and strode away in

the direction of Rosia. Bella, her heart beating fast, watched him until he was out of sight around a bend in the Line Wall. She found that her eyes were misting over with tears; her love for him was so intense a thing, had become almost unbearable, like a thorn piercing her heart with longing.

And, tremblingly, casting modesty to the winds, she told him as much that night, when they met secretly beneath the silver moon at the wall at the end of the garden, looking out across the starlit water of Algeciras Bay, hearing the cicadas clicking in the trees, looking out towards the Spanish sail, those cruisers which still maintained their long vigil over the sea approaches to the Rock. She and Roger were standing in almost the same spot as, so long before, she had stood with Colonel Fitzmaurice the night he had agreed so to arrange matters that Private Roger Carter would not be charged with desertion from his place of duty. Now she was enfolded in Ensign Roger Carter's arms; and she looked up at his strong, brown face and said a little tremulously,

'Oh, my Roger . . . this is such sweet, sweet pain. To be with you is wonderful, my dearest dear . . . yet all the time I am thinking of when we must part!'

He bent his head and kissed her, lingeringly. Then he said gently, 'When this siege is lifted, and times are normal, and when perhaps the regiment will be ordered home . . .' His voice tailed away.

'Yes?' she prompted. 'And then, Roger?'

He seemed all at once sad and pre-occupied. He said glumly, 'I am – afraid for the future. Yes, afraid, Bella dearest. I cannot offer you anything except unhappiness.'

'Why so?'

'I cannot tell you.'

She asked suddenly, her face cradled in the angle of his neck, 'Is this, then, what we spoke of this morning?'

'It is,' he answered after a pause.

'Roger,' she said quietly, 'I think I have a right to know. We . . . we care for each other, you and I . . .'

He didn't answer for a long time and then he said heavily, 'Yes, you are right, dearest heart. You have done so much for me. Yes, you have the right.' He paused again, then went on, 'This will be safe with you, I know that for certain. You will never speak of it to anyone at all. Bella, my dearest,' he said, suddenly holding her very tight to his body. 'I am – not Roger Carter.'

'Not?' She felt her body stiffen in his arms. 'Then – who – who – '

'My father,' he said in a low voice, 'is Sir Charles Conyers-Little, lately commanding the First Guards . . . four years ago I was an Ensign in his regiment at Windsor. I was obliged by my father to send in my papers . . . he charged me with an act of cowardice in refusing to accept a challenge to a duel after I had been wrongly accused of cheating at cards by a brother-officer who wished to bring about my disgrace. Well,' he said without rancour or bitterness, 'that brother officer succeeded, though, to give the devil his due, not precisely in the way he had planned. After that, after I had in effect been dismissed from the First Guards and my commission terminated, I rejoined the army under another name – as now you know!' He paused. 'The name of Conyers-Little is an old one, Bella, but it carries comparatively little money with it, and no money at all that my father would let *me* have. And I had to eat . . . and I knew no other means of livelihood than the profession of arms. Besides, I love the army. It is my life. I should explain that I did not refuse to fight that duel from any cowardly notions, but only because I knew I was a better swordsman than my challenger – and hot tempered, too. I saw no point in the useless shedding of blood. I still do not. Give me a proper enemy to fight, an enemy of my country, and I will fight him, but – ' He shrugged.

'And this your father would not accept?'

'No, my dearest, he would not. He was the Colonel of the First Guards . . . no scandal, no merest whisper of the word cowardice could be allowed to touch his name, so afterwards he himself also sent in his papers. He has never forgiven me, nor ever will. I have no contact with him whatsoever – though not by my wish. By his alone.'

She asked, 'Your being commissioned in the field will not help, Roger dear?'

'No. And in any case I dare not risk the news coming out that Roger Carter is Roger Conyers-Little, who was supposed at the time to have been shipped out to the American colonies and never heard of since. I must not now be exposed as a disgraced Ensign of the Guards. If that should come about, then Roger Carter would quickly be asked to send in his papers once again – or would merely be arbitrarily deprived of his fresh commission, which in any event has yet to be confirmed by Whitehall and by His Majesty . . . a commission which, in effect, that same Roger Carter has obtained under false pretences.'

Bella said stoutly, 'Won by an act of leadership and bravery, Roger, which cancels out the stupid stigma of the unaccepted challenge, surely?'

He said sadly with an ironic laugh, 'Dearest, you do not know the army as I know it!'

'But,' she asked, 'need this make any difference to *us*?'

'Unfortunately, yes – a great deal of difference. I will not offer you insecurity, the certainty that one day my charade must be discovered and all the past revived . . . to see you scorned and spurned by the wives of my brother officers in the line – as you would be, make no mistake about that! Society is so narrow, so vicious, so stupid, my dearest, and of all society the narrowest and the most stupid are those who hold the King's commission – and their wives!'

Bella was crying now; ultimately she would refuse to accept this, but for the moment her defences were down, dissolved in pity for Roger and for herself. He let her have her cry on his shoulder, her face nestled again into the neck of his coat, and then he kissed her passionately, feeling the salt of her tears on his lips. After a time her sobs subsided, but he felt the rapid beat of her heart against his breast. She drew away a little and said,

'Roger, there is yet one thing left . . . which no one need ever know about, and which no one can take from us while you are in the fortress.'

He didn't answer, but he pulled her close again.

'There is a summer house,' she whispered a little later. 'Along to the right here, where it is warm and sheltered – and private. No one will find us there, my love.'

Gently he took her arm and helped her along the path, feeling in his fingers the quiver which ran right through her body.

It was like the melting of a glacier, the end of winter, the rush of summer warmth, of tender music dimly heard, the soft sound of angels' wings in the night . . . never had she known such consummate joy, such ecstasy, such an upsurge of the spirit. He came to her as a passionate and devoted lover, and she received him into her with an outpouring of love and desire such as Antony and Cleopatra had never, never known. The soft and gentle play of his hands as they ran lightly along her limbs and stopped in the area where they played the finest of all tunes on her tautened nerves, the sensuous touch of his flesh, tender and loving on her urgent parts, sent soft shivers of love running through all her body so that she became as a violin upon which he played his cadences of love and joy . . . and when at last dawn broke the sky he drew away from her, his face content and happy, a sigh escaping his lips and his face young and fresh. They lay there together naked and un-ashamed, and she felt as if all her soul had been drawn away, drawn from her body and lodged within the frame of Roger Carter.

He left her soon after that, before the mounting daylight brought its dangers, and made his way, as circumspectly as he had come, out of His Excellency's garden and thence to Hargrave's Barracks for the early parade of the regiment. As Bella stole back inside unseen, the Royal Battery opened on the shattered Spanish lines, as if to remind the enemy, if such a reminder be needed now, that the garrison at Gibraltar was still in being.

24

It was not long, of course, before the Spaniards effected the
necessary repairs to their fortifications, though the garrison
kept up their fire against them continually, harassing the men
at work upon them. By February of the following year, 1782,
the enemy had restored the St Carlos and St Martin's
Batteries, though the latter had been only partly rebuilt, with
five embrasures to open on the town and Water Port. They
were sending across only some one hundred and fifty rounds a
day at this time, but the rate of fire increased rapidly as they
made more and more additions to their advanced works and
were thus able to bring more guns to bear. Their defensive
preparations also progressed.

So the siege went on again, wearily, interminably.

On the 24th March the 97th Regiment was disembarked from
some very welcome transports which had made the passage
through the cruiser cordon, thus reinforcing the garrison.
Long afterwards Bella recalled that day, the day the fresh, fit-
looking soldiers came ashore and marched, as the 74th had
done more than three years before, to their quarters to the beat
of the drum and the shouted commands of the sergeants. She
was able to remember it so clearly, not only because the new
arrivals and the supplies that accompanied them raised the
spirits of the garrison, but for a very personal reason also: it
was the day she first began to suspect that she might be with
child. If she was right – and time alone could tell that – then she
was sure in her heart that the child would be Roger Carter's.
At all events, she prayed that it might be, prayed with all her
heart and soul. Yet she shrank from saying anything of her
suspicions to Roger himself – she didn't really know why. She
both longed and dreaded to bear his child. She felt tremulously

eager to bring a new life into the world, life quickened by Roger, but the thought of giving birth to a helpless baby, a mite howling for sustenance, in this garrison under siege and doubtless in danger once again of attack, was scarcely to be borne, and Bella was distracted with her anxiety – almost, at times, giving way to blind panic. However, it was early days yet and she could be wrong; but if she was not wrong . . . then the time would come when her secret would begin to show. How then would she explain matters to His Excellency – and to Captain Frazer, that dour Scot who would condemn her out of hand, and condemn Roger Carter also, if his name was ever linked with her condition?

Six weeks after that day, at seven o'clock in the morning of 4th May – by which time Bella had become more and more certain of what was happening to her body but had not spoken of it to a soul – there occurred the first complete lull in firing for thirteen months. This respite lasted for twenty-four hours and then it was observed from the garrison that the enemy was making ready some floating batteries for what appeared, at long last, to be the grand assault. Soon after this, the Rock galleries were begun by engineers under one Sergeant Ince, who mined great tunnels into the living rock from above Willis's Battery to below Green's Lodge, in which His Excellency proposed to make a battery; and this system of galleries was greatly extended as the weeks went by.

On 26th May a vessel from Algiers signalled intelligence which confirmed that the final assault was indeed near – that it was in fact universally believed in Spain that the garrison must inevitably be taken before the end of July, of such magnitude were the preparations for attack then being mounted. And that same day upwards of one hundred enemy sail of the line entered Algeciras Bay to anchor off the Spanish shore. Shortly after, they landed some twelve battalions – about nine thousand men, who took up their positions before Gibraltar to reinforce the great assembling army. On succeeding days the besiegers were further reinforced and yet more enemy ships arrived, including some battering-ships. A little later a French convoy of more than sixty sail, laden with troops, entered the bay.

And then, as spring became summer and the garrison watched the ships and men pile up against them, the enemy batteries became totally silent . . . and the garrison wondered, and wondered again.

'They're up to the devil's own tricks,' Eliott said. He stopped for a moment as the skirl of the pipes filled the air mournfully, fading into the distance as a Highland regiment marched towards Grand Parade. He went on, 'According to my information, the Dons intend to mount a combined bombardment by land and sea . . . I suppose that in itself has been obvious enough, but they've got some fiendish new weapons which they mean to employ, so I hear.'

The ADC prompted, 'Yes, Your Excellency?'

Eliott tapped at some papers on his desk. He said, 'I have here a description of the way in which those battering-ships are constructed. They're supposed to be impregnable – incombustible and unsinkable. And by the sound of them, they are!' The General paused. 'They're to be fortified six or seven feet in thickness on the larboard side, with green timber bolted with iron, cork, junk and raw hides . . . they will carry guns of heavy metal, they will be bomb proof on their tops with a descent for the shells to slide off. Now, these vessels, as I understand it, are to be moored with iron chains within half gunshot of the walls. Large boats with mantlets will lie off at some distance, filled with troops, to assist. These mantlets will be hinged so that they can be lowered to facilitate the landing of the men.'

'Is there any indication of the numbers of men to be employed, Your Excellency?'

Eliott nodded. 'Forty thousand! It will be very heavy odds against us, as you can see. The plan is believed to be that the principal attack will in fact be made by sea, and will be covered by a squadron of men-o'-war, with bomb-ketches, floating batteries, gun-boats and mortar-boats.' He rubbed wearily at his eyes, and sighed heavily. Then he seemed to rouse himself with an effort. 'Frazer . . . you will arrange for three sergeants to be posted on the North, King's and South Bastions, to observe and report the enemy's signals in camp and along the coast. All the regiments and corps must be ready at a moment's notice to stand-to. You will also inform Captain Curtis of the Navy that I desire his ships to lower yards and topsails, to be in readiness to act on shore at a moment's notice. We must increase our artillery activity against the enemy lines – I shall speak myself with the Colonel of the Artillery as to that, shortly. For the rest . . . we must strengthen our communications within the garrison, repair the splinter-proofs, and caisson Green's Lodge Battery and the Royal Battery with ship-timbers. And I think it would be as well if the civil inhabitants were to be evacuated towards Europa.' He stood up. 'Pass the word that I shall hold a Council this evening at six o'clock, Frazer. All other matters can be gone into then – and the garrison rendered as impregnable as it lies within our capacity to make it.'

'Yes, Your Excellency.' The aide-de-camp hesitated. 'You . . . speak of evacuating the civil population. What are your intentions with regard to . . . Lady Kilkieran?'

There was a curious look in his eye and Eliott, looking directly at him, saw it. The Governor asked sharply, 'My intentions?'

'Your Excellency . . . she, too, is a civilian.'

'I am aware that that is correct in a strict and narrow sense, Captain Frazer. She is also, however, the widow of a very gallant officer in my command – and has the right to be called gallant herself as well. I therefore regard her as being on the strength of my garrison. She stays where she is – unless she herself requests otherwise, which I consider it most unlikely she will!' He added abruptly, 'Have you any further questions?'

'No, Your Excellency. I understand.'

'Good! That is all, then.'

The ADC, thus dismissed, bowed and left the room. The look on his face, however, was far from pleasant. In the midst of what now promised to be the final act in the long tragedy of the siege, Frazer's mind, hate-filled, was dominated increasingly by one thing and one thing alone: his pathological detestation of Bella Kilkieran. He knew very well that she was laughing at him, at his virtual impotence now that she was His

Excellency's own protégée, and this knowledge inflamed him beyond all capacity to endure. He also strongly suspected that she was seeing a good deal of Ensign Roger Carter – that newly commissioned ranker (as Frazer still sneeringly regarded him) of the 74th.

Possibly that young man could prove her Achilles' heel. Possibly he could be made to be!

Captain Frazer was trembling all over as he made his way through the ante-room.

Just before the Council was due to meet that evening, Bella, walking in the garden alone with her distracted thoughts about what she was now certain was her approaching motherhood, encountered the Lieutenant-Governor, the veteran Lieutenant-General Boyd. His eyes twinkled at her as she greeted him; this pretty young girl was good for old eyes, he felt, and he was oddly moved that evening by her very youth. So young a thing, he reflected sadly, to withstand what was to come on top of the hunger and dangers of the past years . . .

'My dear Lady Bella,' he said gravely, 'I envy His Excellency, having you about his household!'

'La, sir, but you pay a pretty compliment!' She dimpled, pleased to have someone to talk to. 'Tell me: How much longer are we to wait for the Dons?'

Boyd shrugged, his shoulders thin, body haggard and bent beneath his scarlet coat – and bent by more than his years. 'That I really cannot say, Lady Bella,' he answered in a thin voice. 'Their ships are ready yonder, crammed with men, but – '

'So I see.' Bella looked out across the bay towards the assembled fleets, the combined fleets of France and Spain. 'It is indeed a mighty armada, General Boyd. Och, sure, how wonderful it would be . . . if it could be destroyed before it even weighed anchor to cross the bay!'

'Indeed it would be, Lady Bella, but – h'rm – that is the merest dream.'

'Could it not be done with fire-ships?'

Boyd shrugged again, and shook his head. 'No,' he said

wearily. 'Manoeuvring is difficult enough in these restricted waters, and fire-ships could be blown back by a shift of wind into the Water Port or against the Line Wall.'

'But if they should somehow reach the fleets . . . what then?'

Boyd said, 'The battering-ships are said to be incombustible, and I doubt if fire-ships would worry them much. They would severely damage the sail of the line, of course, but all I have said still applies, Lady Bella. We cannot command the winds, and Gibraltar cannot move itself out of the way!'

'I suppose you are right, General Boyd.' Bella turned away, watched the Spanish shore line, purple and red beneath the declining sun. 'But what about the landward batteries? Could they not be destroyed to good effect, as in the sortie?'

'Of course, and are being, dear lady – but by cannon shot!' Boyd laughed with indulgence. 'Even you cannot suggest sending fire-ships against the land batteries?'

'By no means . . . yet to set them afire would be more effective than knocking them about with a cannon?'

'Why, undoubtedly, but – '

She said with energy, 'General Boyd, if you cannot send fire-ships, you can at all events send fire-balls! You can use red-hot shot! Heat your balls until they are red hot, then load them into your cannon and toss them onto the enemy fortifications!' She seized his frayed coat-sleeve. 'General Boyd, we must, we *must* spoil the Spanish designs! You must give this suggestion a trial!'

Boyd started, frowned, pursed his lips. 'Damme, girl,' he said softly after a moment, 'if you haven't taught an old campaigner something after all. Red-hot shot . . . hundreds of balls, and spreading fires on all sides of the line! And attack before they do themselves – carry the offensive to the enemy once again, as we did in the sortie! It's worth the attempt, damned if it isn't!' He laid a hand on her shoulder, a hand that shook with excitement. 'You will excuse me, Lady Bella? I must speak at once with His Excellency. You may well have saved Gibraltar, my dear young lady, with that suggestion!'

25

Next day the Spanish flagship off Algeciras hoisted the English ensign to her main topgallant masthead – with the ensign of Spain floating in triumph above it.

A pointer? The garrison took it as such.

Soon after that, seven barges with crimson awnings rowed from Algeciras to the Orange Grove, returning with other passengers to Algeciras. This being observed from the garrison, it was taken as another indication: the great personages had arrived to watch Gibraltar brought finally to its knees.

The day following, Bella's proposals to Boyd were put into effect and Gibraltar took the initiative. Bella went with Boyd to the northern batteries which had been ordered to open with red-hot shot. She watched the great fires being started and the balls heated until they glowed fiery red. Alive with sparks, they sent out wafts of heat as they were handled by big metal grabs and loaded into the cannon, then swiftly fired against the Spanish works and batteries.

This bombardment was kept up throughout the day with great precision, causing considerable damage and loss to the landward enemy. Glowing fires were seen where the shot landed, and these fires spread with great rapidity along the Spanish lines, and in the late afternooin an ammunition-dump went up with a tremendous explosion; while Fort St Philip was later covered with a great pall of smoke in which the leaping flames could clearly be seen.

As that day ended, the hopes of the garrison were higher than they could have hoped for.

'But the physical damage,' Eliott told Bella during the evening, 'is as nothing when compared to the moral effect ᵒf our fire, my dear . . . I believe de Crillon will be provoked into attacking before he is in all respects ready and this may help a great deal to frustrate the whole enterprise – you would agree, I take it, Boyd?'

He looked across at the Lieutenant-Governor, who nodded. 'I would indeed, sir. I would indeed.'

Eliott rubbed his hands. 'Then we must now prepare a warm reception for the Dons, General! You will please see to it that additional grates for heating shot are made, and distributed along the Line Wall. There may well be an attack from seaward at any time, and we must be ready for this . . .'

And early next morning the enemy did indeed open upon the garrison in earnest.

Following upon a signal of two rockets from the landward forts, the cannonade began at five-thirty with a volley of some sixty shells from all the enemy's mortar batteries, and this was soon backed up with a general bombardment from one hundred and seventy guns of large calibre. It was a tremendous curtain of metal and the firing was extremely powerful – and was directed entirely against the defences; but the damage was not in fact so great as might have been expected from such a train of artillery as the Spaniards had brought up. At the same time nine line-of-battle ships passed along the Line Wall and discharged several broadsides into the garrison, their great sheer bulk almost obliterated by the curling smoke from the guns. The noise was thunderous. Then, rounding Europa, they wore and returned to bombard Rosia and the New Mole. Fifteen smaller craft also approached and opened, but were deflected by fire from the King's Bastion. In the meantime Eliott had ordered the furnaces at the New Mole to be lighted, and the enemy in future to be saluted with red-hot shot to seaward.

That night the attack was broken off except for some shelling from the land batteries, but early next morning the enemy's men-o'-war came in again, to be received this time with a well-supported fire of the heated balls, which made them keep their distance.

After this there came an unexplained period of inactivity.

★

Roger took her face in his hands, tenderly, his own face alight with love and gentleness as they lay close, beneath those lowslung stars, in His Excellency's garden.

He whispered, his lips brushing her ear, 'Do not let us talk about war and fighting tonight, Bella. I have had enough of it to last me for a while . . . let us talk rather of what is to happen when the fighting is over and the siege lifted.' He looked into her eyes. 'What will you do, Bella? Will you remain in the garrison?'

She said, 'I doubt it, Roger. My excuse for remaining will vanish when the first ships come freely in. I wish only to see the siege lifted, as you know.' She sighed. 'Naturally, I must think about how I am to live. Here, I have lived in army quarters and on army rations helped by such money as my husband left behind him when he was killed.'

'He did not leave you well provided for, I gather?'

She shook her head sadly. 'Alas, no . . . dear Kilkieran . . . so much older than I, yet I loved him, Roger! No – Kilkieran lived up to his means and very often beyond, I fear, and there will be very little left when my return to England allows me to settle up his estate.'

'Then,' he asked after a pause, 'what do you propose to do?'

'I don't know, Roger,' she answered a trifle helplessly. 'Truly, I have no idea.'

He pulled her down to him again, and she felt the urgent pulse in his body, the trembling of passion in his limbs. He said thickly, 'I have some ideas, my Bella. You must allow me to – to – '

'Assist me? Is that what you are trying to say?'

He nodded, and started to speak, but she cut him short. She said decisively, 'That I shall not allow, Roger.'

'But why?' He sat up, stroking her hair. 'Is it not customary, for a husband to support his wife?'

She gave a smothered exclamation, found herself shaking a little with emotion, tremulous with a very great joy. She said, 'You mean – you really mean you want – '

'Oh, my dearest!' There was a catch in his voice and his hands went out to her lovingly. 'Surely you could never have imagined I wanted anything else in the world, my love? Have I failed you to that extent, that you did not know?'

'No – not that exactly. But Roger . . . you once said – '

He kissed her on the lips. 'Yes,' he said a moment later, 'I spoke once of not wanting to offer you the insecurity of my position – I confess it. But it has seemed to me on reflection that you cannot in fact be more insecure than you are at this moment – and likely to remain so unless you fall in love with someone more worthy than I – which God forbid! You see,' he added, smiling down at her, 'my mind is really changed after all!'

She couldn't speak, could only look back at him, her love for him filling her eyes. He said softly, his lips caressing her cheek, 'Once all this is over, my dearest Bella, we will marry, here in Gibraltar. The 74th will assuredly be ordered home – and you will come with me, as my wife, to England.'

'And – your father, and the rest?'

Roger gave a quiet laugh. 'The past will lie buried, if we are lucky, and we must pray that we are lucky. That is how it must be. Roger Conyers-Little no longer exists. As for my father, he will never connect Ensign Carter of the 74th of Foot with his son – so nothing will ever be said from that quarter, I'll warrant you! For the rest, we must trust again to luck. I am much changed since the old days and I may not be recognized by those who knew me then.'

'Oh, Roger! No one ever changes so much that his friends do not recognize him, and it cannot be so long since – all that happened.'

'All the same,' he said quietly, 'I have concluded that we must live our lives and not look backward at the shadows. I have given much thought to this.' The young officer took her more tightly in his arms then, kissed her hungrily on the mouth, the eyes, the throat . . . his hand sliding gently, caressingly down her body. She responded to his pressures, her breath coming faster and her breast warm against him. Then, very tenderly, she pushed him away a little.

She said, 'Roger my sweet, I must go inside. I have lingered too long . . . His Excellency may be wondering, or if not him, then Captain Frazer. They have not gone to their beds tonight . . . and Frazer is ever on the watch. They must never know about us, Roger . . . I mean, about what we have done, when we had no right to, other than the right of our love for each other. That should be enough, I know, but – ' She broke off, then seemed to stiffen in his embrace. She whispered, 'Dearest heart, look after yourself tomorrow and every day that this accursed siege lasts! For my sake, my dearest, and – and . . .'

'Yes?' He looked at her, his dark eyes almost luminous, mutely pleading, as she knew, for her body.

She said, 'Nothing, Roger dearest. It was nothing.' Words had been trembling on the very edge of her tongue, but for some reason – perhaps because she did not wish to worry him at this historic moment of imminent and decisive action – she still could not bring herself to tell him that she was going to bear his child. Soon he must find out . . . she had even begun to thicken round her hips and waist but Roger appeared to have noticed no changes yet and neither, so far as she was aware, had anyone else . . . but soon! When she could no longer put it off any longer, then she would tell him and be grateful for the comfort and shared knowledge. She did, in point of fact, long for that shared knowledge and the increased tenderness which she knew he would show towards her; but not yet, not just now.

Next day, observation from the garrison told the defenders that every enemy preparation was now complete and that they must hourly expect the last, the grand assault.

The Land Port and Water Port guards were heavily reinforced, the furnaces and grates lighted again, and the artillery ordered in strength to the batteries. Everything was stand-to now and no off-duty. The enemy bombardment increased that day to four thousand rounds; and a combined French and Spanish Fleet, with no less than ten admirals' flags, hove in sight from the westward. But, though the preparations were immense and the force apparently overwhelming, the enemy seemed to have overlooked entirely the nature of the Gibraltar garrison, who were by this time veterans of siege warfare and had been for a long time thoroughly habituated to the effects of artillery; had been, in fact, prepared by slow degrees for what awaited them now. And Eliott had the utmost confidence in his officers and men, whose spirits had in any case been elevated by the success of the red-hot shot.

Trouble, after that, was not long in coming.

It was heralded by the battering-ships which came down on the Rock in the early morning and moored in their appointed stations. As soon as the first ship dropped her anchors, the fire commenced briskly from the garrison. But the enemy were moored in a little over ten minutes and their cannonade shook the very foundations of the Rock itself. Upwards of four hundred pieces of heavy artillery were now playing simultaneously upon the fortress, the constant gunfire first exacerbating, and then stupefying, the senses. The battering-ships were extremely formidable; the heaviest shells from the garrison rebounded from their tops, whilst the 32-pounder shot was incapable of making any impression whatever on their hulls. Meanwhile, every effort of the garrison's artillery was being concentrated upon these massive battering-ships; the landward guns were being totally disregarded.

The casualties were mounting now, but the confidence of the garrison was undiminished; and, in spite of those mounting casualties and the odds against the garrison, things were already going much better by the afternoon, and they knew that indeed they were to be delivered from the bloody hand of Spain.

26

The garrison's success was, like the success of the sortie before it, almost incredible when it came, though the British troops had always known the Dons to have small stomach for a fight – and that, indeed, had they possessed such stomach they would have mounted an attack long before this. Not the least incredible part of it was the very speed of the enemy's collapse. The bombardment on both sides had been intense throughout the morning and the Rock had suffered badly enough; but the masts of several of the attacking ships had very soon been shot away, while the rigging of all of them was quickly in the greatest confusion, rendering the huge fleet virtually helpless. And then, during the shot-filled afternoon, as the sun blazed down, the enemy flagship and one other ship of the line were set ablaze; towards evening the bombardment once again slackened from landward, while that from the sea almost totally ceased. Distress rockets were now seen to go up from the battering-ships. A little before midnight a wreck floated in below the town Line Wall, filled with dead. Before the next dawn two more ships were set ablaze, one of them being a continuous flame from stem to stern. Shortly after this six other battering-ships were put out of action, and it was obvious after that that the defenders had the measure of the Dons.

At five in the morning the flames reached the magazine of one of the battering-ships to the northward and with a shattering explosion she was gone, to be followed a moment later by another. Of the six ships which were still burning, three blew up before eleven in the morning, while the other three burnt to the water-line. Of the remaining two as yet unburnt, one blew up unexpectedly and the last was burnt during the afternoon by the Navy, who thus put the finishing touches, and in truth very little else, to the victory. Prisoners taken asserted the complete surprise which the use of red-hot shot had caused to the Spanish crews, and they were bitter against their officers for having described the ships as invulnerable. Their admiral, they reported, had quit his flagship with undignified haste a little before midnight, but other officers had retired to safety ashore even earlier than that. Thus had the enemy's craven-ness of spirit negated the stupendous force built up against the garrison . . .

It was now all but over. The Spanish might, the Spanish punch, had been broken. The landward armies had never stirred against the fortress; the sea defeat had taken the guts from them. It had been almost too easy. And it had been almost wholly due to the red-hot shot.

It was after the last of the battering-vessels had been destroyed that Bella heard her name being called urgently.

She was standing on the Line Wall in the lee of a battery, watching a blazing line of enemy ships, when she heard the men shouting above the sounds of the battle, and when she turned she saw a blood-stained sergeant in the ragged uniform of the 74th. He saluted her and said breathlessly,

'Milady, will you please come with me, and quickly – '

She knew at once what had happened, and a hand flew to her breast; but she was able to ask almost stonily, 'What is it, Sergeant?'

'Mr Carter, milady.'

'Is he – bad?'

'I'm afraid so, milady, very bad. He is asking for you . . . there is no time to lose if you are to get to him while he lives.'

'Oh no!' She reached out a hand towards the wall of the battery for support; her knees felt suddenly as if they must give way. 'Take me to him,' she whispered, her face grey with fear. 'Please take me to him . . .'

'Take my hand, milady. Come.' The sergeant stretched out his hand and she came to him almost like a child. He took her arm and she sagged limply against the strength of his body, a terrible blank misery filling her mind. She was scarcely even conscious of the way they took, scarcely conscious of her own stumbling footsteps alongside the sergeant. Her ears were filled with the resumed roar of the landward cannonade, her eyes stung with the acrid smoke of the powder and with tears, and with the dust which rose up around her to the shimmering sun. All she could recall afterwards was reaching Roger's side after that dreadful journey, and then the sight of him, his red coat torn and white with dust, and stained with the blood which welled from his side as he lay on a pile of sacking behind a stout wall which itself shook and trembled to the bombardment.

He was deathly pale and he was drawing difficult, gasping breaths. It was obvious he could not have much longer left to live. Her heart fluttering wildly, Bella dropped to her knees beside him and took his hand. Tears were streaming down her face now, channelling through the clinging sandy dust which overlay everything like a shroud.

'Roger,' she breathed. 'Oh, my dearest, my darling . . .'

He opened his eyes then, weakly, the lids fluttering with scarcely strength enough to keep them up. But she saw the instant recognition, saw his lips move as he tried to speak. She leaned closer, felt the dying breath on her cheeks as she strove to hear, to understand. It was already much too late, however; he gave a long, faint sigh and then his head drooped sideways, his hand fell limp and slack in hers.

It was a long time before the sergeant, and the private who had been left with Roger while the sergeant went for Bella, could lift her away from him. She clung to the body, in a storm of weeping. When this had passed and left her dry and lifeless, with her face as cold and dead-looking as Roger Carter's, the sergeant gently lifted her trembling body and kept hold of her arm. He said something to her, something which she was not conscious of hearing. There was a drumming in her brain, a voice of self-reproach was saying to her over and over again that Roger had wanted her last night and she had refused him, she had refused his last request of her. It kept on and on at her . . . after a while she realized that she was walking, stumbling along the rubble-strewn streets with the cannonade from landward still whistling overhead, and that the sergeant was escorting her to His Excellency's residence.

She summoned all that was left of her will and her determination and stopped dead. She was scarcely conscious even then of her own voice, though she spoke with surprising calmness and almost a detachment. She said, 'Thank you, Sergeant. You have been very kind. Please come no farther now. I shall be all right.'

'But milady – '

'Please!' It was a strangled sound now, very close to a sob being wrenched from her lips. 'I would – rather be alone. Quite alone. You must understand.'

'Why, of course, milady – it'll be as you say.' The NCO let go of her arm and stood there irresolute and concerned. She walked away from him, conscious of his gaze on her back, but when she had gone on a little farther she looked round and he was moving off, no doubt going back to his interrupted duty. She took a turning down what had been a side-street, walking fast now but with no very clear idea of her immediate whereabouts, aimlessly walking, shocked and dazed . . . walking to she knew not where, walking simply to get away, to lose herself in these, the final moments of Gibraltar's long ordeal. She wished for death. Whatever happened, she would not return to His Excellency's household now. She knew she could never face the pretences which she would have to make that Roger Carter's death meant no more to her than that of any other brave soldier lost in battle, and the aide-de-camp's almost open sneers . . . that, and the garden where they had met so often and so happily and where in the end she had refused Roger her comfort, the comfort which no one else in all the world could give him, on the very night before his death; the garden where she had failed to tell him of her suspicion that she was carrying his child. For she felt instinctively – she had no doubts now – that the unborn child was Roger Carter's. And now she must keep that secret to herself; she would not allow herself to hear any criticisms of Roger for what he had done . . . and the best way to make sure of that was to disappear from all the places and people she had known – to join, perhaps, the townspeople and the troops.

Before the sun set that evening, thousands of spectators, of whom Bella was not one, watched from the heights behind the town as the Royal Standard of Spain, which had been intended to fly upon the battlements of the Rock, was brought ashore ignominiously by seamen of the Navy. The following afternoon, many ships in the combined enemy fleets loosed topsails, and several thousand men marched with their colours from the lines to the camps. The land-based fire was still maintained, though at a reduced rate now, and Eliott kept the garrison standing-to and continued to heat shot.

Nevertheless, it was obvious now to the whole garrison that it was merely a matter of time before the Spaniards marched away from their lines altogether. And within a few days the news was received that Lord Howe in HMS *Victory*, with the British Fleet, was preparing to sail to their relief.

Sunk in her misery, Bella heard the tidings; but they conveyed little to her. She had found a place to hide, a mere hole in the ground beyond the shattered South Port and some way up the Rock and here she sustained life almost unwillingly, living on berries and wild onions as the townspeople had done for the greater part of the long siege.

The siege was not over yet; but she who had once wanted nothing more than to see the redcoats march in triumph through the town and fortress, now cared little if she never saw anything of the kind.

27

She had not even attended the militarily splendid funeral quickly held for Roger, who was one of a mere handful of officers killed in the repulse of the grand assault; she would not even reveal herself for that, and indeed if she had many of the garrison eyebrows would have been raised high at the idea of any woman attending a funeral – let alone somebody who had no ties of blood or marriage with the deceased officer. Nevertheless she did make enquiries as to the time of the funeral and from her hide-out she was able to see, far below and through a mist of tears, the snail-like cortège making for the burial ground before the North Front – up there by the Devil's Tower where Kilkieran lay buried also. Dimly she could hear the mournful dirge of the regimental slow march, of the muffled, crêpe-bound drums. Then a little later she heard from the distance – she could no longer see from where she was – the rattle of the muskets as the firing-party paid its last respects to the corpse now settled in the earth; and then again the drums and fifes of the 74th as the burial party came back through the Land Port, swinging along now to a cheerful quickstep.

And that was that. It was all over now.

The past was the past and she knew now that she could have no possible future. Without Roger Carter, there could be none. Her love for him had followed a perhaps curious course: there had been that start like a flash of summer lightning, then a pause . . . and then the gradual build-up to the real intensity of a genuine passion. And then the final break, which had come when all seemed set so fair . . . it had been the cruellest blow. The shock of Roger Carter's death had driven her right into herself and she cared nothing for her life now. She wished that one of the enemy's guns would end it all for her; those guns were firing still. They could yet bring forgetfulness to her . . . and a reunion with Roger Carter's spirit.

That night she made her way back into the town and went towards a wine-house frequented, when there was any wine to sell, by the soldiers. She had no money now, and she would have to beg for such food as was available, such crumbs as fell from other person's mouths. And as the days passed, she would perhaps be driven to other resorts to stifle her hunger.

She didn't care now.

The ADC said stiffly and ominously, 'She has been traced, Your Excellency.'

'Well?'

'It is somewhat as I suggested some days ago. She is living the life of a common harlot in the town, Your Excellency, selling her favours to the troops. The men were at first reluctant to speak; that is why it has taken so long to find her. I was eventually able, however, to gather all the evidence necessary.'

Eliott had started, and his gaunt grey face now took on an angry flush. 'Frazer, what are you saying? You can't mean that!'

The aide-de-camp did not answer; he simply shrugged.

Eliott went on, 'There would be no need whatever for her to come to such a pass – such a total degradation!' His hands shook on the desk. 'If she was in trouble of any kind, she could have come direct to me. She knew that very well.'

'And yet,' Frazer murmured, 'she did *not* in fact come to you, Your Excellency. Instead, she left your household. That we are only too well aware of.'

'I still cannot imagine why she should have left.'

'Ah – but I think perhaps I can, Your Excellency, if you will permit me to say so.' Frazer licked his lips almost salaciously. 'I believe that the Lady Bella was with child, and also – '

'*With child* . . . !' Eliott's head jerked up and he glared at the ADC as though the Scot had taken leave of his senses. 'What makes you say such a thing as that?'

Again Frazer shrugged. 'Your Excellency – her character is common knowledge in the town, I do assure you of that. As to her pregnancy, I have from my own observations formed the suspicion that she might well be with child. Again if you will permit the liberty, I have been somewhat surprised that Your Excellency had not noticed it also, though I confess that the cares and anxieties of conducting this siege will have . . . um . . . left you with little time for such observations, perhaps.' Frazer paused, then added, 'I believe that the father could well have been the man Carter, whom you commissioned, and who was killed recently.'

'Carter . . . Ensign Carter of the 74th?' His Excellency seemed totally dazed.

Frazer nodded.

'You mean – ?'

'I mean, Your Excellency, that she was in the habit of seeing a very great deal of him while she was a member of your household.' The ADC coughed discreetly. 'You will not wish me to go into all the details, Your Excellency, but . . . I have good reason to believe that they were coupling together – in your own grounds.'

'I see.' The General's tone was icy. 'How long have you had this "good reason", Captain Frazer?'

'For some months, Your Excellency – '

'Then why have you not approached me earlier – with the results of your spying?'

Frazer was prepared for this. He said, 'I did not regard it as spying, Your Excellency, but as my simple duty.' He paused, but there was no reaction, and he went on discreetly, 'I did not approach you upon the matter because I had no conclusive or absolute proof, Your Excellency. It would have been monstrously unfair to have come to you on the basis of mere belief, however reasonable or indeed strong that belief may have been . . . wrong both towards Your Excellency and to the two persons most closely concerned. Now, however, the situation has changed, as Your Excellency will, I am sure, agree. It is my clear duty to put all my knowledge at your disposal. Now – it seems to me that the Lady Kilkieran had a very strong attachment to Carter – that is vouched for by others – and it is my belief that his death has driven her, at least temporarily, out of her mind, that in fact she is not wholly responsible for her actions.' He added, 'She was ever a most strange woman . . . and Your Excellency will no doubt recall that many points about the death of Colonel Fitzmaurice remained unexplained. I am of the opinion that Lady Kilkieran knows a good deal more about *that* than she has ever been willing to admit.'

'That has nothing to do with her present case, at all events.' Eliott rubbed at his eyes, looking suddenly years older. He said with difficulty, 'This news – the news you have brought me about her present way of life. You are certain of this, beyond all doubt?'

'I am quite certain, Your Excellency, or I would never have brought it to your notice. The evidence is . . .' Frazer screwed up his eyes '. . . incontrovertible. The way in which she is maintaining herself has been remarked by many of the garrison and by the townspeople. I can bring all the witnesses that Your Excellency may desire.'

'I cannot, cannot believe it!' His Excellency's head drooped as if with fatigue – or sorrow. 'I cannot believe such a thing of Kilkieran's widow.'

Frazer said slyly, 'Indeed, Your Excellency, it *is* hard to believe. But I would ask you to remember that before she was wife to His Lordship of gallant memory, she was daughter to a peasant farmer and a mother who lived a loose life herself . . . Lady Kilkieran was a wild girl from the Connemara bogs, a mannerless, graceless bog dweller.' His voice had become hoarse with hatred, but His Excellency, pre-occupied with the melancholy of the situation, seemed not to notice anything amiss. 'She is merely reverting to her origins. I repeat, Your Excellency, I can bring much evidence before you to bear out all I say.' He produced some sheets of paper which he now placed on the desk in front of the Governor. 'As you will see from this report, Your Excellency, the Colonel of the 74th Regiment himself urges most strongly her expulsion from the fortress by the first ship to enter, regardless of where that ship may be bound. He is explicit on that point. He fears for the discipline of the garrison among other things.' He coughed. 'Anticipating your complete agreement, Your Excellency, I have already drawn up the necessary documents for her despatch. They await only Your Excellency's signature.'

He pushed a sheaf of papers towards the Governor. Eliott looked up at him and snapped, 'Wait, if you please! I shall decide nothing in a hurry, Captain Frazer.' He rose from his desk, heavily, and walked across to the window, where he stood looking out, deep in thought. He gave a heartfelt but almost unconscious sigh. He had formed a very close and affectionate attachment for Bella Kilkieran; that very fact alone made him realize the more sharply how necessary it was for him to put his duty before his personal feelings in so delicate and potentially dangerous a matter as this. It was indeed a matter of the utmost importance to his command. If what he had been told was true – and he could not reasonably doubt the accuracy of the reports that lay on his desk, even though he had for a long time known of his aide-de-camp's personal bias against the girl – if all that was true, then it was his clear duty to relieve the garrison of an undesirable element, the more so as the sea passage could now be considered relatively safe, or at least safer than when last she had left the Rock. To allow the widow of a former commanding officer to behave as Bella was said to be behaving was, of course, utterly unthinkable. In a garrison such as this, still under rigorous siege if no longer threatened with actual attack, morale and discipline could be disastrously undermined by allowing her to stay. And even for the girl's sake . . . yes, undoubtedly she would be better off in England now, rather than remain in disgrace in a garrison where she had been one of the most prominent of the ladies. Especially – if Frazer was right – he could not possibly have a baby being born into the garrison! And further, if it were true that the death of young Carter had hit her so badly, then she would be best away from the scene of so many memories . . . and there was indeed the matter of Fitzmaurice . . . yes, there really was only the one thing to do in all the various circumstances.

One thing was clear enough in all conscience: he should never have allowed himself to be persuaded into letting her remain in the fortress in the first place. All this evidently had its roots in the past and was to some extent the fault of his own weakness . . .

Eliott walked stiffly back to his desk, his face grey and tired and drawn with worry and sadness. In silence he read through the document before him and then he took up a quill. A moment later he laid it down again. He said, 'I am signing nothing pending further enquiries. You will inform the Colonel of the 74th that I wish his presence here at once. You will also inform the senior of the garrison's surgeons that I wish to see him, and that I may require him to carry out a professional examination. You will take steps immediately to inform Lady Bella that I am available now if she should wish to see me. But only if it is her own wish . . . I do not want her *brought* before me. You understand what I mean? I will have no indignity thrust upon her, and I trust her to come to me of her own free will and tell me whatever it is she may wish to tell me. If she wishes to be examined by the surgeon to clear her of the charge which you have brought against her – of pregnancy – then she shall be so examined.'

'Yes, Your Excellency.'

'Then let us bring this matter to a speedy conclusion, Captain Frazer.'

'As you desire, Your Excellency.' Frazer left the room and Eliott sat on, an elderly man puzzled and anxious and uncomprehending, his mind clouded with sheer fatigue and the terrible strain of the recent years of responsibility. It was some half-hour later that the Colonel of the 74th and the senior surgeon presented themselves to His Excellency, having arrived with all despatch from their duties. Eliott was scarcely aware even of their presence; he greeted them perfunctorily, received the Colonel's confirmation in detail of his written report on Lady Bella, and then sat in silence; and they waited, sitting uncomfortably on the gilded chairs, as the minutes became hours and Lady Bella had still not arrived. Officers came and went with papers and orders and His Excellency continued to conduct the affairs of the garrison. Three hours – no less – after the Colonel and the surgeon had come as bidden, Captain Frazer returned to His Excellency's room – alone.

Bowing, he reported that the Lady Kilkieran – whom he had had some difficulty in finding – did not wish to speak with His Excellency on any matter whatsoever.

There was a heavy silence for some moments; then Eliott, more drawn than ever and oddly shrunk now, reached forward and smoothed out the documents which were still on the desk before him. Once again he took up his quill, and this time dipped it in a crystal ink-pot on a silver stand. He scrawled his signature upon the warrant; then reading the document through once again, he penned a couple of alterations and initialled them. As he did so, he said, 'If Lady Kilkieran should change her mind about wishing to see me, I am available at any time before this warrant is executed. *At any time*. You will see that this is brought to her notice.'

'Of course, Your Excellency.'

'And one other thing, of even greater importance to me.' Eliott rapped his desk. 'You spoke of Lady Kilkieran leaving by the first available ship, wherever such a ship might be bound. That is not my order. My order is, and I have amended the warrant accordingly, that Lady Kilkieran shall board, as a passenger, the first ship to clear *for England*. There is to be no mistake about that. Is that fully understood, Captain Frazer?'

'Fully, Your Excellency.' Frazer could at this stage scarcely control the eager shake in his limbs.

'Very well,' Eliott said curtly. 'You will attend to the details. And you will deal with Lady Kilkieran as a lady of rank and widow of a distinguished officer – not as what it is reported to me she is.'

'Your Excellency, I – '

The Governor lifted his hand. 'I no longer disbelieve you, Frazer, for had it been otherwise she would have come to me. Nevertheless, I have stated my wishes – and they are to be obeyed. Is that, too, understood?'

'Certainly, Your Excellency.' The ADC reached out for the sand and lightly dusted some over the wet ink of the Governor's signature and amendments. When the ink was quite dry he blew gently at the sand and gathered up the papers. Then he bowed to His Excellency and the two officers and left the room. There was a world of satisfaction in his dark, satanic eyes now. This time there would certainly be no mistake. The Lady Kilkieran would never return to Gibraltar now . . . and though the order about sailing to England and

England only would be obeyed, Frazer knew he could safely put a reasonably wide interpretation on the order as to *how* the woman was to be expelled from the garrison. As to her passage, that, of course, was entirely within the province of the Captain of whichever King's ship took her away from the Rock.

Frazer had dutifully carried out his orders to tell Bella that she could see the Governor; there was, from his point of view, no reason why he should not, for he was on safe ground. The reports were in their entire basis true, and he had a cast-iron case. And Bella's refusal to see His Excellency had also been truthfully reported by the ADC. She could not have faced Eliott, could not possibly have borne the look which she dreaded to see on his kindly, trusting face.

Frazer had, however, neglected to inform her that she was to be deported – that, he thought, would be better left until a ship was ready for her in case she should find some subterfuge for remaining. But Bella was beyond subterfuge now; she was almost at the end of her tether. She was thin, haggard, wretched-looking beyond anything that mere hunger could do to her. Her beauty was gone now, though it could recover; it was still not too late for that, but she cared nothing now for matters of that sort. She lived in an unfeeling daze for most of the time, in a complete agony of mind for the rest of it, thinking continually of Roger, re-living in detail all those brief occasions when she had been able to be with him. Her afflicted mind, accumulatively played upon by months of the greatest danger and hardship, carried her back also to Fitzmaurice and to Kilkieran . . . and, occasionally, to the great affairs of state which she had attended with the latter, both in London before the regiment had been ordered overseas, and here in Gibraltar on a lesser scale prior to the siege. There had been the balls, the dinners, the levees and the receptions, glittering functions all, bright with the splendour of the officers' uniforms, colourful with orders and decorations, and the dresses of the women . . . she was living now entirely in the past, and it never occurred to her, in her shocked state, actually to contrast that glorious past with the degradation of the present – of which, for most of the time at any rate, she was scarcely aware. She wandered from place to place, returning sometimes to her hide-out on the heights, living almost like an animal. She took her meagre food where she could find it, or where she gave her favours listlessly to the men of the garrison for a share in their own pitiful rations . . . and wondered why she bothered to keep alive, since she had no wish to live – unless, perhaps, it was that she still in her innermost heart (and quite sub-consciously) wanted to see that final triumphant moment when the siege would be lifted forever and the ships and armies would come in with all of England's might behind them. Apart from this one slender and submerged thread she was a mere shadow, an automaton to be used by the redcoats as the fancy took them . . .

One evening there was news in the air, the kind of news at which Bella would so short a while ago have exulted. From her cave she had seen, during the afternoon, the sails of a British man-o'-war making into Algeciras Bay and had heard the shots exchanged, harmlessly, with what remained of the combined fleets of France and Spain. Later she had gone down into the town and had heard, without understanding, the wild rejoicings as the soldiers celebrated noisily and the towns-people flocked back once again to the ruins of their homes, braving the shot from Spain. She soon learned that the sail which she had seen was His Majesty's Frigate *Latona* and that her Captain had reported to His Excellency that the van of Lord Howe's fleet was already within the Strait.

Soon after that the fleet itself could be seen driving, like Rodney's force so long before, past Europa on the current into the Mediterranean. A little later the enemy fleets weighed and left to engage Lord Howe; and two days later, by which time the enemy camp was breaking up and sixteen battalions had already marched away, it was published in Garrison Orders that Lord Howe had made contact with the French and Spanish Fleets and that the British Fleet, inferior in numbers as it was, had shattered that of Admiral Cordova.

Next day HMS *Latona* received orders for home, and the Governor's aide-de-camp at once went aboard for a personal and private word with her Captain – whom as it happened he had met upon earlier occasions.

28

Frazer looked speculatively across the cabin at Captain Smyth. Smyth looked like a barrel – corpulent but compact, tough and leather faced and with small, pig-like eyes, and he had a reputation for a high degree of ruthlessness. He sat now with his thick legs apart and his paunch drooping down between his knees. Frazer envied him his evident good health, which must come in part from the good food with which he filled that paunch . . . but then, now that Lord Howe was returning victoriously to Gibraltar to fill Algeciras Bay with British sail, it would not be long before a food convoy entered.

Smyth said angrily, 'A damned woman aboard my ship's a damned nuisance, and you can tell His Excellency so for all I care.' He took a large pinch of snuff, noisily.

Frazer nodded; he knew Smyth, and he knew he had to be tactful. He said, 'Your objections will naturally be conveyed to His Excellency, but . . . he is most anxious to get rid of this woman, sir. And yours is the only ship returning to England in the foreseeable future.' He shook his head mournfully. 'Of course, if you really do feel unable . . . this woman, I am bound to admit, may give trouble . . .'

'Unable?' the naval Captain snapped, his small eyes staring unblinkingly at the Governor's ADC. 'Who the hell said I was *unable*? It's merely that I don't like it. And as for trouble . . . why, damme, man, I'm well accustomed to trouble and to having a damned short way with anyone who causes it – man or woman! Tell me now – in what way do you expect her to give trouble?'

Frazer said briefly, 'She is a harlot, sir. An undesirable.'

'Harlot – hey?' Smyth's small eyes narrowed still further. 'With a name like that? Come, come, my dear feller, I'm not to be trifled with, y'know – '

'Quite, sir, quite. That is fully understood. But I am telling you nothing more nor less than the truth. You see, it is her origins which count more than the status which she has since acquired by her marriage with Lord Kilkieran – if I make myself clear?' There was no answer, and he went on with a shrug, 'She is undeniably beautiful . . . or was. Kilkieran was suborned by her looks, no doubt – or her wiles! But since his death, and the deaths of certain of her – um – protectors, she has reverted to what she was before her marriage into the nobility. She is now living the life of a common prostitute among the soldiers.'

'And you're asking me to take this woman aboard a ship full of sailors who haven't yet set eyes on a woman since we left Portsmouth, and but for her – but for her, mark you! – would not do so until we reach Portsmouth again?'

Frazer spread his hands. 'His Excellency will understand perfectly if you feel . . . reluctant to accept the responsibility for any unrest which may be caused to your crew, sir . . . but he will not be pleased.'

'The devil he won't!' Captain Smyth flushed angrily. 'I care very little for his pleasure or displeasure, my dear fellow. I am answerable to my Lord Howe and my Lords Commissioners, not to the Governor of Gibraltar. However,' he added, leaning forward heavily, 'I have never yet shirked a responsibility.' He stared fixedly at Frazer for some thirty seconds after that and then said, 'Very well. I'll tell my First Lieutenant to make arrangements for her passage.'

'Thank you, sir, thank you very much. His Excellency will be much relieved.' Frazer leaned forward then, his adam's apple wobbling in his long, sunburned throat. 'If I may say so – do not hesitate to use any force that you may think necessary. I assure you that no questions will ever be asked from this garrison, whatever becomes of her. I shall see to that. The woman has been a continual trouble-maker ever since Kilkieran died early in the siege. We shall all be delighted to see the last of her.'

'I think I see.' Smyth drummed his fingers on the table-top and looked at the ADC narrowly. 'I think I understand what you are not committing to words. Well, my dear feller, you

196

can leave it all to me, I assure you. Now, then. I sail at first light tomorrow. The woman is to be aboard by midnight tonight. No later.'

'That I can guarantee, Captain Smyth.' Frazer got to his feet, keeping his tall, skinny body bent almost double in the confined space between decks. Smyth accompanied the soldier to the ship's side, where a bosun's chair was ready to lower him to a waiting boat to be pulled inshore to the Water Port. Frazer noted with some interest the brisk alertness of Smyth's officers and men when their Captain appeared on deck. He had noted before that Smyth's ships' companies were frightened of him, much more so than he had ever noticed aboard other ships.

Captain Smyth was undoubtedly a martinet, and so much the better for that.

It was not easy to find Bella. When they eventually did so, it was after dark and she was aimlessly wandering the streets of the town, picking her way over the rubble and the heaps of stones, stopping now and then in doorways to bargain with some of the soldiers. 'They' were the ADC himself, a sergeant, and two privates of foot with bayonets fixed. The sergeant was carrying a lantern.

She ran when she saw the escort, for she had guessed very accurately what it must mean. She ran away like a wild thing, very fast and with the whites of her eyes shining as if she were deranged. Had sheer hunger not forced her from her hide-out, she would never have ventured into the town until the *Latona* had sailed away. She ran, but she had not the strength left to cover more than some twenty yards before she fell, a huddled heap in the dust. Frazer gave an order and the sergeant lifted her gently to her feet, where she swayed back against him for a moment or two and then, finding some hidden reserves, pushed him away and stood, with her back straight, facing Frazer.

Frazer said formally, 'Lady Kilkieran, I have here a warrant from His Excellency ordering me to conduct you to His Majesty's Frigate *Latona* for passage home to England.' Glancing round, he saw that a crowd had collected, a crowd composed of both townspeople and soldiers. He went on coldly, 'If you have any possessions which you wish to collect together, I can allow you thirty minutes. These men will accompany you to – wherever you are living.'

She gave a high-sounding laugh and with difficulty bit back tears of mortification and hopelessness. This man of all men must never see her weaken in her hour of total defeat. She said cuttingly, 'Damn you, Captain Frazer. You must know very well that I have no home, and no possessions that I would wish to take with me – except for my memories of better men than *you* will ever be! Neither you nor anyone else can deprive me of them, even if I intended to leave Gibraltar, which I do not.'

Frazer bowed ironically. 'Your protest is noted and will be conveyed to His Excellency – in due course. For now, you will accompany me to the Water Port. I must execute my warrant, and you are most decidedly going to leave Gibraltar.'

She stared at him, not moving. She said in a low voice, 'So you have got your way in the end, Captain Frazer.'

'I think so,' he answered. 'This will not be like last time.'

'So you say. Who do these orders come from – His Excellency, you said?'

'Of course.' His face looked devilish in the lantern's flickering light.

'Och, but engineered by you, I have no doubt!' She went on staring at him, still unmoving; and after a while his eyes dropped. Her own eyes were bright now, and her face was hectically flushed. She said, 'I demand to see His Excellency, Captain Frazer.'

Frazer retorted smugly, 'You cannot. You have already had your chance, and you refused – '

'But you did not tell me why His Excellency wanted – '

Frazer brushed that aside. 'His Excellency has said that he will not see you now.'

'I do not believe you!' she said hotly. 'In any case it is my right. I do not intend to be denied.'

He shook his head. 'I am afraid you have no right to anything any longer in this garrison. His Excellency's only responsibility towards you now is to see that you are given a passage home in such safety as is possible.' He paused. 'That is all there is left to say, Lady Kilkieran. As from the moment my warrant was signed, you ceased to be on the strength of the garrison of Gibraltar.'

'So I am an outlaw?'

'In effect – yes.'

'I still refuse to go.' Bella looked at the soldiers, sweating and ill at ease in the lantern's glow. They did not like their duty this night. Beyond, on the fringes of the pool of light, she saw the ragged garments, the thin yellow faces of the mob of townspeople and soldiers, heard the beginnings of a curious growl coming from their throats. Frazer, it seemed, had also noticed this. He called up the sergeant.

He said, 'Sergeant, muster all soldiers off duty and present among the crowd. They are to place themselves under your command and form column with bayonets fixed. Lady Kilkieran will proceed with a Captain's escort . . . and fire will be opened upon the mob if they attempt to interfere in any way. Is that clear?'

The sergeant saluted. 'Yes, sir,' he said, and turned away. He disappeared beyond the lantern's pool of light but his voice could be heard bellowing at the soldiers. and in ones and twos they mustered, their faces grim, their eyes avoiding Bella. In a dead silence except for their footfalls and the clanking of arms and equipment, and the orders of the sergeant, they formed into column. The moment they were ready Frazer nodded at the sergeant and the procession moved through what was now a clamouring mob, forcing their way through with Bella inside a hedge of red and steel on which the lantern glittered with its yellow flame. They went along those broken, ghostly streets with the mob running and pushing beside them, still giving that curiously baleful howl, with an occasional oath as one of the soldiers, hustled too far, jabbed with a lowered bayonet-point. A few stones and jagged rocks were flung, but Frazer held his fire in case worse should ensue, and the columns moved ahead . . . as they neared the Water Port the mob thickened, was joined by more and more soldiers who recognized Lady Bella in the middle of the marching men. They gave her a ragged cheer, and she waved back at them. They shouted encouraging remarks, remarks to which the

ADC, his face flaming angrily, was obliged to turn a prudently deaf ear. Those men, like the townspeople, knew all about the Lady Bella's heroism in escaping across the neutral ground at risk of her life, to bring news to the garrison of the Dons' intentions – news which had led to the brilliantly successful sortie against the enemy, which she had herself suggested and then so gallantly if insubordinately accompanied. They remembered how she had tended the sick, how she had interceded with His Excellency to get them extra meat. And somehow word had also got around that it was she who had first suggested to General Boyd that red-hot shot be tried against the enemy in the grand assault. All this, they were never to forget. Degraded, dishonoured, cast out she might be, but to the defenders of Gibraltar she was to be forever more than that; she was a woman who had bravely, and without necessity of orders, undergone the same dangers and the same privations as themselves and who had contributed much to the success which was to come to British arms – and had remained in good heart throughout.

So, cheered all the last of the way, she neared the Water Port. There the columns were halted and turned into line. Bella was ordered to step forward, and was then formally handed over to a lieutenant of the Navy in charge of the boat's crew from the *Latona*.

At once, in an atmosphere charged with emotion and menace, the boat was pulled away by the seamen. The escort was turned about to aim their muskets into the crowd, who had looked like rushing the jetty at the last moment. Seeing the danger Bella called out in a tear-choked voice,

'My friends . . . I do not wish you to make any trouble for yourselves. I am sad to leave you, but I am happy to be going home to my own country now . . . there must be no enmity in your hearts towards your Governor, who is a great man and a good one, or towards the soldiers who brought me here. They have done no more than their simple duty. I wish you all God speed and a bright future . . .'

She choked to a stop and turned her back on the receding Water Port, the tears streaming unchecked down her cheeks now. She knew in her heart that the ADC had been right: this would not be like last time.

She would never see Gibraltar again now, that great Rock where all her cherished past lay buried.

They sailed away at dawn, making along the Line Wall, past Rosia, towards Europa. Off Europa they turned westward into the Strait and, with a keen wind behind them bellying out the canvas above their heads, they headed through to leave Carnera and the Spanish lines to starboard. Bella stood on deck as the Rock dwindled, tears coursing down her haggard cheeks until, as the wind freshened beyond Tarifa, she was roughly pushed out of the way and ordered below by a bosun's mate who was wielding a tarred rope's-end on the naked backs of seamen straining on sheets and tacks. She was cold and miserable and sick, and she was shivering with a terrible, intense violence.

She grew worse, more and more listless as the weary, wind-tossed days passed. Despite fairly adequate food now, the years of siege had seriously weakened her and she was in no condition to withstand the continual seasickness and the sudden drop in temperature – nor the veiled brutalities of Captain Smyth and the more sadistic of his officers and petty officers. She was given no privacy and indeed she was accorded the ultimate indignity of no more than a gun-deck hammock in which to sleep. And some of the bosun's mates, affecting not to know who was in that hammock, used their rope's-ends and their canes on her cringing body as readily as they used them on the seamen when the hands were turned out in the early dawns for their watches . . . dawns filled with flung spray and foul oaths and coarse, greasy naked bodies blundering into hers as men fought in the confined and claustrophobic spaces to lash up and stow their hammocks before the bosun's mates came in amongst them again with those swinging tarred ropes which bit and stung and cut. Captain Smyth had deliberately berthed Bella with the men, with what cruel purpose in mind she could only guess – but to guess correctly was not a very difficult task!

And the men – tough, hard bitten, press-ganged many of them, woman-crazy all of them – made the most of their unexpected good fortune. She was still young, still barely twenty-three years of age. The few who complained about her pinched and sickly looks did not realize that she had been a wild-eyed beauty so short a time before, or indeed that they were inflicting the final degradation and humiliation on a woman who had been, if for so short a while, a member of the nobility of England, and a brave defender of Gibraltar almost to the last . . . and so they took their pleasures brutally and lustfully and Bella was left a sobbing, huddled husk, nakedly cringing in the lee of the cannon along the gun-decks. It was clear that her vile treatment, coupled with her continual sickness and bouts of shivering as if with some raging fever, was wearing her down fast.

Seven days out from Gibraltar Lady Bella Kilkieran died from cold and fever and exhaustion and callous treatment, as well as from a broken heart; and was sewn into canvas by the sailmaker's mates. That day the final notation of her short life was made in the Log of His Majesty's Frigate *Latona* and signed with a flourish by Captain Henry William Foster Smyth of the Royal Navy:

This day died from privations undergone during the siege of the Fortress of Gibraltar, Bella, Lady Kilkieran. Body committed to the deep in Latitude 42° 18' North, Longitude 14° 43' West.

It was not until 2nd February 1783 that letters from the Duc de Crillon informed His Excellency of Gibraltar that preliminaries of a general peace had been signed between Great Britain, France and Spain. So at last the long bombardment totally ceased; and three days later the Duc de Crillon informed His Excellency that the blockade by sea was as of that date discontinued. A placard was published in the garrison signifying that the port of Gibraltar was, once again, free and open.

At noon an elevated gun was wantonly fired over the Spanish lines, and this was the last shot fired in the siege – which had lasted three years, seven months, and twelve days. That same afternoon, as a spontaneous act of joy at deliverance, the Land Port was ceremonially opened and left open for the first time since the siege had begun; in the evening a concourse of wildly cheering townspeople and soldiers, beside themselves with joy and triumph, celebrated throughout the garrison, letting off fireworks and shouting themselves hoarse. Next evening a great parade was held on the Red Sands where the tattered but glorious colours of the regiments were marched past His Excellency.

As the drums and fifes went by, Eliott's face was troubled and sad. Here, on these very Red Sands, Bella Kilkieran had formed up with his columns – if he had but known it then – to attack the might of Spain, a spirit brave and unafraid . . . When the pipes of his Highland regiments faded behind the English soldiers into the shadows of the closing day, echoing and echoing again off the great, grey-brown Rock of Gibraltar, martial and throbbing with overtones of glory and victory and yet at the same time weird and sad, His Excellency turned to General Boyd. He said simply but heavily, 'Thank God! Thank God for His deliverance . . . and thank Him too for Bella Kilkieran. I can wish only one thing more, Boyd – that she had been spared to be among us to see this day, as she had always wished. To see the 74th march past in triumph!'

The veteran Lieutenant-Governor of the fortress lifted a shaking hand to his eyes, his uniform sleeve showing up ragged and torn and threadbare. 'Amen,' he said in his thin, old-man's voice. 'Truly, sir, she was a woman of great courage.'

'She was more than that.' The pipes were still echoing off the Rock, sending their still defiant messages throbbing out across Algeciras Bay. 'That young woman was . . . a lady of the line, Boyd. Yes – a lady of the line! She served as truly and as well as any of the men under my command.'

Eliott stayed there a little longer, not speaking; then he turned away and walked unseeingly through the lines of senior officers as if in a dream. Silently, they made way for him, recognizing and respecting his preoccupation in this, the moment of official victory. He went slowly towards a commissariat cart, and the driver leaped down and stood at attention beside the head of the transport mule.

'Drive me to the North Front,' Eliott said abruptly.

'Sir!'

The man helped His Excellency into the cart, mounted himself and whipped up the skinny mule. Ahead of them, the pipes and drums marched on, the reverberating sound seeming to fill the still pregnant air with noise, a noise of war and death and savagery that beat about the ears of the listeners. Eliott himself scarcely heard it. When he reached the North Front he directed the commissarist driver to the burial ground, and there he made for two graves: Kilkieran's and Roger Carter's. He stayed for some time at each, looking down at the mounds of earth, his lips moving in silent and humble prayer.

He moved away at last. Someone had brought up a skinny horse. Eliott mounted and touched spurs to the animal's side, and slowly, dispiritedly, the horse ambled off towards the Land Port and His Excellency's residence, with the aide-de-camp, Captain Frazer, at a respectful distance behind. Curiously, Frazer looked no happier than he had looked during the siege . . .

The sun was almost down now, and the pipes had stopped their lament. In Hargrave's Barracks, or what was left of them, the 74th Regiment was lining up for a meal. And there, too, three people were being especially remembered in this hour of glory, and most particularly of them all, Bella Kilkieran.